'... I'll get to the point of me bec[...]
It all started with my last bit of troubl[...]
Bit of trouble! That's a right giggle. I couldn't be in
more trouble. I'm up to my charm pits on a murder
rap. It don't sound much in cold print, but believe
you me the law takes a dim view of it.'

In the only language he knows, a mixture of the
dialect of London's slumland and of cockney rhyming
slang, James Auchinleck Grant sits down at the age
of nineteen to record the tragic origins and results of
a short and brutish life. Brought up in a loveless
home, sharply confident in (though grotesquely mis-
informed about) his capacity to compete and survive,
he first and always seeks easy money in whatever
criminal partnership can find value in his services.
Last of these is Shy Ronnie, ruthless gang-leader and
protection racketeer.

The 'Auk's' life, as he writes it, becames a picar-
esque tour of London's criminal haunts and characters: a world of complete brutality and sentimentality,
giving rise to situations of weird comedy and sudden
endings. For Auk everything is physical, financial or
prestigious: morals and manners do not exist.

In its scenes from criminal life, in the energy and
compassion which it brings to its descriptions of London's lost souls, this first novel is memorable. Some
of the courtroom scenes during the Auk's trial are as
stirring and pathetic as some of the episodes that
precede it are bizarre: such as the gathering of the
criminal world at the cemetery to do honour to
Cornelius Murphy, 'the best getaway driver in the
business', who had killed himself while being chased
by the law after a warehouse job. *Swansong for a
Rare Bird* is an entry for the Macmillan/Panther first
crime novel competition.

To Barbara

Chapter One

My name is James Auchinleck Grant and I was born in a putty-coloured block of flats with a khazi in the back yard that was shared by three families who all seemed to want to use it at the same time. Especially in the morning, when everyone hammered on the door bawling 'Hurry up. You fallen down the hole?' Not very polite I'll admit, but when you've got a bus or tube to catch and your bladder's near your eyes there's no time for good manners. Still we never came to a punch-up often. My best trick was to climb out the window at the back while they waited and nip over the wall and go to school. It made a laugh leaving them all yelling their nuts off and kicking the door and getting no answer.

Our block was five floors high and split into about 20 flats. The higher up you lived the posher you was. The rents also went up with the number of stairs you had to climb. Our rent was the lowest – we lived in the basement. You didn't see much sunlight, but if you hid behind the curtains you could get a fair old view of the birds' legs and sometimes even their pants as they passed. Mostly they was old bags, but now and again a decent bint would stroll by and that made the waiting worth while. It also made up a bit for having to have the light on most of the time.

The flats – we never called them nothing else although there was a posh name on the rent book – was only a short walk from Leicester Square. That gave my Old Man the half-baked notion that he could tell everyone he had a flat in the West End of London. He'd got the gift of the gab all right and more than his share of animal cunning. He seemed to think he was conning people into thinking he had a film star pad among the big wigs with a butler to open the door for him when he got back from his job as a warehouse labourer.

My Old Lady on the other hand had more sense. She called it the black hole of Calcutta and said it was so dark down there you couldn't see a tanner on a sweep's arse when the light was off.

But to get back to the Old Man. He was in the army as a young bloke and Jesus, didn't he let you know it! At some time or other he served under General Auchinleck in the desert so you don't need a cartload of clues to know how I get my stupid name. He named me after his army mucker and I'll never forgive him for it. The way he talked about the army – and he did nothing else – you'd have thought the General called him aside every five minutes to ask his advice before making the slightest move. 'I say, Private Grant, what say we do a flanking movement.' The war's over for everybody else but my Old Man. The shot shit and shells are still flying as far as he is concerned. He's like a dog with two tails when he gets into a shooting gallery. Only it isn't a shooting gallery to him – it's a battle field and those little coloured ping pong balls bobbing up and down on jets of water are Germans in Jack boots, and those white elephants that go across the back of the booth are Panzer tanks.

The war had been over some years when the Old Lady had me, but I've heard so much about the bloody thing I could write a book. It might be a bit one-sided of course – the Old Man makes out he was behind victory. I'm what they call in those magazines the Old Lady buries her nose in a love baby. You see, the Old Man left his wife to go off with my mum, and as he didn't see the point in making the same mistake twice they never got hitched. They've never told me themselves, but a lot of other people have. Mind you, they didn't tell me out of no sense of duty. They did it when they lost their rag and wanted to nark me. Frankly I couldn't give a monkey's. A copper who was feeling my collar one night called me a 'right little bastard'. He's the only copper I've met who spoke the truth.

Love baby! If I sound micky-taking you'll have to

8

pardon me, because the amount of love in our house you could stick up a dog's jacksie and he wouldn't even yelp. But I'll give the Old Man his due; he liked his oats. When you're all living on top of each other you can't help finding that much out. The times he's kept me awake when the horn was fighting a losing battle with 10 pints of mild and bitter!

I don't want to waste no time on him though, so I'll get to the point of me becoming a writer. It all started with my last bit of trouble with the law. Bit of trouble! That's a right giggle. I couldn't be in more trouble. I'm up to my charm pits on a murder rap. It don't sound much in cold print but believe you me the law takes a dim view of it.

Anyways, my Legal Aid solicitor come to see me on the first day of my remand to tell me that a big Sunday newspaper would like to pay for my defence, just so long as I wrote my life story for them. It smelt to me, but my shyster legal eagle said I should take the offer because with the lolly a newspaper had I would get the best mouthpiece in the land when I got to be weighed off. On Legal Aid I wouldn't do so well. It seems that our legal profession ain't much different to our flats. The higher you are the more it costs. Not that I needed much talking into doing it. The prospect of being topped is off-putting to say the least. With a bit of luck I might just get life. Now ten years is a long time to be out of circulation, and I'd rather be shagging a bird than doing it. But it's a lot better than the eight o'clock walk.

The way my solicitor put it was that with a real big lawyer I stood a fair chance of a not guilty. That's what the paper was out to get. Then they wanted my life story. Natural enough I agreed to do the story. A rather flash Harry of a reporter briefed me as to what they wanted. I was to tell the story dead straight and he'd knock it into shape. The idea behind it was to prick the conscience of the nation – anyhow, that's how he put it – for allowing me to end up in the dock in the first place.

He said it wasn't my fault, it was the lousy world we live in that was all to blame for it.

9

But the newspaper dropped me like a hot spud because my life story wasn't worth a candle after a better one cropped up for them. A young bag killed her sugar daddy with poisoned gin. So they signed the Tom up instead.

That left me with a whole heap of crap I'd been writing for them since I first was nicked. I didn't see no point in doing all that for nothing so I decided to go right on ahead with it.

I had nothing to lose. Even so, it turned out to be a much harder job than I thought it would. I'm not exactly dumb and if my Old Man had let me stay on at school longer I might have done all right for myself, but he needed the loot I could earn out working. To be dead honest, I can't say I minded leaving school as it was always a bit of a pain in the arse to me. Still cutting off my reading and writing like that don't exactly make me a big threat to Hadley Chase. The most I'd ever written before was essays like 'A Day in the Life of a Sixpence' and 'How I spent my summer holidays'. I'm not even much of a hand at writing letters as the only time I've had to was when we went on holidays from school and had to sit down and write home twice a week, and I even skived on that when I could. So far as I can remember all I ever said was 'Hope this finds you as well as it leaves me. Please send me half a dollar.' Still, everyone's got to start.

One thing that helped was some tips I remember from our English teacher who always said start at the front, have a middle and then an end. And that's just what I aim to do. I'm O.K. about the beginning and the middle, but the end is still up in the air kind of. I'm just keeping my fingers crossed that it'll be a happy one. By that I mean I really hope I'll only get life which I can do standing on my head. On the other hand, they might top me. I just don't know the answer to that one because I'm writing this as I go along and at the moment it's even stephens I'll con my way out of it with no more than a big helping of porridge. At least I ain't got long to go before finding out.

So let's get back to the start. My early baby days we can skip for the simple reason I can't remember nothing about it. So you're all in for a disappointment if you think I'm going to tell you what I thought when the Old Lady wheeled me through the park. Knowing her, I shouldn't think she bothered.

The first clear memory I really have is one of proper disgust for the Old Man. This was when I realised what a mutt he was for naming me after his general pal. That took a lot of living down, believe you me. I had to belt a few kids to spread the message that anyone who took the Michael out of me had better be tougher and rougher. Those fights taught me something valuable though – most people hate to get hurt. Me, I didn't care. Even when I was getting a good duffing up I just kept on going; as a result I never lost a punch-up.

As I said earlier, I wasn't the brightest kid at school but I certainly wasn't the dumbest, and one day sticks in my mind like you know what on an army blanket. That was when I found out that if you use your loaf you'll always come out smelling of roses. You see we was having wood-work lesson with this bloke who liked to run his class like an army drill ground. At the end of each lesson we knew exactly what he was going to say. We had those long wooden work benches with a vice on each side and when the lesson was over Puffer – we called him that because his name was Train – would biff a little brass bell on his desk and shout 'Atten-shun.'

Then off he'd go like a parrot week after week. 'Put your book, wood and pencil on the inside end' – ping – 'and the outside boys sweep down' – ping. Then came another order 'Commence.' We was all expected to grab these dust pans and brooms and clear up the wood shavings. Only this day I beat him to it. Just as he pinged I shouted 'Commence' before he even had a chance to. The whole class burst out laughing and looked at me. I must say I felt 10 feet tall and there was a soppy grin on my face that I just couldn't wipe off. Puffer naturally didn't see the comic side of it. He dashed down the workshop and grabbed me by the earhole and yanked me to the blackboard. After a couple of right-handers – and they hurt believe me because those years of wood-work had made his hands like oak – he got started. 'Boys, I want you to look at a relic from a bygone age. The great Auk. An extinct bird that perished because it was bone-headed. I predict a similar sticky end for this Auk here.' With that he gave me another clout and sent me back to my bench. By then he was getting the laughs and I was looking a right mug. That might have suited old Puffer who was laughing his nut off at the respect the boys was now showing to him. So real loudly I called him a name that had the whole class laughing, only at *him* this time. Honest they was really splitting their sides. I can't tell you what I called him because I'm told they would never allow it to appear in print. Not that it matters anyway. They wasn't laughing at me no more. Old Puffer did his walnut. He went purple instead of red. 'Come here,' he hollered. I didn't budge an inch though. 'Not on your Nelly,' I told him. That did it. Because just then I looked round the class to see if I'd raised another laugh, and next thing I knew a lump of wood had whacked me on the bonce. Old Puffer had flung it at me with all his might. Some silly nit even shouted, 'Bloody good shot, sir.'

I'll have you, you bastard, I said to myself. So I clasped a hand to my eye and started yelling blue murder. 'Oh my eye. I'm blinded.'

You could have heard a feather drop it was so quiet. As I swayed up and down in pretended agony yelling my swede off I thought, 'I've got you now all right.'

I could hear old Puffer's voice saying, 'Now stop it James. That's quite enough. You're not hurt. Now be a big boy.'

Then I noticed the change in his tone as I kept moaning.

'Here James, let me look.' I felt his hand on my shoulder and I pushed him away screaming even louder. I knew no one would hear as the wood-work shop was down at the back of the playground where you wouldn't hear a H-bomb go off.

'Don't touch me, please sir,' I screamed.

You could almost hear the tears in his voice. 'James, you must let me look. I won't hurt you.' I piled on the agony at that. 'You're going to beat me, I know.'

'James. I want to help. You may need a doctor.' I put him through the mangle a little longer then. With my hands still over my eyes I whispered, 'Don't worry sir. I won't tell no-one. You can't help having a bad temper.'

'But James, please. I haven't a hasty temper. I'm a mild man really. You must admit you drove me to it, James. Now isn't that true?'

I snivelled a little more and told him, 'If the headmaster gets to hear of this sir, he may not think that way.'

Anyhows, to cut a long story short he cleared the class pronto. He still didn't forget to ping his bell and shout 'atten-shun' though. Then he made me sit at his desk and we had another little wrestling match while he tried to see what damage he'd done.

I made certain he didn't get my hand away. When he got near it I just yelled a little longer and he let go. We sat there for quite a while as he flapped around like an old hen that's dropped a square egg. But I didn't let up. In the end I whispered, 'I think I'll be all right now sir.' I got up then and staggered towards the door like I had a bullet in my back. I was pretending to myself I'd been ambushed and not just clobbered with a bit of wood.

'Here James, let me run you home in my car.'

'Oh no sir, please don't do that. My Old Man might ask questions. So I'd rather you didn't sir,' I told him.

Then I felt him shoving something into my trouser pocket. I had a pretty shrewd idea what it was. I was right too. When I got out I found he'd dropped me five bob.

As I walked – hand still over my eye – down the flight of wooden steps that led from the work shop to the play-ground, the other boys were waiting. 'How's it go?' they asked.

I felt I was about six feet tall as I took my hand from my eye and gave them all a big wink and a thumbs up sign. Then they all began to cheer and shout, 'Good old Auk.' And you know something, I never minded them calling me it at all. In fact, I liked it.

Next day I went to school with a big patch over my eye

like Nelson. Puffer went out of his way to be nice to me – including dropping me a tosheroon. I'll admit I felt sorry for him because he was dead scared of being called before the Head. But I never eased up on him. Instead I asked him if I could be let off early as I had to go to the eye hospital again. He even wanted to run me in the car. I wouldn't let him though, and I took myself off to the flea pit and had a couple of hours with the U.S. 7th Cavalry.

That little how-do-you-do may sound nothing. But it taught me something valuable. When you have someone by the short and curlies don't let go. That's one of the best lessons I learned. It has turned out to be more help than knowing how long it takes for a bath to empty when you have the plug out and both hot and cold taps going. I ask you, who would be daft enough to do that in a bathroom? Anyways, we didn't have no bath in the black hole.

Chapter Two

When I was a kid people in motors always used to put my back up. It don't now of course, but I used to wonder then where they got their money from because I certainly never had none. It was as scarce in our house as pigeon's milk. Blokes with birds in cars, especially them sports ones where the dolly sat with her head wrapped in a scarf covered with horses' heads, really got my rag up. Just for a giggle I used to stroll right in front of them. They'd hoot like billy-o but I just kept on until they finally had to slam their brakes on. In some daft way I felt a little more equal after that.

But I learned the hard way not to overdo it.

One morning out of the corner of my eye I saw this big car with a flag on the bonnet, and a driver in uniform in front, coming down our street at a hell of a lick. I ambled easy across the street whistling like a kettle. I kept my head to the front but one eye on him. Then it came – a hoot that sounded like the Queen Mary. I still kept on though. Then wham it smacked me right up the rear bumper. I saw myself getting enough insurance to buy me a car and a driver too, so I lay on the road bellowing my head off. That driver was a hard case though. He whipped out of that car, grabbed my ear and gave me a real painful toe up the bottle and glass, then turfed me out of the way. Before I could get a word out it was off up the road blasting away like a destroyer after a U boat. Still, it only confirmed what the Old Man was always saying – there's one law for the rich and another for us.

Being always so short on the spondulicks it's no wonder I'd stoop to anything to get a bob or two.

Now our landlord was a real old miser who'd skin a turd if he thought there was anything in it. He was tighter than a duck's arse which, as you know, is watertight. To save himself a few bob he had a separate switch for every light on our landings, and our caretaker's job was to go up every night at lighting-up time and switch them on with his special key. He was bone idle and another war bitching hero who said his gammy leg stopped him climbing up. To prove he was a hero, he always wore a little silver medal in his button-hole and Christ help anyone who asked him how he was crippled. They had a run down for nix on the whole of the war. Everyone had to be grateful to our porter. He won the war. Him and my Old Man that is.

Anyways, I was grateful for that gammy leg, as rather than go up and down the apples and pears he paid me to do it. I liked the money but hated the job. You see, I always did it arse about face. I used to run up to the top through all those coal black landings, then switch on the top floor and the others on the way down. Every corner had a man waiting with a big axe to chop my nut in two like a coconut. And all the whistling and talking to the bloke I pretended was with me didn't drive them away. I can't recall a night when I didn't think someone was lying in ambush for me. Come to think of it, I'm still a bit windy of the dark. Years later I still whistled when I went down dark alleys. Not that I was *too* scared. A shiv in your pocket can work marvels.

One night though I told old gammy leg I got the wind-up and he burst out laughing. Why didn't I switch the bottom light on first, then I wouldn't have to be in the dark at all, he said. Now that shook me rigid. I thought he was too dozy to work that out. It just goes to show though. Never underestimate no one.

Although I did this job every night, I was clued up enough to know it wasn't going to make me a Charlie Clore. I'd never fell for that bilge the millionaires trot out to hard-up geezers – look after the pennies and the pounds will look after themselves. You can talk that kind of bull from the back seat of a gold-plated Rolls-Royce, but I'd like to hear old Clore say it after a week of running up and down those stairs.

It's a fair old time ago now, but I can still recall the first

16

quid I ever held in my hand. I never had no chance to spend it though. I ended up in the Juvenile Court charged with stealing instead. Or, as the copper who prosecuted me told the Court, petty larceny. I don't know whether that fancy phrase was to make me feel a bit better about being nicked or not. If it was it certainly didn't work.

It all happened like this. There was a scruffy little sweet shop at the end of the street which was owned by a weirdy old Jewboy called Glickberg. He was a funny old geezer who used to stand at the doorway in a old blue suit that had more grub down the front than I've had hot dinners. His titfer was an old bowler that was so green with age it could have done with mowing. Inside though there was a out of this world stock of sweets; sherbert fountains, bars of fruit and nut, bulls eyes, liquorice pipes with red bobbly tops to look like flame, gob stoppers that changed colour, and bubble gum. You name it, he had it.

Well one day I was walking past when he nipped out and grabbed me by the elbow. He made me jump like a bird does when you run your finger down her back.

'Knock it off. I haven't done nothing,' I told him.

It's funny, for such a weird looking old coot he had quite a nice voice. You could tell he wasn't English mind. Quite apart from him looking dirty, I mean.

He didn't beat about the bush at all. 'Little boy, would you like some sweets?'

I'd been clued up to old men like him from some of the big blokes who played pitch and toss on the corner. 'Get stuffed grandad. I'll call a copper if you don't knock it off,' I said. Right angry I sounded. I wasn't really though.

Instead of being narked, he just burst out laughing and shook so much I thought the grub would fall off of the front of his coat.

'You don't understand me, boy. I want you to light my gas stove and fire for me.'

Now that was a odd thing for a grown up man to ask. 'Come off it. You look strong enough to strike a match mate,' I told him.

Then he went on to say that because he was a Jew boy he

wasn't allowed to light the gas at certain times and this was one of them. He sounded straight enough to me. Anyways, I fancied some sweets. So I followed the sound of his squeaky old shoes down into the kitchen where he gave me a box of matches as if they were made of gold and told me to light the gas. When it was over he squeaked back into the shop and thanked me as if I'd saved him from drowning. Waving his hands round the shop like it was Aladdin's cave he said, 'Little boy, please tell me what you would like.'

I had a quick gander round the shop and pointed to a slab of thick toffee. 'I'll have some of that.'

'Of course,' he said, and got a tiny hammer that wouldn't have knocked a tin-tack into a pound of butter and bashed the toffee into little squares. I left him smiling his head off. I was laughing too. It had given me a great idea.

I waited till next Saturday before I passed the shop again. There he was outside, still in the same clothes and still wearing the shoes that could do with an oiling.

'Morning Mr Glickberg. Want the gas lit?'

He showed his rotten teeth – they looked like some of his sweets – in a big grin. 'I appreciate your kindness little boy. Come in.'

Now I didn't go much on his 'little boy' kick as I was anything but little. Still, I didn't want to ruin my plans because the old man said the wrong thing. Anyway, I lit the gas and sure enough in the shop he said, 'Little boy, what would you like?'

'Some of those,' I told him, pointing to some acid drops in a big glass jar up on the shelf behind the counter.

'Then you shall have them.'

Puffing like a pair of bellows he dragged some step ladders out of a corner and started climbing up. You'd have thought he was going up the side of Everest the noise he made.

When he was up the top and wrestling with the jar I made my move. I nipped round the counter and opened the drawer that was the till. The money was in hollowed-out bowls of wood and I had a quid in my pocket before he'd got the jar down.

I learned another lesson that day. If you're going to nick anything you need to have eyes in the seat of your pants. As I picked up my bag of sweets I heard a voice say, 'I saw him with my own eyes Mr Glickberg.'

I turned round and there was this fat old bird, Mrs Hempy, still in her slippers yelling blue murder. 'I just did see him. He's swiped a quid from your till.'

Chapter Three

The Juvenile Court was a bit of a let down to put it mild. All week I'd been kind of getting ready for it in my imagination. I'd find myself sloping off into thoughts of how I would play it . . . real cool and tough. I'd lay in my kip in the morning, hands behind my head working it all out. It wasn't a bad game really. My eyes would nearly close as they slipped the cuffs on me and dragged me into the dock. I'd shrug my shoulders and push the cops away and walk in, head as high as a randy dog's tail. Then when I'd been sent down I'd move up to the end of the bed and pretend the bars was a cell. Even the screws had to admit I could take it without squealing.

It wasn't like that at all though. They made the Old Man come along with me and I had to wear my Sunday suit and my hair was all plastered down with water, and it kept dripping down the back of my neck. The Old Man didn't take no extra care though. He put on a clean shirt but didn't bother to put a collar and tie on. Made me that mad, honest. I've always liked to take a pride in my dress and it griped me to see the Old Man with his collar stud showing in the front.

The Juvenile Court turned out to be a great barn of a place with a big draughty corridor and a lot of snivelling kids sitting on benches wiping their snotty noses on the back of their hands. Inside was a big copper with a long list and as we arrived he checked the names off and told us to sit down.

I gave my name and the copper said, 'Is your dad here?' I looked round and saw he was and wasn't really, if you get what I mean. He was sitting on the bench puffing at a fag miles away. I could tell by the look in his eyes that he was on his Jack-Jones on the battlefield knocking out a Panzer division and getting a medal from the Queen for it. The copper gave him a nudge in the Kelly and pointed to a notice on the wall which said 'No Smoking'.

I thought that was a bit of a liberty seeing as how the copper was having a sly drag himself. But he was better at it than the Old Man. Years of crafty dragging on the beat had given him the knack of being able to smoke without being seen.

The copper, a big bloke with a row of medal ribbons and boozer's cheeks, sat down by the Old Man and told him not to worry too much.

'It's not like a court really, and for one thing your neighbours won't get to hear of the lad's trouble. There's a strict rule governing the Juvenile Court. No names are ever allowed to be published. Not under any circumstances.'

If the copper expected some thanks from the Old Man he was unlucky. Instead he got an earful of what my Old Man thought of them.

It chirped me up though. I was glad the local rag wouldn't have nothing in it. I didn't relish the idea of my mates reading what a cock-up I'd made of everything.

Waiting for your turn was a bit like going to see the doctor really. The only difference was that instead of someone shouting 'Next please' another bogey came out and shouted your name and ticked another list. There was so many lists around it looked like a laundry.

When we went in I was a bit browned off as it wasn't like a court at all. Just a small room with green and white walls and a table with green stuff on the top like you see on snooker tables. In front of that was two chairs. Behind the table was two old blokes and a woman with a pair of Bristol City's on her that looked like melons with spikes on. But what got me was her titfer. All cherries and blue plums. There was enough fruit on it to keep a coster going for weeks. They all sat there sucking their pencils and looking like the team in 'What's my Line?'

Me and the Old Man were plonked down on the two chairs and someone read out from a piece of paper that I was before the court for nicking the money. I don't know why he bothered. Me and the Old Man knew full well why we was there.

Then the woman – she wasn't even a judge, just a chairman – says like syrup of figs, 'James. You know why you are here?'

Before I had a chance to speak the copper gave me a nudge in the ribs that almost knocked the wind out of me. 'Stand up when the chairman addresses you.'

I wasn't going to argue. I stood up. It was real comic. I felt just like that kid in the painting hanging on the classroom wall; I thought any minute now she's going to ask me, 'When did you last see your father?' She didn't. She just gave me a lot of cobblers about me not being there to be punished but to be helped.

Next that old bag Mrs Hempy was called in to have her say and then the copper who knocked me off had a natter about me denying it and how he found the quid in my pocket. Then the bird with the fruity hat told the Old Man to stand up. It was worth turning up just for that, because she gave him a ripe old rollicking. 'Mr Grant,' she said. 'This is a serious matter. One would have thought you would have come properly attired for it. Instead you haven't even put on a tie. It's really not good enough.'

I thought for a minute he was going to do his nut. 'It ain't no good going on at me missus. I ain't the one who nicked anything. He's the one you want to have a go at. If I ain't got a tie on it's because I've been worried sick about this.'

Well, you had to give it to him. He didn't care who he dropped in it so long as it wasn't him. The magistrates seemed satisfied although I knew for a dead cert that the Old Man couldn't have cared less if they'd sent me to Devil's Island with a one way ticket.

The three heads behind the table got together for a quick natter that no-one else could hear.

Then the woman turned to the copper. 'Is there anything else we ought to hear?'

The copper said, 'Mr Glickberg would like to say something.'

They all went into a huddle again and decided that the old Jewboy should be allowed in. I thought ain't that rosy. Things hadn't been looking too bad, now he comes along to twist the knife.

When the old boy shuffled in I didn't recognise him. He was all dressed up like a dog's dinner. He took the bible in his left hand, stuck his right one on top of his bowler and promised to tell the truth.

'I think the little boy should be getting another fresh chance.' He kept shrugging his shoulders like he had a bed bug up his coat. He probably did.

'I think he's now more than sorry. The money I have not lost. I want to say that. Thank you.'

'Thank *you*,' they all replied.

'You have been *most* helpful Mr Glickberg,' said the bird with the fruit hat. 'The bench will retire,' she said.

When they came back she said, 'After careful consideration the case will be adjourned for one week. Meanwhile, we would like to have a psychiatric report on James.'

She made it sound like a Bob Martin's powder. Outside old Glickberg tried to shake the Old Man's hand. But the Old Man didn't want to know.

'You want to get back to Israel,' he told him.

The old boy patted me on the head and said, 'I am sorry little boy. Now you cannot light the gas again.'

I thought to myself, you don't know how lucky you are mate. I wouldn't make the same mistake again. I'd make certain I wasn't being watched next time.

Chapter Four

I thought it would be like on the telly. Me lying back on a black leather sofa while the head shrinker sat behind me asking questions and writing things down in a book. It was nothing like that at all though. As soon as I arrived at the hospital I got the message that he was in no dying hurry to see me because I drank four cups of tea and smoked four coffin nails in the lav before I was taken to his room. When I went through the door he was already looking at his watch. He was a real toady looking gink who hadn't even bothered to put his white coat on. Now a wink is as good as a nod to a blind horse where I come from, and I knew straight away he was as bored as armholes as I was about the whole thing.

He pulled a sheet of paper towards him across this big desk and told me, 'I see your full name is James Auchinleck Grant. Rather a mouthful. Would you like to tell me why?'

'Not really,' I said.

'And why not,' he asked. The look on his fizzog suggested I had let out something as important as a state secret.

'It stands to reason,' I said. 'Would you? It's so bloody daft.'

'Do you always swear?' he asked me.

'Who was swearing?' I asked real puzzled.

'Well it wasn't me,' he said.

'It wasn't me neither,' I told him.

He was dead set on needling me before we'd even started, and I was getting quite snotty.

'All right, all right,' he said in a God help me be patient voice. 'If you'd rather not talk about your name we won't,' he said.

'Look, I don't mind talking about it one bit,' I said. 'If you're really interested. I don't like being rude but the amount of time you kept me farting about outside I thought you was busy.'

Now don't ask me why but he got narked, and he pressed down so hard on his pencil that he snapped the lead off of it. He obviously did it quite a lot though because he had a half pint glass in front of him full of yellow sharpened pencils. 'Playing the bloody fool won't help you at all – you should realise that,' he shouted.

'Who's swearing now?' I asked. 'Not me.'

If looks could kill. You'd have thought I was something he stepped into on the pavement . . . I thought I'd better play the choirboy until he had come off the boil.

'I'm sorry sir, but I get brassed off with people taking the Michael out of me through my name.'

'That's all right, I understand. Now we are getting somewhere. I don't really want to hear about it now. I don't need to.'

Cross my heart, I never said a word. Here we'd spent 15 minutes arguing about it and then he finally turns round and tells me he don't want to hear anyway. I just thought if anyone needs a head shrinker it ain't me, mate.

I sat there getting saddle sore while he wrote something down on the sheet. Don't ask me what he wrote because he didn't bother to even tell me. And he said *I* was jude.

When he looked up again he fixed me with his leery look and says, 'Do you masturbate?' Just like that, right out of the blue.

I thought to myself, ain't they all the same. Our headmaster was always on about boys pulling their pudding. He seemed to think it was responsible for everything from nits in your head to bad handwriting. Well, I knew our Head thought it was 'abominable' and while I don't know what that means it certainly ain't something to crow about. From the way he said it the trick cyclist had the same views as our Head. There's no point in making a rod for your own back, so I played it close to the chest.

'I'm sorry sir, I don't understand you.'

'That's all right. Perfectly all right. No reason why you should. Let me put it another way. Do you ever play with yourself?'

'No sir. I have a lot of friends.'

Bang went the end of another pencil. 'You know damn well what I mean.' I'll give him his due though. He didn't take a swipe at me. He just tapped the desk with the bottom of a new pencil like someone calling a meeting to order. 'Well answer me. Do you?'

It was a daft question, because of the hundreds of kids he must have asked none of them could have been balmy enough to tell the truth. I wasn't no exception. 'No sir,' I said.

'I know that isn't true, of course,' he said. Which to tell the truth made me wonder why I was there in the first place. If he didn't believe me, we wasn't going to get anywhere fast.

'I don't have to tell no lies,' I said all quasimodo. That's a foreign saying we have when someone gives you the hump. I don't know what it means but round our way everyone says it.

I'll hand it to him. The bloke could sigh. 'These aren't trick questions. I'm asking them for a purpose,' he said. 'The answers you give will assist the court. Because what you tell me will aid me in preparing my report. I'm here to help.'

Now if he hadn't said those last four words I might have believed him. But I knew even then that anyone who used words like that was out to screw your nuts off.

'I don't do it, sir, because it's bad for you.'

'Who ever told you that?' he asked, sounding real scared.

'Our Head, and my Mum. You get hairs in the middle of your hands and you go blind and mad.'

Another pencil went for a Burton. 'That is rubbish, absolute rubbish. People who say things like that are unaware of the great harm they can do,' he told me.

'Do you mean it's all right then?'

I was getting really interested. Get out of that, I thought. 'Don't misunderstand me, and I'm not saying it's all right. All I'm saying is that you shouldn't worry too much about it if you do – occasionally. How can I put it? It's like drink. The odd beer is perfectly safe, but too much makes you a drunkard. You see what I mean?'

'Yes sir.' I didn't, naturally; who would? I knew if you drank too much you got boozed out of your head. But what you ended up as if you let too much dirty water off your chest with the five fingered widow was a mystery to me.

'Anyway sir. Our Head says there's no need for it if you play plenty of games and have cold baths.'

He grabbed at the *out* like my Old Man grabbing a pint before last orders. 'You like games then? That's encouraging. They are character forming. They are also an outlet for aggressive tendencies. What do you like best?'

'Bedlam's good,' I said.

'What?' He made it sound as if I'd said croquet.

'Bedlam. We play it against the milk shop. That's the best place, see? Because he always boards his windows up at night as they get broken so much, see, and that makes it good as you can bash up against it without ruining the game – or smashing his window.'

I tried to explain the rules to him, but Bedlam's like most games, you got to play it really before you know what it's about. I had a go but the witch doctor couldn't cotton on. It's simple really. You just chalk a square on the pavement and that's Bedlam. Three blokes are locked inside and the other gang sets guard and has to stop you breaking in and springing them out. It's an excuse for a punch-up really.

I might as well have been talking to a deaf eskimo. He just nodded and said, 'Very interesting. What about organised games though? Such as cricket or football?'

Well, cricket is a game I can talk about or play for hours. I told him about the Test Matches we had. Mind you, there was only one batsman and the wicket was this grating in the middle of the road. Blimey, on a hot day a terrible pen and ink used to come up from it. But you got used to it and anyway no one ever stayed in that long. Twenty-two yard away from the grating was a lamp post and that was where we bowled from. We knew it was the right distance 'cos some workmen measured it for us once with a big chain. We had some smashing matches, I told him. But I never told him we used to give ourselves the names of famous batters and bowlers. To us it seemed all right, but it sounds soppy when you tell it to someone else.

I might have guessed I was wasting my time though. All the head shrinker said was, 'You shouldn't play in the streets. Aren't there any parks nearby?'

Just about then this nurse came in with a cup of coffee for him and two biscuits in the saucer. I didn't get offered none. Still I thought, that's the end of this little lot. But not on your Nelly. He dunked the biscuits in the coffee and sucked them like a kid with a mushy rusk and started off about the books I read.

'Well, to be honest I'm not a great one for books,' I said. 'Micky Spillane I go a bomb on, but frankly I like those murder magazines best. You know the ones that show you the cops at work round the stiff. At least you know it's all true. The pictures prove it.'

That got him busy with his pencil once again, and when he looks up he asks me, 'Dickens now. Have you read him?'

I hadn't, but the way he said it made me think I ought to say yes. It's funny, but something seems to happen to people when they talk about Dickens. It comes out like God or the Royal Family or the Archbishop of Canterbury. I know everyone rates him strictly top ten, but to me he's dead corny. I remember we had David something or other at school and it gave me the squitters. All the blokes seemed to be saying werry good and werry sorry. I don't believe no one talks like that.

Still, the head shrinker seemed pleased when I said yes. He nodded his head at me as if I was a dog which had just balanced a knob of sugar on its nose.

Then he said right out of the blue: 'Oscar Wilde – Now what about him?'

Now I don't go red easy, but I felt my face going like beetroot. I thought to myself, 'He's got sex on the brain'.

28

It was awkward, I tell you. Because all I know about Oscar is a poem about him and a cabin boy. I felt pretty certain he wouldn't want me to repeat that.

'You're blushing,' he said.

'Course I am,' I said. 'Wouldn't you if someone started asking you questions about a ginger beer?'

Crikey, there goes another pencil I said to myself. If he goes on at that rate with every patient he must work through a pine forest by the end of the day, I thought.

'Grant, I have met some foul minded illiterates in my time but you leave them all standing,' he told me.

I didn't understand a word of what he said, but I could tell by the tone of his voice he wasn't paying me no compliment.

'What, may I ask, is a ginger beer?' he asked.

As he said it he took out a nice new sharpened pencil and I thought to myself 'Now don't go saying anything to upset him'.

'A ginger beer, sir, is a queer, a poove, an iron hoove, sir. It's rhyming slang, sir.' I was scattering the sirs like pepper on a bag of fish and chips. If I was going to nark him I might as well do it politely.

'Grant. For your edification,' – by Jesus, he could drag out some long ones – 'Oscar Wilde was a famous writer. It's tragic that you seem to have heard the least important aspects of his life.'

I could see I was fighting a losing battle with the old know-all. As if it was my fault that his mate Oscar was a bum bandit.

Anyway, two hours, ten pencils and fifty million questions later it was all over. He didn't even bother to get up when he said, 'You can go now Grant.'

Stopping at the door I asked him, 'What happens now?'

'I will send my report to the Juvenile Court. They will then take the appropriate action.'

'What will that be sir?'

'Probably probation.'

'Thanks sir, that's not too bad really.'

'No. That's because they'll ignore my report. If they

didn't it would be slow asphyxia.'

I didn't get the words, but I got the tune all right. I said, 'Thank you sir,' and tried to make it sound as near to balls as I could.

Outside, I got on top of a Number 11 and got a weed out. Then I found I had no matches, so I squeezed next to a bloke who was having a drag. 'Got a light mate?'

'Certainly not,' he said. 'You're far too young to be smoking.' So I had to go back to my seat and sit there with the fag in my lips. By the time I got to the stop near home it was too soggy to smoke, so I had to drop it in the used ticket box. Still, I managed to dodge paying my fare.

Chapter Five

The trick cyclist was dead right. The Juvenile Court took no notice of his report and I was put on probation for two years. When I went back to the Juvenile Court a fortnight after seeing the head shrinker the same old trout with big knockers was sitting in charge. She fingered through a pile of papers in front of her and said, 'James, the psychiatrist's report was far from favourable, far from favourable. In fact, I will go so far as to say he was very unimpressed. But my colleagues and I —' she gave a nod to each of them to make sure I didn't think she was nattering about someone else – 'still feel there is plenty of promise in you. Given the right encouragement you can become a credit to society.'

I thought for one minute we would all be waving flags and singing a chorus from 'Land of Hope and Glory'. You could almost see the lump in her throat.

'I must make this clear however. If during that period you misbehave in *any* way you will be brought back here, and this offence will also be considered when we come to dealing with you. If on the other hand you are a good boy you will hear no more from us. The Probation Officer will see you afterwards and just remember from now on he is your best friend.'

Well, it wasn't too bad I suppose. The trouble was the Probation Officer. He turned out to be a real bind. I was put off the first time I met him in his office, round the back of the court.

A ripe creep. He wore those thick itchy grey flannels and a sports coat that had all three buttons done up. Not my idea of a sharp dresser at all. What's more, he had one of those white tube things which he kept sticking up his hooter and sniffing.

He kept nattering on about youth clubs and society and I

31

don't mean the co-op. Still, like most do-gooders he was quite happy if you just kept telling him he was dead right and you'd learned your lesson the hard way. The trouble is I didn't know what the lesson was and he didn't bother to tell me. He was too busy clearing his nose.

Fortunately, he saw no reason why I shouldn't go on the school journey, and it was agreed I could start my prob when I got back. That really meant a lot to me because the school journey was the best part of the whole year at school. You see we'd all been paying a couple of bob a week to the Headmaster for it. Frankly I didn't care how I got the money just so long as I did. My holiday was paid for in returned beer bottles, old iron and car washes. Not to mention the odd bob I nicked from the Old Man when he got sloshed and emptied his pockets on to the sideboard at night.

As a matter of course he used to go off at the Old Lady and accuse her something rotten. Not that she minded though. She knew he was too stoned to remember how much he had anyway. The rows naturally suited me. They were at each other's throats like a couple of Draculas so that it never struck them it might have been me. He used to break even stephen though by helping himself from her purse or swiping a few bob from the stand-by float she kept in an empty tea tin.

Every year we used to set off from outside the school around eight in the morning. Then we all turned up with our duffle bags and suitcases and a great big chara would be parked in the kerb. Some of the posher kids had blazers and caps but most of us wore jeans and T shirts. Me, I always think a uniform is a dead loss 'cos if you get spotted doing something wrong a blazer and cap is a dead giveaway.

Before we were allowed to pile on the bus and fight for the back seats the Head used to read us the riot act in the school hall. It was the same crap year after year so we didn't really have to listen. We got reminded of the school motto, to always keep the honour of the school, not to damage crops and to always say good morning to the people in the village we was going to. The way our Head talked about the country people, I always felt we ought to take along a boxful of mirrors and beads. He made them sound like niggers with bones in their noses. I went to the village three times in all and I never once saw anyone with a spear let alone a bone.

If you'd ever seen our school you'd understand why we was always so happy to get away. It was five floors high and the colour of horse manure. There was a playground on the roof and one on the ground. But what you noticed more than anything was the wire. There was this high wire everywhere and it wasn't to keep people out if you ask me. All the time I was there I never heard of anyone trying to break in. I knew lots of kids though who sloped off during the morning break. No one ever noticed you had gone, because once you had answered your name when the register was called you were there for the day even if you'd skipped.

Apart from the wire the tops of the walls were covered in thousands of broken bottles which had been stuck in cement when it was soft. The bottles didn't worry us though 'cos on top of the ground floor lav we had hidden one of those real thick coal sacks we nicked from a lorry once. If you slung that on top of the glass you never got cut.

Mind you, if you were ever caught going over the top you were in for it. Six on each hand and the whole school turned out and made to watch it in the main hall. It was quite a rigmarole actually when someone got the cane. It was always done after morning prayers when everyone was sitting cross legged on the brown lino in the big hall. The Head, who was the only one who seemed to enjoy it, always did the whacking. What a right to-do it was. His desk was up on a platform under this glass case where they kept the book with all the names of old boys who'd got knocked off in the wars. In his desk he kept another book, a thick brown one. He wrote your name in it if you got a whacking and sent it off to head office wherever that was. First though he'd get his cane out and give it a few practice swipes while he told you who was in for it. Not that he needed to tell us,

33

we all knew. You couldn't keep a thing like that quiet.

It was only a little cane, no bigger than a Charlie Chaplin walking stick, but it didn't half hurt and I'm speaking from experience. There was a rumour that he used to pickle it in vinegar to make it sting more, but no one ever actually saw him doing it.

Once when I got my six on each, my mate gave me some orange peel to rub on my hands. He told me it wouldn't hurt then. Maybe he gave me the wrong kind of orange, that's all I can say because it really did hurt. Mind you, the build-up didn't do your nerves any good either. You had to go up this platform while the Head swished his cane and told everyone why you were getting clobbered. Then he'd say, 'Right hand up. Higher. Higher.'

If you didn't go high he'd tap your hand up from underneath with the cane, and that didn't feel like a powder puff neither. Some clever kids used to take their hands away at the last minute but that always seemed to me to be half baked as the Head tried to squeeze in a couple of extras thinking no one would notice.

After he'd had his morning exercise he used to write your name down in the book and you were allowed to go back to your seat.

As you shuffled your way through the rows of sitting kids with your hands under your arm they'd all whisper, 'Did it hurt?'

I never knew a kid at our school who didn't say, 'No. Didn't even feel it.' One time I got it my fingers swelled up like a bunch of Fyffes and when I got home my Old Man was proper narked. 'He's not allowed to do that you know. There's a law against it.' Like most things the Old Man said, it was about as useful as the Pope's balls.

He was a funny gink, our Head. When he whacked you like you was a door mat on a clothes line he seemed to be loving it. Yet other times he could be as soft as a wet fag end. Like on Armistice Day when we all piled into the hall while he took the Book of Remembrance from the glass case and read all the names out. You'll never credit it but he used to cry his eyeballs out. Once he had to have it in the playground on the roof, as someone dropped a stink bomb right in the middle of 'Time like an ever rolling stream bears all its sons away'. It smelt like a herd of elephants had farted together after a banquet of pickled onions. But it never lasted long. He was back to the old routine in no time at all.

The Head never used to come on the school journey himself and I can't remember any of the kids crying over that. I don't suppose he cried himself because we really ran the teachers ragged for the fortnight we were away. Three of them came with us that year – old Beaky who was a real weirdy who used to hand you a pair of scissors when you put your hand up to leave the room, and Whiskers the young bloke who used to get piles sitting in the rain outside Parliament moaning about the H bomb. He used to try and get us interested in banning the bomb. Me, I was always in favour of dropping the bloody thing provided it landed on our school and blew it to Kingdom come.

The other teacher was this Miss Frimley who wasn't a bad looker except she had this white moustache and a bee in her bonnet about clean shoes. She used to have an inspection every morning and keep a league table of results. If your shoes were O.K. you'd get a little blue star, if they wasn't you'd get a lecture. If you wonder how anyone can give a lecture on dirty shoes then you don't know Miss Frimley. She and my Old Man would have got on well together because she could turn a pair of shoes into a history of the British army. It seems if only we'd used a bit more Cherry Blossom we'd still have an empire. Still, it did make us keep our shoes clean if nothing else. One of the kids used to claim that she and Whiskers used to have it off during the dinner hour in one of the classrooms. No one could ever prove it though. I never believed it myself; for one thing old Whiskers' shoes were too dirty for her.

It used to take us all day in the coach to get to the village where we stayed, but the journey was one of the best parts as we used to have a sing-song until we lost our voices. It

35

was like being let out of a cage and as a result we used to do some real potty things. The coach would no sooner get round the corner and out would come the grub – sandwiches and bottles of Coke. The nosh was always finished before we even saw a tree, and we used to arrive starving.

At the village all the women who was going to put us up used to be waiting at the war memorial. Me and four others were dead lucky. We were billeted out at this big farm. The others were all shacked up in little houses around the main drag.

The only trouble with the farm was it was a long walk in the mornings down to the hall where we had prayers. Yet we never noticed the journey as we used to sing all the way at the top of our voices and people would come out and watch.

Our favourite song went like this:

> *We are the London boys*
> *We know our manners*
> *We spend our tanners,*
> *We are respected wherever we go.*
> *Marching down the frog and toad*
> *Doors and windows open wide*
> *Up a specky apple goes*
> *Hits a copper on the nose*
> *We are the London boys.*

It had a smashing tune but there's no way of letting you know how it went. We did spend our tanners too. I had a nice little wrinkle which no one tumbled the whole two weeks I was away. You see there were five telephone boxes around the village. Three outside the post office, one in the Red Lion car park and the other was outside the public library. The second day I was there I tore up my exercise books which I was supposed to use for sticking in flowers and leaves. Then I bunged up the chute in the phone boxes so that anyone pressing button B didn't get his money back. It was amazing how much money you would rake in because a lot of the villagers used to make long distance phone calls. Now of course they've done away with most of the old boxes and you can't work the fiddle on S.T.D. boxes.

This farmer whose name I can't recall was a real decent bloke, he used to let us do anything we liked providing we didn't do any damage. I used to borrow his big air gun and go ratting in the barn for hours on end. He took that away though when I accidentally on purpose put a slug up the rear of his big tabby which used to creep into the barn and bitch up the shooting by scaring the rats off. I knew then that I took after the Old Man because I really used to be miles away when I shot those rats, only they wasn't rats they were the Sheriff's posse who'd got me holed up in this barn after I'd robbed Wells Fargo. One day I was pretending I had been winged in the leg and I was dragging myself over the bales of hay shouting 'Come and git me' when the farmer came in. I felt a real Charlie. When I look back now I can't help feeling that if the truth was known that's the real reason I shot his cat.

I remember one day when he gave me this big ball of thick black cotton and asked me to protect his peas from the birds. Well, when I finished there was still a lot left over so me and the other kids went down to this little street where a lot of the other kids were billeted. When it was dark we linked all the knockers together with the cotton and then we waited for the last bus to come through. You've never seen anything like it. As the bus went through all the knockers bashed down and people came to the front doors. You should have seen their faces. They must have thought the place was haunted until they found the cotton next morning.

My best mucker was Ginger Bailey and we always did everything together. Ginger's old lady was a widow though, and she was always writing to him. If she could have managed it she'd have had a card waiting for him as the coach arrived. Remember, do keep dry. Remember to change your socks. Have you got everything? Poor old Ginge. She made him promise to write home every other day. School orders was twice a week when they gave you a post card to fill in. Sometimes I never sent mine. It didn't seem worth wasting the stamp money. It's not as if my Mum and the Old Man didn't know where I was.

It wasn't all larking about, we had to do a lot of work as the school journey wasn't during the proper summer holiday. We didn't break up till we got back. So a lot of the time we had lessons, not arithmetic and geography but nature lessons. Off we'd go into the woods to find leaves and flowers and write down the birds we saw. I could never see the point in it myself. Where I lived there weren't any trees and the birds were the kind who never laid eggs. They only got laid. Anyway, I couldn't do it because I'd used my book to bung up the phone boxes.

Ginger and I often used to slink off down to the canal which ran past this factory. We didn't have any swim suits but we used to stand below the bridge as the workers came out for lunch and shout, 'Penny in the water and I'll do a long dive.'

The secret was to dive in as soon as the money hit the water. If you didn't you never could find it in the thick mud on the bottom and the weeds wrapped round your legs. Ginger was a bit on the shy side though, and he would stick his hand over his J.T. and go like a beetroot when the girls shouted out, 'Watch your worm. Here comes a blackbird.'

'He'll bite off more than he can chew,' I shouted back when they had a go at me, and the dollies giggled and chucked some more money in. After a couple of trips Ginge bought himself a pair of trunks. I never knew why.

When we went back in the coach the mums were waiting outside the school like a lot of coal miners' wives in those films you see of pit disasters. The kids were brown and cheesed off with having to come home and the mums were whiter than their old men's shirts and glad to have them back. That is until the novelty wore off – which in my case was about 24 hours.

Me, I could have stayed in the country for ever. Coming home was no joy I can tell you. I was on probation remember, and I had to be home at nine every night and report to the Probation Officer twice a week.

The only consolation I could see in it all was that I was due to leave school soon and I aimed to get the softest number possible with the least amount of work. That makes sense to me – you don't graft away all day to make money for someone else.

Chapter Six

Probation was a doddle really, and it didn't make much difference to me, after all two years is nothing when you compare it with what I'm lumbered with now. I used my loaf and soon got on the right side of the Prob-O. All he ever wanted out of life was the happy belief that you was doing what he wanted and trying to be a good citizen. That's not difficult with a geezer who meets you half way with his questions, is it? Our sessions in his crummy little office always went the same way. I knew what he wanted me to say, so I said it.

'Come in James, and how are we this evening? Are we keeping out of mischief?'

'Yes sir.'

'That's good. That is good. Really encouraging, James,' he told me.

Mind you, it wasn't all plain sailing. Sometimes I felt I was up the creek without a paddle. 'I'm worried James about one thing. You don't seem able to hold a job down for long.'

He could say that again. Since I'd left school I'd had more jobs than he'd had hot dinners. The Prob-O just couldn't understand it at all. Nor could you expect him to – he'd been sitting in the same crappy little office for twenty years, wearing the same old itchy flannels and sports coat I bet, and bashing his head against a brick wall. No matter how long he sat there he would never cotton on that villainy wasn't the terrible thing he thought it was. If he'd lived in our street instead of catching the tube to Cockfosters every night he'd have realised that the blokes who got the most out of the rat race were the villains. They had the cars, they had the dames, they had the sharp suits and enough green backs to make the geegees fun and not the answer to their

40

prayers. I've seen too many blokes who've spent a lifetime at one firm. What do they have to show at the end of it, I ask you? A gold fountain pen to fill the pools in with, and a letter of thanks from the boss saying he hopes they enjoy retirement. Which is the last thing they want anyway, because they can't afford to give up work.

I won't deny I *did* have a lot of jobs. There are jobs and jobs though, and I'm not sorry one little bit that I told so many foremen to stuff them. Mind you, I put a lot of the blame on the youth employment for sending me after them. Before you went for a job they'd already marked your card. I'm sure they tipped the wink to the firms they sent you to because at one the gaffer said to me, 'I see you're unreliable with money.' Now in the eyes of a boss that's even worse than not being punctual. Anyway, the result was you only got taken on by those firms where they wanted a lot of humping and heaving done. And those kind of people can get knotted as far as I'm concerned.

You take for instance the job they sent me to at the warehouse. I could tell from the minute I arrived that the foreman had it in for me. My job was to lift these great big boxes on to the lorries which delivered them C.O.D. all over the place. The first morning he pointed to a pile as high as Big Ben and said to me, 'Get that little lot on that lorry, then you have lunch – an hour. Not a minute less, not a minute more.'

Well, I stuck my transistor on top of the boxes and tuned in to a pop show and got weaving. That didn't suit the foreman though, he had to keep popping in and bitching about my slowness. 'You want to sleep with boxing gloves on son. Then you wouldn't be so tired,' he told me.

At half past twelve my old kelly was rumbling and I fancied a pie and chips, so I put my coat on and clocked off. He was waiting for me though. 'I said when that pile was all loaded up, not before.'

So I had to go back and start grafting again. When he came back to check up I was walking around with my J.T. hanging out. 'And just what do you think you're up to, Grant?' he asked.

'Nothing,' I said. 'Only if I got to work like a horse I might as well look like one.' It's a corny gag and it didn't even raise a laugh. 'Get your cards,' he said.

'I don't need to,' I told him. 'I haven't even had time to hand them in yet.'

Of course the Prob-O was choked, but I smoothed him over. 'It wasn't my fault sir. I've done my best to keep my nose clean but how can I when people keep throwing up that I'm on probation?'

The Prob-O was most narked because he really felt the world owed his boys a living. If only bosses would give them big fat salaries and the key to the safe they would finally turn out trumps as 'decent citizens'. You can't tell a bloke like that what a load of cobblers he's talking because they really believe it.

So when I told him about getting the bullet once again I had to put the ball back in the foreman's court.

The Prob-O really did overtime on his sniffing stick, he was that choked. 'He shouldn't do that. It's quite wrong. It undoes all the good work we are trying to accomplish. I'll see to it that no more of my lads are sent there.'

I didn't see that the foreman was going to argue with him and go down on his knees begging him to change his mind.

Still, I finally got one job that I stuck to for over a year and that saw me through my probation period.

Once I got the Prob-O off my back I didn't bother any more about getting a regular job. I went on National Assistance and ponced about doing tax free stints that brought in a few quid each week. On Saturday afternoons I used to work with 'Harry the Watchman'. That doesn't mean he looked after property. He got the name from the racket he used to run outside the gates at football matches. Harry used to have a big brown suitcase full of little envelopes like the ones you get wages in and we used to fill these with cotton wool and a ring that was worth sweet fanny adams.

Then we used to motor up to Spurs or the Gunners and wait for the suckers to come out. Sometimes we did Chelsea but not often. Harry didn't like the ground. I never knew what difference it made because Harry never went inside. But he was funny like that. He took a real pride in his work, and somehow Chelsea's ground put him off his stroke.

Harry used to plonk his case on a trestle and give a spiel that soon got the crowds round. Most of the envelopes, he told the suckers, had a ten bob note or a pound and a gold watch in them. To prove he wasn't kidding he used to bust a couple of envelopes open and pull out the lolly and watches.

My job was to push through the crowd and offer him my half dollar. The patter was always the same. Harry would say, 'Shove off kid, I don't want your old lady around here accusing me of robbing the cradle. I don't mind taking money from the suckers, but not children.'

Of course the sportsmen who'd just spent a pleasant 90 minutes chucking Guinness bottles at the ref and knocking hell out of each other on the terraces didn't like that one little bit. Some mug would always fall. 'Here, let the kid have a go. I'll pay.'

Well, you don't need a telescope to see what happened next. I'd take a pick and sure enough there was a watch or a greenback inside.

Then I always used to say, 'Can I have another go mister? I got lots of money now.'

Harry took the loss like the good sportsman he wasn't. 'Sorry son. Mustn't be greedy. Let these other gentlemen have a chance. What you can do though is earn yourself a couple of bob by standing on the corner keeping cave for the coppers.'

And off I'd go and from then on it was money for old rope as the mugs bought the cotton wool and their half-penny rings. When it began to get dicey because no one had got a prize I used to rush back and say, 'Mister, there's a copper coming.'

Harry would set off up the road like a bull was trying its horns out on the seat of his trousers. Everyone would think what a lousy rat he was and they were so busy shouting up the street after him that they never noticed that the coppers never turned up. Of course, I'd go straight off and meet

Harry because we'd always arranged a meet before we set out. He used to shell out a couple of greenbacks every time I helped, and that could mount up because apart from football matches we often did the dog tracks as well.

Sometimes I did the same thing when Harry was running a 'find the lady' school. I could tell you how it works but it wouldn't be fair to Harry. He's still got a living to make.

Of course, a job like that don't last for ever. I got too big and Harry said he was sorry but he'd have to get a new boy. Mind you, I'd lasted much longer than any other of his stooges. Harry always put the age limit at sixteen and I was 17 when the partnership busted. He slipped me a fiver and sounded real cheesed off. 'Sorry, kid, but the ventriloquist must be bigger than his dummy. Unless they feel sorry for a kid the mugs don't shell out.'

I won't say I wasn't a bit choked at splitting up – I was, but I didn't crawl into a corner and give up the ghost. Life's like a bird I say, you've got to get on top of it.

'Tell you what I'll do Auk,' said Harry. 'Meet me in The Boot on Saturday and I'll arrange a meet with Shy Ronnie.' The Boot was a big boozer called 'The Duke of Wellington' but no one ever called it that. If you'd asked for 'The Wellington' no one would have known what you were talking about. They would though if you asked for Shy Ronnie.

Shy Ronnie was a real big time villain. Strictly league division one. For a front, he ran a secondhand car firm but everyone knew his real dough came from villainy. He had more rackets than a tennis champion – and there were plenty of strings attached too.

You might think he was a quiet geezer from his name, in fact he was a loud mouth and as flashy as a pearly king's waistcoat. That's why they gave him his name. Mind you, no one ever used it in front of him. Ronnie ran a mob and he wouldn't think twice about getting one of them to learn you some manners with a knuckle full of pennies.

He was a funny geezer all right. He had all this dough, a big Rolls-Royce, and a whopping house in the country where Queen Elizabeth was sure to have kipped, but he couldn't keep away from The Boot. My Old Man once said that he hated going home to his big house because the people in the village were too toffee-nosed for him. It didn't matter how much he gave the British Legion or the local Tories, they still wouldn't have him round for tea and crumpets.

Well, come Sat. night I really tarted up. First I put on the kettle and had a real close shave because I'd reached the stage where I had to shave nearly every day. Then I locked the kitchen door and stripped off and had a good wash up and down in the zinc bath we kept on a hook on the wall. Now I may not be the cat's whiskers when it comes to looks. I certainly ain't handsome enough to sell toothpaste on the telly, but I dress real sharp. My best suit was this Italian drag I bought down the Charing Cross Road. It was really with it . . . dark blue with little bits of flashing silver running down the stripes and nipped right in at the waist. The trousers were slick hip huggers that fitted so well I didn't even need a belt although I shoved on one with a big buckle just for decoration. My best shirt was reddy mauve with stripes as thick as your finger and a button-down collar that looked a bit like a parson's until you put a fancy pin in. Last, I put on my Italian winkle pickers. I had to put them on last because my trouser bottoms were so narrow I couldn't get them on over my pickers.

Then I borrowed the Old Lady's mirror and set my titfer at a right ritzy slant. I was proud of that hat. It was a Sunset Boulevard straw with a striped band and a real narrow brim. Now a hat suits me even if I say so myself, because I've never been one to let my hair grow like a bird's. I like it short – though not as short as it is now – with a nice parting and a bit of a blow wave in the front. Then I sloshed the old fizzog with a handful of after-shave. Nothing cissy, mind you, it couldn't be with a label called 'Big Game Hunter' on it.

Saturday night at The Boot was *the* night of the week. Everyone was well breeched and in their glad rags. The blokes who rolled their own during the week were all dragging at tailor mades, and when I strolled inside the smoke

45

was so thick I thought there'd been a tear gas raid. The women were all tarted up too, and knocking the stuffing out of gin and tonics and starboard lights. By Monday they'd be back on the stout, but they never minded. Spend it while you've got it, they said.

Trade was so brisk the guvnor had to take in about four part-timers to cope. He didn't like doing it, though, because you can never trust them, so he had big mirrors on the ceiling above the bars then you could spot if any of them tried to short change you.

Up on the stage Gloria was bashing out all the latest pop numbers on the joanna and everyone was shanted up enough to want to sing. Actually, Gloria was a bloke called Sidney who was as queer as a clockwork orange but he could certainly punish the ivories. There was already half a dozen browns on top of the joanna and you could tell from the way he was playing he was already well away.

It was the one night that made life worth while for him because the rest of the week he was up to his elbows in greasy water washing dishes in a posh hotel. He was camp all right and he could play like Winifred Atwell and when he was Mozart and Liszt enough he wasn't playing in The Boot any more but at the Palladium with the spotlights on him. And up in the main box the Royal Family were clapping and singing their heads off. The trouble was every Saturday ended the same for him, bombed out of his mind and bawling his eyeballs out. Still, someone always ran him home to his stinky little bed-sitter and put him to kip. Then he'd cry himself to sleep with this horrible ginger cat of his kipping right by his face. I know this because I went home with him once.

I had a bit of a job picking anyone out when I went in, it was so smoky. Then I saw Harry waving his hand at me. He was sitting with Shy Ronnie at a table right under the piano. They had two birds with them who looked real corkers. You could tell from their clothes they were different to the other bints.

Shy Ronnie was laughing so much you could see a mouthful of gold. Some card said he'd insured his teeth for two grand. He had class though. He was smoking a big cigar and wearing a suit you could have played draughts on.

I tilted my hat back and waded through the crowd nearly knocking old Biddy Ann over in the process. She was a funny old bird who mopped up the tables whenever someone sloshed beer over them. The trouble was she couldn't keep off the red biddy and by the end of the night she managed to spill more wallop than she mopped up.

When I got to the table, Harry said, 'This is Auk, Ronnie.'

Shy Ronnie flicked about an inch of ash down the front of one of the birds and said, 'He smells like a whore's handbag. Anyway, is he old enough to be here?'

Shy Ronnie or not, I wasn't having any urine extracted. 'Knock it off,' I told him. 'That's after shave. Big Game Hunter.'

The bird was saying, 'Do you mind,' and shaking her knockers about as if she'd got a bit of hot coal down her bra.

Shy Ronnie told her, 'Belt up,' and to me, 'Park yourself.' I took a pew and he said, 'What'll you have?'

'Pint of M. and B.'

He called the barman over because on Saturday you could order from the tables. 'A crème de menthe, a mother's ruin, two large gold watches and a pint of mild and bitter,' he said.

Then he stuck out his hand and I noticed that between each knuckle he'd got a fiver all neatly folded up.

'You look like a pox doctor's clerk in that whistle and flute,' he said.

Now I'm pretty thick skinned about most things, but I wasn't having that. When it comes to the wise cracking I'm as sharp as the next geezer. 'Get stuffed. At least I ain't a walking draught board.'

Harry looked as if he was going to break out in a rash. 'Easy, Auk. Ronnie ain't used to being spoken to like that.'

I thought of the mobsters and the bike chains and took a quick gander at the door to make certain I could get out quick. But Ronnie didn't mind. 'He's all right. I like a kid with spirit. Don't worry son, the suit is O.K. I'm just ribbing.'

Suddenly he turned away and shouted like a Sergeant Major to Sidney.

'Oh Gloria. Do you know the arse is hanging out of your trousers.' Well, we all knew what was coming because it happened every Saturday night. Gloria swung round on the stool and said, 'No, but you hum it and I'll pick up the tune.' Naturally, everyone laughed like a drain. Even me, though I'd fallen out of the cradle laughing at the joke.

Then just as if he had never said it, Ronnie turned to me and said, 'Harry tells me you're looking for some work.'

That wasn't strictly true. I was looking for money. I wanted easy street and I'd seen enough of the rat race to know that hard work is strictly for the canaries. 'I don't want no labouring,' I said.

'You've got the shoulders for it, lad,' he said. 'But don't worry, I think we'll line something easier up. Come round to the office on Monday morning I'll see what we can fix up.'

And he never said any more about it after that. We just got down to some real solid boozing. After a couple of hours though, I was feeling shanted and the two birds were giggling at everything.

I couldn't keep my eyes off one of the dollies. She had on these red kinky boots and a skirt that was so short she'd have caught a cold in the throat if there was any draught around. And her blouse was so low cut you could see her boots when she leant forward. What a pair she had. They were all bunched up so tight she couldn't have got a fourpenny stamp down sideways. When she wasn't leaning forward she was leaning backwards. I didn't know where to put my eyes.

Soon we was all well away and singing our heads off. The heat was something awful though, and I knew the Big Game Hunter was fighting a losing battle with my arm pits. I had a sly sniff when no one was looking and wished I'd stuck the bottle in my pocket when I left home.

Suddenly the bird started playing kneesey kneesey with me under the table and I was dead scared that Ronnie would spot us because I wasn't really sure what the score was with him and her.

But as the Old Man used to say, a standing one's got no conscience, so I decided it was in for a penny in for a pound, and I put my arm round her pretending we were having a duet like. Ronnie didn't give a dicky bird. 'Here, look at those two. They'll be giving an exhibish any minute,' he shouted.

I asked the bird what was her name.

'Rosanna,' she said.

'That's a posh monica for round here. Still, it's a nice handle,' I told her.

She bent over and sent the old temperature up to boiling. Then she whispered, 'I'll let you into a little secret. Actually, you see my real name is Doris. Rosanna is my professional name.'

'What, you on the stage then?'

'I suppose you could say I was in a way. I'm a kind of performer,' she said.

Obviously she didn't want to say any more about it, because when I asked her what kind of performer she just tapped me on the tip of my hooter with her finger and said, 'Curiosity killed the cat.'

Not that it worried me. I wanted to have a leak so bad I couldn't think of anything else. But the slash house in The Boot was right down a steep flight of wooden stairs and I wasn't sure the old legs would make it. But I got to my feet without knocking the table over and said, 'Back in a jiff. Got to strain off.'

That made Rosanna laugh. 'You're kinda cute,' she said.

I made the door all right but then the steps came up and smacked me right in the kisser. I reckon I got to the bottom in one bounce. I hung on to the cistern while I watered the horse. Then I gave my head such a clout I thought I was in the planetarium. Of course I lost my titfer and had to crawl round on all fours in the dark before I could find it. The bending couldn't have mixed too well with the beer because

I honked my ring up – I just hoped I'd missed my hat. Anyway, it was washable, and I felt too rough to care.

When I finally made it up the stairs again the others were just leaving and Gloria was just starting to snivel.

Shy Ronnie just said, 'Lost your hat, Auk? Hop in the motor, we'll run you home.'

In the back seat of the Rolls Rosanna started trying to bite the end off my earhole. Frankly, I couldn't have cared less. When I piled out at the flats I felt her stuffing a bit of paper in my hand. I tried to read it when I got inside the main door, but the words were doing the twist so I gave it up.

Then I took another short cut down the stairs to the flat and would have kipped outside if the Old Man hadn't stepped on me as he came in, bombed out of his mind on boiler makers.

Chapter Seven

I woke up next morning with a mouth like a navvy's sock and a head that felt as if there was a Salvation Army drummer inside. My best whistle was in a big heap on the floor and I could just see the heel of one of my pickers sticking out of the trouser leg.

The Old Man was already up and nose deep in the Rhino Horn. Don't ask me why, but that's what we always called the *News of the World* round our way.

Although it was Sunday morning I knew I wouldn't be able to enjoy a lie in. The Sally Ann drummer had teamed up with a squad of clog dancers. I just had to get up. Otherwise I would have pegged out. No kidding.

As far as the Old Man was concerned I could have been a mummy in the British Museum, so I shouted to him, 'Oi Rommel, give us a hand to put the bed up.'

It was like talking to a brick wall. Now, normally I could fold the bed up without no trouble, but my nut felt like a jelly fish in a rough sea. The Old Man wasn't doing anything more active than turning pages over as far as I could see. I still had to do it on my jack jones though. Well, I made it after an all-in wrestling bout and finally got it upright. Then I put the clip on and covered it with the fancy cloth so that you wouldn't know it was a bed standing against the wall. Mind you, it was no great shakes as a bed, and taking it down in the morning and putting it up at night made kipping a real bind. If we hadn't have had a fold up though you wouldn't have been able to move around in the kitchen. As it was you only needed half a dozen people in there to make it feel like the tube in the rush hour.

The Old Man came to life. 'You must be bloody proud of yourself,' he shouted in his parade ground voice.

I didn't even jump to attention. I'd heard it all before.

Ten million times.

'Just look at you. Eyes like fag holes in an army blanket.'
Trust him to bring the army into it.

'What a spectacle. I ask you. You should have seen
yourself. You was bouncing around this room like a ping-
pong ball trying to get your fancy pants off.'

I knew it was no good rowing with him, but I just
couldn't help it.

'Why don't you belt up just for once,' I told him.

When he got to rabbiting like that there was only one
way to shut him up. Give him a taste of his own medicine.

'I don't know how you got the nerve to talk like that. You
were so boozed you trod on me.'

'Quite right too,' he said. 'If you want to act like a
bloody door mat you expect to get treated like one. I'm not
saying I didn't have a few. I did, and I'm the first to admit
it. But no one had to put *me* to bed. I ask you, a boy of your
age being tucked in by his Dad.'

'So I had a few shants,' I said.

'Listen, cloth ears,' he said. 'No one minds if you have a
few, just so long as you can hold it. Just remember this: on
parade, on parade. Off parade, off parade. Get it?'

Don't ask me what I was supposed to get. The Old Man
was always saying things like that. The thing was not to
make the mistake of asking him what he was talking about,
because he would really give you an ear bashing and at the
end you'd be no wiser.

'You give me a pain in the goolies,' I told him and
collected my togs together and went to the wash-house to
clean them up.

I cheered up a bit in there. The whistle wasn't half as
bad as I thought it would be.

When I came to put everything back in the pockets I
come across this note that Doris had slipped into my mitt.
Her writing wouldn't have won no contests but at least I
was now in a fit state to read it.

It just said, 'Come and see me when you're lonely
handsome – Rosanna (Doris).' Underneath she'd wrote her
address.

I was in two minds as to whether I really wanted to get lumbered with a doll who couldn't make up her mind what her name was. But when I remembered what she looked like sitting in the pub I decided it was worth the candle. I was a bit windy though about calling round. You won't believe this but I had never had my end away. I knew what it was all about of course, and everyone else thought I was clued up on the subject, but the truth was I'd never actually done it. Not even a knee trembler, honest.

I still felt too rough to belt round there straight away and anyhow I didn't want to miss Sunday dinner. Whatever might be wrong with the Old Lady she certainly pulled the stops out for Sunday nosh. Not like the rest of the week at all when the grub was left over a saucepan till the gravy all dried up and left a brown ring round the plate that was so hard you needed a road drill to get it off. No, on Sunday she really let rip. Roast beef and a really big Yorkshire and baked spuds with greens and sometimes even peas. You can keep a bit of tail waiting and it won't get cold, but you can't take liberties with a good dinner, I always say.

You should have seen the Old Man tuck in to the Yorkshire. Only he never called it that, he always called it zizz pud, 'cos after two helpings he had to get his head down for the afternoon.

That's all beside the point really. Quite apart from the grub stakes it was a bit early in the day to start thinking about getting your leg over. Who wants chocolates before breakfast?

Don't get me wrong, now, I wasn't making no excuses. I wanted to see her all right. What I was honestly worried about was going round when I wasn't feeling like I could do justice to myself. I didn't want to bitch things up because I had hung one on last night.

The trouble was that I wasn't getting to feel any better as the morning went on. In fact I was feeling worse.

Even the Old Man couldn't stand it any more. 'You going to mope around here like a wet dream all day?' he asked me. 'What you need is the hair of the dog.'

Well, it couldn't make me feel any worse I thought. So I

53

tucked into a big plate of bubble and squeak and decided to go round to The Boot for a couple of shants. I didn't exactly go round there like an Olympic runner though, because I was worried in case the guvnor was umpty about the night before. The last thing I wanted was a slanging match over the counter. To be honest with you, I still couldn't remember much about it, but what I could made the short hairs on my neck start creeping. Just like when the barber runs his open razor round your neck at the end of a short back and sides.

It didn't help much either when I looked at my money and found I was nearly stony. It came back to me slowly that I'd really played the money-no-object boyo. I'd bought three rounds for Ronnie and the two birds, which left me with a ten bob note, a handful of silver and four fags.

I gave the Old Man one of the weeds and lit it before trying to put the arm on him. Polite, because I needed him, I said, 'Dad. Lend us a bar till tomorrow.'

'Don't call me Dad,' he said without even bothering to look up. 'The only time you call me that is when you want something. Anyhow, what makes you think I can afford to go lending you a pound? What with the rent and what have you I don't have a penny left for myself.'

It wasn't worth wasting my time. When he was in that mood I stood as much chance of getting a loan from him as I did from a pawn broker with no hands. All that crap about the rent didn't fool me one bit. I knew he spent so much on himself that we were in arrears. I'd been home many times when he made the Old Lady go to the door and tell the rent man he wasn't in and to come back later. She thought it fooled him, but it didn't. The rent man was too bone idle to argue and knew it was a waste of time coming back anyway. He just let the arrears pile up until the landlord got browned off and gave us notice to quit. Somehow or other the Old Man always managed to make up the money then.

Once his snout was back in the paper I nipped into the kitchen and lifted a quid from the Old Lady's tea caddy.

It's mean gits like the Old Man who turn people into thieves.

I walked slowly round to The Boot taking great big deep breaths of air. Not that it helped. The air around our way was so lousy it was likely to do more harm than good.

The usual Sunday morning crowd was in the saloon bar. Most of the women hadn't dressed properly and their hair was still in curlers and they had slippers instead of shoes on. They had just nipped out to knock back a few while the grub was in the oven.

Fred the guvnor was polishing glasses and holding them up to the light just like they was diamonds. I spun a half dollar in the air and slapped my hand over it as it hit the counter. 'Pint of bit.'

'Sorry Auk. Nothing doing,' he said without taking his eyes off the glasses.

'What's eating you?' I asked, knowing full well what it was.

'The licensing laws give me the right to refuse anyone a drink. I don't have to give any explanation. What's more, I'm not going to,' said Fred.

I knew it was no good arguing with him because when I was under age he often used to get like that. He just used to point up to this car number plate he had above the bar with RU 18 on it. And that was that.

I put up with it then 'cos I didn't have a leg to stand on; now he was pulling a new one on me. I began to feel a real Charlie so I started to whistle just like as if I didn't care a fart. Then his missus, a big fat blonde in black satin and phoney pearls as big as chickens' eggs came up. 'Leave him be, Fred, and serve him. He looks like he could do with it.'

The guvnor pulled me a pint with a look like he hoped it would poison me, dead slow. 'One, that's all,' he said.

His missus gave me an old-fashioned look and patted my head. 'You shouldn't drink like that, Auk. It'll do you no good in the long run. You could be such a nice lad. I do hate to see it,' she said.

Even from the sound of her voice I knew she felt a bit

sorry for me. Now when someone is sorry for you it gives you the edge over them, so I thought I'd get her on my side a little bit more.

'I'm sorry about last night, really. It was just that the Old Lady took a turn for the worse and I was worried, and then on top of that I had to see Shy Ronnie about a job. I was so screwed up I got a bit boozed.'

She did one of her cluck cluck acts with her false teeth and said, 'That's all right luvvy, forget all about it. I just hope your Mum gets better.'

The guvnor – they didn't call him Big Ears for nothing – said to her, 'Lay off it old girl. His mother's perfectly all right. She was in the Public last night.'

'Yes, but she didn't want to come in,' I told him. 'She felt too queer. And that's a fact. The Old Man wanted her to keep him company. That's why she came out. Another pint please.' I got the order in sharpish while his missus was still there.

The guvnor shook his head like a cart horse whose nose bag's slipped, grabbed my money and said over his shoulder, 'I don't care if you drink yourself into an early grave son, just don't come the old soldier with me. I'm too long in the tooth for that kind of caper. I'm warning you, if you come in here, behave yourself. I had the job of cleaning up after you last night.'

His missus jerked her head towards him and dropped a big wink. 'Take no notice of him. He got out of bed the wrong side this morning. See me when you're ready to go Auk. I cleaned your hat up for you. It's been in the airing cupboard all night. It looks as good as new.'

As the boozer filled up people bought me drinks and we got to nattering. The next thing I knew the guvnor was sticking a towel over the pump handles and shouting, 'That's your lot. Time ladies and gentlemen *please*.'

It had been a jolly good session but I was back to square one with only ten bob to my name. Still, I felt on top of the world and even if my legs were acting like I was on a ship, the Salvation Army band had gone. All the worry about how I would cope with Doris had vanished. I just didn't care any more if it was the first time or not.

Back home the Old Man was just dozing off and my grub was on top of a saucepan. The Old Lady was real cheesed. 'If it's cold it's your own fault, you dirty stop out,' she said.

The Old Man came to just long enough to bawl me out. 'The sooner they bring back conscription the better,' he said, then fell asleep.

After sloshing most of the bottle of Big Game Hunter over myself I wobbled round to the address Doris had given me. Once I was nearly there I stopped a cab as I wanted to impress her like. I clambered in and gave him the address like I always used taxis. But he turned out to be a real mean turd.

'Out buster,' was all he said.

I was having a bit of trouble getting the words out clear, but I managed, 'Whatyer mean *Out*?'

'Like I said, *out*. Before I get the meter down we'll be there. It's Shanks's pony for you mate.'

It wasn't far, so I didn't mind. When I got there I had a real shock. Pleasant though. It was a great big block of flats with a garden in the front and a fountain in the middle with water belting out of a torch thing held by a naked dame.

The pond even had a whacking big goldfish in it, and I couldn't help thinking it might be worth making a call there one night and netting the lot. You could always flog goldfish to Tattooed Ted who runs a fair stall at Hampstead, and gives them away as prizes. I never knew why he was always short of fish to be honest with you, because not many people won them. His stall was as bent as a dog's back leg.

Doris lived on the fourth floor and there was a lift that didn't even need an attendant to take you up. You just pressed a button and that was that. Her milk was still outside when I pressed the button that set off a load of bells as loud as Big Ben. In the middle of the door was a little bit of glass no bigger than a torch bulb, but it must have been some kind of spy hole because Doris shouted through the letter box, 'Be with you in a jiffy, Auk.'

Next minute there was Doris – or Rosanna, take your pick – standing there in this long dressing gown thing. Only it wasn'a a thick woolly one but thin and lacy, like the ones you see those posh birds on the films wearing. Even though she wasn't dressed she was made up to kill with that dark blue stuff round her eyes and enough lipstick on to ruin a million collars.

Grabbing my arm like I'd just come back from the war or something she pulled me inside. 'This is a lovely surprise. You were so sloshed last night I never imagined you'd remember.'

'Course I didn't forget,' I said and I lifted my Sunset Boulevard just like they did in those clapped-out old Spring in Park Lane movies.

'I see you got your hat back Auk. I'm so pleased.'

Reminding me of last night made me feel like belting her one, but I didn't see no point in mucking things up so early in the game.

Doris's pad was really something to rave about. There wasn't even a fire in it yet it was as warm as a watchman's hut – just these radiator things round the walls. In the middle was this coffee table that was so long you could have kipped on it. And although there was a sofa and armchairs there was still lots of room left. But what got me was this big booze cabinet in the corner. When you lifted the lid a light went on and all the bottles and glasses came popping up on a glass shelf.

On one wall was a long row of ducks all flying after each other like they wanted to peck each other's arses. Doris obviously had loot.

Walking across the carpet was like trudging through a snow drift but I made it without snow shoes. Then I skimmed my titfer hoping to make one of the ducks as a hat rack but I missed.

Doris was still clinging to my arm as if it was a life belt. 'It *really* is nice to see you. Have you eaten?'

'Yes thanks,' I said. Frankly, I had a bit of the wind-up as I'd never been in such a posh drum before. 'I noshed at home, Rosanna.'

'Not Rosanna. Doris when I'm at home,' she said and gave me a playful jab in the ribs that set the roast beef and beer into competition.

'Knock it off, Doris,' I said, feeling a trifle narked.

With that she just grabbed me round the neck and planted a smacker on my mouth that left so much lipstick behind you could have scraped it off with a putty knife.

'Go on. That couldn't hurt a great big cuddly boy like you,' she said. 'I'm glad you've eaten though. I have too. Now, how about a drink?'

'Don't mind if I do,' I answered back.

'What'll you have? Martini? Scotch? Gin? You name it, I've got it,' she said.

Before going over to the drink box she had to give me another mauling.

'What about a Martini?' she asked.

Now I didn't want to let on that I didn't know what the hell it was. I only know from the flicks that butlers hand them round on silver trays. If it was good enough for them, it would certainly do for yours truly.

'Suit me down to the ground,' I said and started worrying whether I should stand there in the middle of the room or park my pants on one of the seats.

Doris was fiddling with bottles like she was a chemist or something. 'Dry or dry dry?' she asked me.

'As it comes will do me fine, Doris,' I called back.

I was still standing in the middle of the room like a spare prick at a wedding when she came over with two glasses. 'If that doesn't put some lead in your pencil Auk, I don't know what will,' she said.

Then she linked arms with me and somehow or other I was drinking her drink and she was drinking mine. I couldn't help thinking how tight-fisted she was because they was such small glasses, a lot less than half a pint even. But what a kick they had! I thought for one minute the top of my nut was going to blow clean off. I'd said, 'Down the hatch,' and knocked it back in one.

'Take it easy,' she said in a way that made me think she was worried about me dropping dead on her carpet. 'Have

59

another one and drink it *slowly*. I want to talk.'

Somehow I made the sofa without *too* much trouble. Doris filled up again and sat down beside me. I realised she didn't have a stitch on under the coat thing because she stretched her legs out and hooked her toes round the coffee table and dragged it over to the sofa. She tapped her glass against mine and said, 'Cheers, darling. Now drink up.'

'Listen,' I said. 'You were just moaning that I was drinking too quick. Make your mind up.'

'I have,' she said. And with that she was all over me. Now I knew from the car ride that she was partial to my earholes, but I didn't expect her to act like she hadn't had a square meal in months. 'Lay off,' I told her. 'I thought you said you'd eaten.'

'Auk' – yum – 'you're so' – 'young' – yum – 'and clean and nice' – yum. She went rabbiting on taking a bite between each word.

'Listen Doris, this suit won't be worth wearing if you go on like this all the time,' I told her through a mouthful of hair.

'I'll buy you another one. Lots of suits. Shirts, cuff links, shoes, ties, hats, everything. How about that?'

I was getting right panicky because I had never had anything like this before, and I wasn't coping too well. Doris was now turning the back of my neck into a third course.

What's more, I was a little suspicious. 'What's the catch?' I asked. 'Why all this cobblers about clothes?'

'There's no catch, darling. I like you. Really I do,' she said, returning to my lug holes again. 'It's that you're so . . . well, *you*.'

Whatever I had been expecting her to say it certainly wasn't that. I ask you, if I wasn't me, who the hell could I be?

'Let's not talk here,' she said and jumped up like she'd been singed with a blow lamp. She then grabbed my hand and pulled me up just as if we were going to dance the Conga on our own. We belted across the room and she managed to pick up a bottle from the cabinet without even slowing down. *And* take the white telephone off the hook.

'In here. It's more homely,' she said.

Homely! You can say that again. With knobs on. Because the next thing I knew we were in her bedroom. Cut my throat if I tell a lie. It made the Savoy look like a doss house. Most of it was taken up with this bed that was so big you could have played the cup final on it. And *glass*. There was glass everywhere. It was all round the walls and even the ceiling had a great big mirror on it.

Right by the side of the bed was half an elephant's leg all hollowed out and filled with school canes and those whips you see toffee-nosed birds belting their horses with when they trot round Hyde Park. But before I had a chance to have a proper gander Doris was on the bed and out of the lacy thing she was wearing. 'Make yourself comfortable, Auk,' she said, patting the sheets by her side.

Mate! If I tell you I didn't know what to do, I am telling the whole truth and nothing but. Doris was starkers in her birthday suit. I realised then that though I was a new boy to it, dear old Doris was no stranger to the pork dagger.

It sounds soppy I know, but I panicked. I looked at the watch I didn't have on and said, 'Blimey, Doris. I must rush. Got a date with my girl friend.'

'No you haven't,' she said, and put a wrist lock on me that would have got a submission in any wrestling match I've ever watched.

'Throw your things on the chair, and stop being silly,' she said. She sounded like someone talking to a puppy that hasn't been house trained.

I wanted to, and yet I didn't want to if you know what I mean. Letting you into a secret, I'd often imagined a time like this. *Now* I had this horrible feeling that if I let this slide I wouldn't get another chance. On the other hand, I was dead scared I was going to make a right rooster of it.

Doris stuck her arm over the edge of the bed, grabbed the bottle and took a long swig.

'You'd better go home then Auk,' she said all sulky like. 'I forgot, you're still only a boy really.'

That did it for me. It was like a red rag to a bull to be called that. I whipped off my clothes like I was going for a dip in the public swimming baths and did a fair old swallow dive on to the bed. But all Doris could say was, 'Aren't you going to take your socks off?'

It's a funny thing, but for some reason or other I had deliberately kept them on. I knew it wasn't because my feet were dirty or pongy because I had washed up and down before meeting Shy Ronnie. Somehow, I didn't feel quite so *starkers* with them on. Not that it mattered because Doris *made* me take them off.

I don't really like talking about the rest. Those Martinis and the lunchtime wallop had done something to me and the more I worried about it the badder it got. Doris didn't even get narked, and that made it even worse. I was going to rush out of the flat, honest, because any moment now I thought Doris was going to crease herself laughing.

'The trouble is,' I told her, 'I just don't fancy you.'

'You will in a minute,' she said, all sexy voiced. 'Just relax and let Doris sort it out. I'm the snake charmer from old Baghdad.'

Any other time I might have felt like laughing. Now I just felt like a bloody good cry I can tell you straight.

Then what Doris started to do made me feel proper shy. I knew the French did it but I never knew people did it here. Those mirrors didn't help none either, 'cos whichever way I looked I could see us both. I was real glad no one else could.

If it had been up to me I would have smashed the lot of them because at one stage we was struggling so much we rolled off the bed. When I looked up I thought what a bloody silly picture we made up there on the ceiling.

Doris hauled me back up on the bed and started all over again. 'Look,' I told her. 'It's no good. I haven't got anything with me. I'm not putting no-one in the family way.' By now I was shouting my head off.

But Doris kept on and on until she rolled on her back and told me, 'Good boy Auk, you're ready now.' And I was.

It should have been dead easy, but it wasn't. I just couldn't find it and in the end Doris had to help.

Then she complained like hell that I had been in too

much of a hurry, but honestly I couldn't have cared less. At least I made it.

She soon calmed down though, and the next time was a lot better.

I stayed there the whole night and when I woke up I remembered I had to see Ronnie. As Doris made me breakfast I asked her about all those canes in the elephant's leg. She just gave me a peck and said, 'They're for naughty boys who can't be men.'

I didn't have a clue what she meant so I just said, 'O.K. Ask a silly question, get a silly answer.'

Before she would let me leave I had to promise to see her the next Sunday. I promised, but didn't mean it.

On the way down in the lift I found she had stuck a couple of fivers in my back pocket which cheered me up no end. I took a taxi to Shy Ronnie's office and even before I reached there I knew I would be going back to see her.

Only I wondered if she was on the level about all the things she'd promised me. It seemed worth finding out. What's more, I knew I could cope now, and a bird with a pad like that was worth keeping in with.

Chapter Eight

Shy Ronnie's showroom was on a main drag about ten minute away from my place. It was a brand new building, all strip lights and flashy dressed salesmen with suede shoes and fag holders. There were rows of motors in the windows and even on the pavement outside. All of them had signs on like 'One owner – low mileage' or 'Quick sale – bargain. Owner going abroad.'

As I pushed through the swing doors a salesman who was all teeth and tash was spinning a line of bull to a young couple holding hands by a second-hand car.

'I'm glad you like this one,' he was saying. 'Speaking personally, and I'd get shot if the boss heard me, this is the car I would recommend if my closest friend came in. Just one owner – an old lady who only used it to run to the shops in.'

The couple must have been stark raving bonkers to go to Shy Ronnie for a car. Everyone where I lived knew they'd been doctored with lead, sawdust and real thick oil, and you were lucky if you got the motor home before it collapsed or caught fire. Still, if they wanted to chuck their savings down the drain that was their funeral. Come to think of it, if they bought the car it probably would be. It was no skin off my nose. There's one born every minute. So I went right through the showroom up to this desk where a young bird was sitting plugging lines into a switchboard.

I began to feel like I was the invisible man the way she kept ignoring me. She would have let me take root if I hadn't flicked my dog end over the counter and hit her on the bonce with it.

Crikey, she started shaking her hair like it was going up in smoke any minute. 'How *dare* you?' she said in a voice that sounded like she'd got a mouthful of camphor balls.

'How dare I what?' I said, taking off her voice.

'Throw a lighted cigarette end at me,' she said, cold as charity.

'What d'you expect? I've been standing here so long someone's hung a hat on me.'

'There is no need to be rude. Who are you, and what do you want?'

'Not you, that's a cert. I've got a meet with your guvnor and he'll be choked if he finds out you kept me waiting. So you'd better pull your finger out.'

You could see from her face that she couldn't make up her mind how important I was. So she got all toffee nosed and said, 'What is your name? I'll ring through.'

Then she pointed to a door and told me to go to the second floor and take the first door on the right.

Shy Ronnie was sitting back in a big black armchair looking just like one of those fat-gutted chink statues you see in junk shops, except he had one of his broom handle cigars stuck in his north and south.

'Hullo Auk. Take a pew,' he said. There was a stiff back chair near the desk and another armchair just like his in the corner, so I took the armchair.

'Make yourself comfortable,' he said, kind of sarky like. 'Help yourself to a cigar too.'

In front of him there was a box as big as a suitcase, so I dug in. With that he started laughing so loud he broke into a fit of coughing and went as blue as the back end of a baboon. 'You've got plenty of brass, Auk, I'll say that for you.'

'Make your mind up. I'll put it back if you like.'

'No, keep it now you've got it. There's plenty more where that came from.'

The cigar was in a kind of metal tube and when I took it out it was wrapped up in cork so thin you could have rolled a fag with it. It even had his name printed in gold on it. He certainly had class, all right.

'Still want to work for me?' he asked.

'Depends on what you're offering. I'm not going into the slave trade though. Not for you or no one.'

65

It was better I thought to put my cards on the table before he started offering me a job down one of his pits up to my crutch in grease, doctoring one of his clapped-out motors.

'You don't have to worry one little bit. I wouldn't let you near my workshops, I only employ experts. Christ, they need to be to get some of the junk even moving.'

That was encouraging. 'What you got in mind then? I'm all ears.'

'Listen, I like you Auk, but if any of this ever gets beyond these four walls I'll send someone round to cut your ears off and pin them to the seat of your pants so every time you sit down you'll get earache. O.K.?'

There was a big smile on his fat face, but I knew he wasn't horsing.

I tried to make it sound as if I couldn't care less, but the cigar smoke was getting in my eyes and I felt like choking because I'd inhaled which you shouldn't with a cigar. 'You don't have to put the bite on. I know the score. I'm like the three monkeys.'

And I couldn't help thinking he really must like me otherwise he wouldn't be shooting his mouth off.

'This isn't my only business as you probably know. I got other connections. I won't bore you with it all, but at the moment I'm on the look out for a good rent man. Now, you're a good beefy boy and that's what I need. Someone they won't want to argue with or fall into arrears with. O.K.?'

Actually, I felt a bit let down. 'Nix. Not for me. I got bigger plans than trotting round crummy flats collecting rent.'

'One needs to dot the *i*s and cross the *t*s with you, I see, lad. It's not that kind of rent at all. Perhaps I should have said insurance. You see Auk, there are a load of clubs, shops, barrows and what have you that pay me money to ensure they are kept free of trouble. The contributions naturally vary according to the size of the concern. With me now?'

'I'm not that dumb. You should have said protection in

the first place,' I told him.

'As I said, I prefer the word insurance. We never mention the other thing around here,' said Ronnie. 'You won't have to do anything if someone doesn't pay. Just tell me. I'll make sure they see sense. O.K.?'

'O.K.,' I said, and couldn't help thinking that this habit of Ronnie's saying O.K. every few seconds was catching like the measles. 'What about wages?'

'How about £25 a week, and I'll put you on the staff as a junior salesman?'

'Make it thirty and a car and I'm on,' I said, not thinking for one second he'd agree. Still, there's no harm in trying as the constipated old woman kept saying.

'O.K. you're on. We won't quarrel about the odd nicker. Call in tomorrow and I'll have everything lined up. I want to introduce you to Gorgeous George – only don't ever let him hear you call him that. He'll take you round and introduce you to our clients. O.K.?'

'O.K.,' I said, feeling for once like I was really someone. Even the cigar began to taste all right. So I hitched up my trousers, crossed my knees and leant back and enjoyed the life to come. Then I thought of the faces in our street when I rolled up in my own motor and parked outside the flats. I decided I'd give a kid a bob to keep an eye on it and see no one let the tyres down like I used to.

Shy Ronnie brought me back to earth. 'Hey, don't go crashing your fat swede in that chair. I've got business to attend to. Go home to bed if you've got a hangover.'

'Do me a big favour *please*.' I thought I might as well make him sit up and take notice. 'I was on the nest all night and I feel a bit ropy that's all.' From the look on his face I could tell he was impressed.

'You youngsters. You could learn us old uns a thing or two and no mistake. Who was the lady?'

'Just someone I met, that's all,' I said, trying to make it sound as if it was something that happened to me every twenty minutes. I didn't see no point in filling him in too much about my private life.

Then all of a sudden he threw back his frog's head and

67

started laughing. 'Oh my dear God. Doris,' he said.

He was laughing so much he had to wipe his eyes with his silk hankie.

'What's so funny about that?' I asked.

'Take no notice of me. I can see the funny side – you can't,' he said, and still went on shaking and wobbling like a bowl of jellied eels. 'Tried to ring her up myself all yesterday, but the phone was off the hook. Thought she had a client. As a matter of fact I was going to pop round.'

'What you mean, client?'

'Like you, Doris works for me. She's on the payroll, Auk. One of my best girls believe you me.' Then he looked at me with this who-are-you-kidding look. 'Don't tell me you didn't tumble she was on the game? I'd have thought that palace of varieties of hers would have let on she was a Tom.'

It could have been the cigar, I don't know. But all of a sudden I felt like death warmed up. Screwing a Tom is bad enough, but it's even worse when she belongs to your boss. Never mind, he was still laughing his bonce off, so at least he wouldn't be sending anyone round with a shiv to see I didn't get my oats again. I still had the wind-up though. I could see myself out of work before I'd even started.

'Sorry about that, Ronnie. I wouldn't have gone if I'd known. Straight up and no kid.'

'Don't worry about it. A slice off a cut loaf is never missed, son. Go round whenever you feel like some grumble and grunt. If Doris has taken a shine to you, all well and good. Better to keep it in the family I always say. I must say, I can understand her fancying a big lad like you after all the dirty pervs she has to cope with.'

As you have gathered, I'm clued up on most things but I hadn't the vaguest what he was on about. So I just nodded and said, 'I'm with you all the way there, Ronnie.'

'Glad to hear that,' he said. 'I've never forced a girl into it yet, and that's the honest. You ask any of them. They can pull out any time as far as Ronnie is concerned. That goes for Doris, too.'

Just then a well dressed geezer busted in. You could have

shaved a three day growth off with the crease in his trousers. In a proper posh voice he said, 'Excuse me barging in, sir, but we have a dissatisfied client in the showroom. Thought I'd better have a little tête-à-tête with you first.'

'What's his beef?' Ronnie asked him.

'Quite unjustifiably,' said the tailor's dummy, 'he is complaining that the car I sold him broke down on the way to the coast. He's now moaning that it will cost him sixty pounds to get it back on the road.'

'And what am I supposed to do about it?' Ronnie asked him.

'That is my point. You see he is complaining that we have broken the guarantee.'

'What guarantee? He hasn't got one. Tell him to read the small print on the form he signed.'

Old fancy pants put his oar in again. 'I did suggest to him that while we could not accept any responsibility, we were prepared to buy the car back for, say, twenty pounds less than he paid, and sell him a similar model but in better condition for an additional forty pounds. Would that meet with your approval, sir?'

'Sure, and give him a cigar to show there's no ill feeling on our part,' said Ronnie. 'I'll tell you what, give him a couple of cigars.'

And the salesman went out hugging the two cigars like they was made of 14 carat gold.

Ronnie turned to me then and said, 'O.K. I'll see you tomorrow.'

As I was going out he called after me, 'There's only one thing Auk. See that our Doris don't give you a cold in your J.T.'

I didn't need no crystal ball to know what he was talking about. For one horrible moment it felt like someone had dropped an ice cube down my shirt. It didn't last though. It's only worry that killed the cat, I say.

Downstairs the teeth and tash salesman was thumbing through a pile of fivers that would have choked a hippo. There was an empty space where the car the old woman did her shopping in had been.

At another table a young bloke sat with Ronnie's cigar stuck in his mouth busy signing a new H.P. form. I couldn't help noticing that fancy pants was puffing at the other cigar.

The frump behind the switchboard called 'Goodbye' as I passed. There's never no point in making enemies out of people you might want to use some time, so I ambled back.

If I say she was a frump, I don't mean she was a *bad* looker. It was just that she hadn't the vaguest how to do her hair or what to wear.

'I hear you are coming to work for us,' and I could tell from her voice she didn't live local.

'That's right. Start tomorrow.'

'Good. I'll show you where we have our lunch. It's very clean and wholesome and quite inexpensive.'

Just for a sec I thought she was having me on, but I realised that was the way she always talked. It was nice really, and a change from the birds I knew who never talked about anything but noshing. I like posh talk myself. I said I would take her up on it some time, and on the way out I took a swift gander at her pins. She may have looked a straight Jane and no nonsense, but she had a fair old pair of hams on her.

Next morning Ronnie gave me Gorgeous George's address to go to and told me he would take me on the rounds.

Gorgeous lived in a rank seedy pad in the basement of a big tumbling down house off the Bayswater Road. When I got there he was sitting on the edge of his bed in his vest and pants playing 'Home Sweet Home' on an accordion. Although he wasn't even dressed, he had this turned down black trilby on his head and a fag dangling from his mouth which was all twisted down at the corner where someone had given him a fistful of knuckle duster. He was one of the ugliest bleeders you ever saw, with a face that had more lines on it than a road map.

They were all reminders of the time he was gone over by

a mob-handed bunch of shivvers. They chopped him to ribbons with their razors when they trapped him in the passage of a house. It took a doctor all night plus ten quarts of blood and about fifty miles of cat gut to put his mug together again. They'd made a good job of it, but he still wasn't no oil painting. Naturally, he got nicknamed Gorgeous after that.

Ever since then George had lived in this basement pad because he had an emergency exit through the window and up the area steps. And he had forked out £150 on his own early warning system. A burglar alarm firm had fitted hidden wires under the lino outside the flat so whenever anyone walked down the passage it sounded like the whole of London's fire brigade had been called out.

When I called the bells didn't ring for very long so George had obviously been tipped off that I would call. The room smelt like the bat house at the zoo and there was a whacking great fire blazing in the hearth. Which wasn't bad considering it was the middle of summer. George didn't seem to notice it. The heat or the pong.

'Blimey, you must be cold-blooded George to want a fire,' I said.

George stopped playing – and that was no heart-break neither – buttoned up the squeeze box and put it carefully on top of the wardrobe where there was ten more trilbies exactly like the one he was wearing.

'You can share my little secret. I'm roasting alive, mate. That there little blaze ain't for warmth, it's for protection.' His bashed-up old mouth made him look like a ventriloquist because he didn't even move his lips one little bit.

'When the alarm goes off I get a shovel full of hot coal and stand by to heave it over anyone who busts in. By the time they've cooled off I'll be out of the window, up the stairs and away. Right.'

George wasn't the most talkative gink alive. He didn't even ask what I wanted. He just went to his wardrobe and took out a clean shirt. Inside, hanging up in a row were about eight suits all the same colour as his hats.

Gorgeous took his time over dressing, trying on about

71

fifty ties before he got the right one. 'Auk, ain't it?' he asked.

'Right first time,' I answered.

'Good. We'll pile into the motor straight away and do the milk round then.'

His car was one of those American jobs, as long as an aircraft carrier and just about as wide. No sooner had we piled in than he switched on the steam radio to Woman's Hour.

'My favourite programme, this,' he said. 'You hear some good talks you know. Only a couple of weeks ago there was one on badgers. Bet you didn't know they bury their dead. Now own up you didn't. Not many people do,' he said.

I'd survive without knowing that, I thought, but I didn't make a murmur because George was a real hard case. He was so mean I bet he even enjoyed cutting himself shaving.

'Bet you didn't know too that they marry for life. Badgers do. Just like swans and human beings,' he said. 'Nocturnal too, they are.'

During the day we took in about fifty odd drums – all kinds of places – clubs, betting shops, stalls, pin table arcades and gambling casinos. Everyone seemed genuinely pleased to see George, and after a little chat at each one he was handed an envelope which he tucked in his brief case. And he *never* left without shaking hands.

But you could tell there was a real mean streak in him, because at one fruit stall near a railway station the bloke who ran it said he couldn't manage it this week as prices had gone up at the market.

Gorgeous just said, 'That's all right mate. You can't get blood out of a stone. Everyone goes through a thin time. Just do what you can and that's all any of us can expect.'

Then he leant over to swipe an apple and the whole barrow somehow got tilted up and there was fruit all over the road. Gorgeous said, 'Oops a daisy. Now how did that happen?' and he began to squash the fruit with his feet.

The barrow boy looked like he was going to burst into tears.

Gorgeous took a big bite out of the apple and stuck the

core in the bloke's top pocket. 'He'll be calling in future,' he said, pointing to me. 'Remember the face.'

Apart from that, we never had no trouble to talk of. Mind you, George got the flavour for rum and black after we'd been in a few drinking clubs. It seemed to be the routine to have one set up ready for him as he walked in, and after a while he was as tight as a fiddler's bitch. Not that it showed in his walk or talk or anything. It was just his attitude. Like at one bar when he suddenly turned round on me and said, 'Who the hell are you? You been following me around all day. Now scarper. Take a ball of chalk sharpish.'

Straight up, I felt a proper nana when he turned his back on me and called up another rum and black. That went down without touching the sides. Then he turned and said, 'You're an unsociable so and so. Don't say a word and won't have a drink. If you're working with me mate, you'll have to be a lot less off-handed, a lot less.'

As we went on I cottoned on that he couldn't help it and didn't mean it. Maybe it was the clobberings he had taken that had got him all mixed up. I got used to him giving me the bum's rush one minute and the next telling me what a great future I had.

Our very last call was a club named 'The Pink Penguin' which was down an alley off of Goodge Street. Gorgeous hammered on the door and a white faced yobo looked out of this little square hole which appeared all of a sudden in the middle. 'Come on in, George.' He said it like he really meant it.

Inside it was very posh with ritzy red chairs and a smashing bar and lots of lights made to look like candles. Naturally, there was a rum and black waiting ready on the bar. A foreign looking character behind the bar held out his mitt to George who shook it like they was meeting for the first time for a hundred years. I couldn't help spotting that his fingers were all missing about an inch from the tips. Gorgeous caught me staring and said, 'Caught them in a bacon slicer, didn't you Frank?'

Frank grinned and said like a parrot, 'That's right

73

George. Caught them in a bacon slicer.' He laughed as if it was the funniest thing he'd ever heard.

After the envelope was passed over George had a couple more snorts and was all ready to go when he said out of the blue like, 'Frank, hand us that bottle of scotch.'

'Sure,' said Frank. And George promptly smashed it on the floor and walked out without saying another word.

Back in the jalopy I couldn't help saying. 'What you do that for, George? He paid didn't he?'

George said, 'Frank's a hard case, mate. He has to be reminded every now and then. See those fingers? He never caught them in no slicer. I did that with a chopper. He wouldn't pay the rent because he thought he was big enough to get away with it. Now you must never allow that, 'cos a bargain is a bargain. Even if it's not in writing. I strolled in one night when he had closed up and was doing the tills.

' "Frank," I said, "you've been naughty." And I sang "Hold your hand out you naughty boy". I'll never forget the look on his kisser. He thought it was some kind of game. He held his mitt out and whack. He's never missed since.'

Before we knocked off proper George paid the money into the office. Then he took me to his local. In the saloon this old cow with holes in her stockings put the bite on him for a bar. Gorgeous coughed up without a murmur. He even stood her a drink.

'You'd never credit it, would you, but that old slag used to be a real looker.'

On an old upright in the corner a skinny bloke was knocking seven bells out of 'Nelly Dean'. George called for two large scotches in one glass and took it over. 'Play "Bless this House" or I'll stick this somewhere that'll make you play standing up for the rest of your natural.'

Within fifty seconds the whole boozer was singing it with George's voice louder than anyone's. I could have sworn he was crying.

After it was over and he'd almost killed the pianist with a friendly slap on the back he bought me a pint. 'If there's one thing I love it's good music,' he said to me. 'You just can't beat it.' Then suddenly he got all starry-eyed and told

74

me how he came to play the squeeze box.

'I was doing a five stretch and Ronnie sent me this accordion loaded with snout. Wonderful present, mind you, but when I finished smoking it I was left with the squeeze box and four years still to do. I didn't have no option but to learn to play it. I've never regretted it mind you.'

By closing time, George had forgotten who I was again. 'If you keep tailing me I'll chop you up for cat's meat,' he said. 'Now shove off.'

He could get knotted as far as I was concerned because he was too stoned to drive me home anyway. There was also the danger that he might start singing again. So I decided to catch a taxi and go home.

The last words I heard as I slipped through the curtains that kept the draught out was George shouting, 'Where's my mate? What've you bastards done with my mate?'

Chapter Nine

Bang on the dot of ten I called round to the office next morning. After all the Nelson's blood he'd stashed away the night before, I was surprised to see Gorgeous already there. Shy Ronnie on the other hand looked as if he hadn't left the chair since I left. He was obviously one of those up with the lark geezers because I spotted two cigar ends in the ashtray and the one he was sharpening his teeth on had about two miles of ash on the end.

George didn't say a dicky bird when I ambled in. He just flicked the brim of his black titfer with two fingers like you see cowboys do. Ronnie though shouted as if I was two blocks away, 'Put a shine on your pants, Auk.'

This time I had to take the stiff back chair because they both had the armchairs. Still, I was near the cigar box.

Suddenly George said, 'I've just been telling Ronnie here that he's made a real find in you. Worth your weight in Tom Foolery.' Now it really griped me when George went on rabbiting like that ... saying Ronnie here I mean. After all, it's not as if there was a whole army of them falling around the room. And all that slang was so old it went out with the ark.

'I was just saying,' he went on, 'that I think I ought to run you round the manor a few more times then you'll be O.K. to take over. No point in rushing the hand over of a responsible number like this. We owe it to the customers to get to know you first.'

Ronnie nodded like he was having to decide about giving some nigger country their freedom. 'He's dead right, Auk. I don't see no point in you being dumped in the deep end. Right.'

I looked at George's beat-up fizzog and thought that if he could do it so could I. After all, he'd shown me what to

76

do if anyone got stroppy. My age didn't worry me neither. Billy the Kid was even younger than me when he was in his prime, and no one could say he was a slouch. Still, there didn't seem no point in bitching.

'I'm easy either way,' I told them both. 'I think I can handle it O.K. though.' I looked down at my nails just to make it look like I was casual.

'I bet you can, lad. I bet you can,' said Ronnie. 'But we won't push your luck. Have a couple more trips. Then it's all yours. What say you, George?'

George looked like he'd been asked to work out in his head how long it would take ten million Irish labourers to dig their way down to Australia. First he tipped his hat over his eyes, then he cracked his knuckles and even went for a short stroll round the room before saying, 'Can't do no great harm. If there's any argy bargy, me and the lads can soon sort it out.'

The *lads* were the strong armed mob called Ronnie's Regulars. They were a ripe bunch of villains, who kept in the background until there was any bother. They didn't have to be called in much. They were like crabs on your rocks – you didn't have to see them to know they was around.

It went so quiet then that you could almost have heard the cigar ash drop all over the front of Ronnie's waistcoat. As he brushed it off with his big mitt he had a real moan. 'You know something. There's a fortune waiting for the bloke who can make cigar ash drop off in a solid lump. It might be good for carpets but it mucks your clothes up, no mistake about it.'

Frankly, I didn't see no real point hanging around while he raved on, so I said to him, 'What's on the me and you today?'

'Nothing at all. Take the day off. There won't be a dicky bird doing till the next collection. You'll just have to get used to the routine Auk. This is a bit like the army – lots of waiting around before the next exercise. O.K. George?'

It was O.K. with George – as usual. 'If he's at too much of a loose end Ronnie, I could show him round a couple of the near beers. Let him get the feel, if that's O.K. with you.'

It was, so I was told that one night I could watch the running of one of Ronnie's clip houses. They was an even better investment than television. You didn't need no licence to print your own money. The mugs gave it to you in fistfuls.

'I'll mosey then if it's O.K. with you,' I said and headed for the door. I thought I might call in at the flea pit and take in the new gangster film which was all about this Yank who kept a pool full of crocodiles which he fed with the geezers who double-crossed him.

As I got through the door Ronnie called me back, 'Just one thing, Auk. You shedding a tear for Doris yet?'

Now I did wish he wouldn't keep on like that because ever since he'd first mentioned it I found I kept looking at the old J.T. to see if I had caught a cold. Every few minutes I was nipping into the bog just to have a quick dekko. It was early days yet, but he'd put the wind up me, no kid. I didn't want my nose dropping off or anything like that.

I was still thinking about it when I walked through the showroom, and I was miles away until I heard Miss Frump shout across, 'Mr Grant, do you want to take me up on that luncheon invitation?'

'Hiya sex bomb,' I said to her as I walked to her desk. She hadn't improved much since the last time I saw her, but as my Old Man used to say, you don't look at the mantelpiece when you poke the fire. Actually, she didn't look *too* bad although no one was going to go leaping off Tower Bridge if she had turned them down. As I had nothing to do I didn't see no real harm in punishing myself with her company for an hour or so.

'Tell you what,' I told her. 'Let's skip your noshery and I'll take you out for some grub. How's that? I'm all right for the necessary. So it can be on me this time.'

'I'd love to,' she said. 'May I make a suggestion? You won't be offended I hope.'

Honestly, that's just how she talked. You can go off people real quick. I didn't mind her making a suggestion and I wasn't going to be offended about it. After all I didn't have to agree to it.

Well, her idea was to go to this little wop place where they actually wore penguin get-up and they saved money on the lighting by having candles stuck in the tops of bottles. And the dirty sods didn't bother to clean them ever because the wax had dripped all down the side until it was a couple of inches thick. I'd always kept clear of those places myself because I like to see what nosh I'm putting away. You get in some of these wop places and before you know it you're digging in to some poor old lady's tabby that disappeared the night before. Me, I'm a great one for the old cod and chips as it's one thing you can't muck about with. You can't go lassoing a bit of rock salmon down a dark alley. If you think I'm making it up let me tell you that I had a mate who had chicken once and found some fur on it.

As she started putting on her coat – a big fluffy thing with a high collar – she started off again. 'I think you'll like this place. It's only a short bus ride and we'll be back in plenty of time.'

'We'll grab a cab,' I told her. 'Buses is for the hicks from the sticks.'

It didn't take long to get a cab and as I piled in she tugged me by the back of the coat and gave me a real old-fashioned look. 'What's eating you?' I asked her. 'Don't you like the look of the driver or something?'

'You should let a lady enter first,' she said. 'It's very bad manners.'

'Look mate. Who's paying for this cab, you or me?' I asked. So I got back in and said, 'If you're coming you'd better let him know where to. He ain't a thought reader you know.'

Like most birds she didn't want to lose out on a nosh-up so she gave the driver the address and got in and then went off into a huff. She sat all huddled up in the corner staring out of the window and acting like I got a dose of leprosy or something. Me, I just lit up a weed and stared out of the other window at the birds walking along the pavement.

The next thing she had moved closer to me and was

79

saying, 'If we are going out to lunch it would be a good idea if we introduced each other. My name is Pamela. My friends call me Pam. What's yours?'

'You can call me Auk, everyone else does.'

The way she looked at me you'd have thought I'd said my name was King Farouk or something. 'Auk. That's a funny name. Surely that's not your real name.'

'Look, I don't go a bundle on Pamela,' I told her. 'But I'm not extracting the urine, am I? Now that's what people call me and if you don't like it you can either lump it or get out. I'm easy. Dead easy, see?'

'As you wish,' she said, and from her voice I knew I was right back in cold storage. 'If I had known you were going to be so unpleasant I wouldn't have come,' she said.

'Look, knock it off for god's sake,' I told her. 'I haven't done nothing. I can't say a thing without you going off the handle.'

That's done it, I thought to myself, because she picked up her bag and gloves and was hammering on the window to the driver and shouting, 'Stop, stop.' I thought I'd made a right ricket of it but she just pulled back the sliding door and told him, 'This will do us fine.' I felt glad she hadn't shoved off because I was feeling peckish and anyway I didn't like the idea of any bird, not even a crummy one like Pamela, giving me the old heave ho.

We managed to get into the noshery in the end, but not before she'd had another go at me for letting her get out of the cab first.

'You want to make up your mind for once,' I told her. 'When I get *in* first I'm wrong, and when I get *out* last I'm still wrong.'

Then while I was paying the driver she went into a great long lecture about manners making man. I'd just about had enough so I told her to belt up or be belted. That quietened her down but not for long, oh no. She soon found something to pick holes in. I'd been sitting at the table a couple of minutes and she still hadn't joined me, and when I looked up there she was standing by the coat hangers looking like little orphan Annie, pointing to her own coat which she still had on. 'Aren't you going to help a lady with her coat, Auk?' She said it all sweet like which as you know is how a dolly talks when she wants to tear you off a strip.

'Hang it up and stop poncing about,' I yelled back. Poor old Pam, she went as red as a tomato and hung her coat up without saying another word. Now if only she'd done that in the first place there wouldn't have been no problem.

After the waiter had pulled the chair back for her to sit down and done a bit of sweeping up with the white rag he had over his arm, he handed us a menu that was not much bigger than the *Daily Mirror*. Next thing I knew there was another greasy wop standing at my elbow. 'How many of you blokes are needed to get grub for two?' I asked, rather snooty. 'There's only going to be one tip mate and if you want to split it down the middle that's O.K. by me.' He showed me his teeth which he got on *our* National Health.

'I am the wine waiter sir. Would you like to order some drinks?'

I realised I'd dropped a real clanger but I wasn't going to show out on it. 'I know that, mate, but there's still only going to be one tip. Now, what you got?'

Well, he stubbed this finger that hadn't seen a nail file for years on something I couldn't make out on the list because it was foreign, and told me, 'That is a very nice red wine, sir. Or this – a very nice white wine.'

I'm a strictly beer man so I hadn't the foggiest what he was nattering about, but I thought I'd better act as if I did so I said, 'What other colours you got?' I don't know whether you've ever noticed it but foreigners can get very stroppy when they've only been here a dog watch and act like they was the same as us. Because the next minute this waiter was bending down to his knees laughing his head off and saying, 'Oh sir, very funny. Yes sir, I like that – "Any other colours".'

The other waiter thought it was funny too and he had to use his white cloth to wipe the tears away. Now I didn't mind anyone having a good giggle but I like to know what it's all about. So I gave the wine bloke a sharp tap on the shins with the toe of my winkle picker. He really had something to cry over then. 'Oops, sorry Antonio,' I said to him. 'My foot slipped. Now you just tell me what's so funny and we can all join in.'

Dear little Pamela as usual was doing her nut and sticking her oar in. She was up from the table and rolling up his trouser leg as if I'd whacked it with a sledge hammer. And all the time she's saying, 'Don't worry at all, we'll have the red.'

Red, white or blue, I couldn't have given a monkey's. All I wanted was a drink and some grub.

'For Christ's sake sit down,' I bellowed at her. 'He ain't going to lose his leg. Anyway it was an accident. Look, Antonio, when you've finished playing hop scotch we'll have a bottle of the red like she says. Then maybe your oppo can rustle up some grub, eh?'

Now there's one thing about waiters. You just can't offend them if there's a tip in the offing. Before you knew it, old Hopalong Cassidy had limped off to get the wine while his mate was bashing Pamela's shell-like with ideas about what we should eat.

I couldn't understand a dicky bird about what he was saying. He couldn't mention any of the grub without making with his paws like a music conductor. So I left it all to Pamela.

Actually, when it turned up it wasn't a bad nosh at all and the red biddy went down a real treat. The bill didn't though. When I looked at it I almost went through the roof. The only thing that stopped me was the glass grapes they'd hung all over the place. I didn't want to cut myself to ribbons.

The bill came to three quid and I put five bob on the plate. After all, it wasn't bad. But like all wops he didn't think the tip was enough. He kept giving me a real hard-up look and limped so bad you'd have thought he spent a week in a bear trap. Me, I'd have left it at that but for Pamela, she was having a go at my shins and muttering, 'It should be at least ten per cent, Auk.' She felt so strongly about it that she took some dough out of her purse and stuck it on the plate with mine. That was O.K. with me, and I didn't even point out that's what the Yanks did and bitched it up for everyone else.

Thankfully we didn't have to go through all the cobblers of who puts whose coat on because one of the wops held it up for her and the silly nit gave him another tanner, honest. Me, I can't stand anyone helping me on with my coat. It's like those posh bogs where you go for a jimmy riddle and the geezer insists on brushing down your coat collar. Now I've heard about blokes who splash their boots but never their collars. That's life though. You'll always find some smart alec making a job out of nothing.

On the pavement outside Pam was hopping from one foot to another and looking at her watch all the time. 'Oh dear,' she kept saying, 'I'll be late back.' Now if she said it once she said it twelve million times.

We finally got a cab and were no sooner inside than she turned on the old tape recorder again. 'Really Auk. You behaved quite abominably to those two poor waiters. They were only doing their job. You could be such a *nice* boy if you didn't go out of your way to be so thoroughly unpleasant.'

Well, when a bird gets on that track there's not a lot you can do about it. Of course if you know them well enough a good whack sometimes helps, but with Pamela you never knew which way she would take it. I mean, any bird who gets hot under her briefs because you get into a cab first is likely to have a fit and head for the nearest convent if you belted her.

'Look Pam, you'll have to take me as you find me. If you think I'm going to turn into St Paul you've got another think coming,' I said to her. And just to show I wasn't really narked I slipped my arm round her shoulder and she didn't seem to mind that at all, in fact she leant against me all soppy like. Not for long though. 'Cos when I let the old mitt slide down smooth and sly to get a handful of Robin Redbreast she got all quivery and jumpy. 'Now please stop it, Auk. I'm not like that at all. Anyway, the driver can see us.' And she started fussing around with her hair which I hadn't even touched. Not that I was really interested at that time of day but you know what it's like, a doll expects you to. And if you don't she may think there's something queer about you and spread it round the manor.

The drive wasn't long enough for me to really get any real work done, but I'd done enough to know that dear old Pam had a pair that would have been pushed for space in a bowler hat. You wouldn't have thought so though to look at her. She was a right funny bird and no mistake. Most birds with a pair of Charlies like hers would have broadcast it, but not Pam. She seemed to dress like she was ashamed of them.

Once I paid off the driver she could hardly wait to get back to her plugs and earphones. 'We'll have to tie up again some time, eh?' I said, trying to make it sound as if it was the last thing I wanted.

'I'd love that. I really would,' she said. 'I don't suppose you'd like to join me tonight. I'm going to the ballet.'

I was at a loose end in the evening so I said to her, 'Sounds great to me.'

'Wonderful,' she said. 'I'll meet you here at five thirty.'

There was a fair old wait until five thirty, but I never minded really. I thought I'd nip into the snooker hall above the tailor's shop and flog the reds. Now, a lot of blokes didn't like Barney's but it was the drum to go to if you wanted a real good game of snooker. Mind you, the characters up there ought to have been good, they spent most of their lives bashing around the reds and the colours. But it was no place to go if you had an umpty pair of bellows. The air was so thick with fag smoke you could break your hooter if you walked in too quick. The smoke was like a brick wall. And the illuminations wasn't too hot neither. The only time you could ever really see anyone's face was when they was taking a shot under the lights over the tables. The rest of the time you only knew who you was gassing to by the sound of his voice. Mind you, the lousy lights was essential to Barney who ran a tea and coffee stall at the end. No one could see what he put in the urns or the sandwiches. If they could have done they'd have lynched him for sure. Still, it was a good place to waste a couple of hours, also to pick up a couple of oncers if a sucker happened to drop in.

I happened to be lucky too as there was a lonely looking bloke wanting someone to play with. I could tell from his rig out that he wasn't one of the boys, and from the way he held the cue I knew at once at Joe Davis was still all right for a while. To be honest, I wasn't hard up for the lettuce, but it's dead balmy to stand up a dead cert opportunity to increase the bank account. The real secret though is not show out too quick. So I sat down on the wooden seat by the table and watched him making a fanny of himself. I'd got a cue down and when he finally did get a red in a pocket I thumped the floor like he made a ton break.

The way his face lit up you'd have thought I just pinned the V.C. on him. He turned round and said, 'Fancy a couple of quick frames?'

'Not me, thanks,' I said, trying to make it sound like Freddie Trueman had asked me to play cricket with him. 'I'm not in the same league mate. I'm a strict bash 'em and hope for the best player.'

'Not to worry,' he said. 'I'll give you a couple of blacks. How about that?'

'O.K. But don't get narked if I bitch the game up. There's only one thing though. Let's keep the stakes low. No more than five bob a corner.'

I thought he was going to bore a hole right through the chalk he was so busy working on the tip. 'Actually, I wasn't thinking of money at all, but if you don't mind a wee gamble.'

He was so lousy it was harder losing against him than it would have been beating the world champ. I mis-cued, went in off, played jump shots on to the floor, hit his ball. You name it, I did it. Then he only just beat me.

Three frames later and 15 bob the worse off I put the bite on. 'Tell you what mate. I fancy my chances on a last frame for the frog and toad. Let's make a real game of it. You on?'

The poor sucker's eyes lit up like the jack box in a one-arm bandit. 'I'm game. But I don't like doing it.' Then because he obviously thought I was going to back out, he said quickly, 'Tell you what, let's make it a couple of quid.'

'Make it a fiver as far as I'm concerned. I'm not worried about the loot, mate. I had a lucky run on the geegees.'

'A fiver it is,' he said, and he was already setting up the reds in the triangle. 'God bless you,' he said as he put the green, brown and yellow in place. 'That's the only way I can remember,' he said with a soppy grin.

Now when you pull a con in a snooker hall you got to be ready for the explosion that comes at the end when he realises he's been taken to the cleaners. So I bawled up the hall, 'Someone come and mark for us, we got a big bet on here.'

The boys knew exactly what was on when I said that. I didn't need to write them no letter of explanation, and soon we had a nice little crowd round the table and I made certain one of them was holding the money.

We spun a penny for who was to break, and I won. I rolled a slow break back up the table that nestled right behind the reds without even breaking them. From then on he didn't know whether to shit, shave or shampoo. I took three blacks, a pink and a blue and then decided it was time to let him have a go. There was no point in rubbing his nose in it. He got a couple of reds and a brown, and from then on that was his little lot. As I took the ten quid from the stake-holder he did his nut. 'You chiselling little rat. You conned me. I thought you said you couldn't play. Here, give me that money back.'

'Hold on matey,' I said, all indignant. 'You never said that when you copped my money, now did you?'

'That's soon settled,' he went on. 'Here, take your fifteen bob back.'

'Sorry cock, we don't play those rules here. A bet's a bet in this school. Ain't that right fellows?' I said, looking at the mob round the table.

They didn't say a dicky bird but just nodded their heads. The poor sucker took one look at the faces and sensibly decided that he wasn't going to argue. He put his coat on and walked towards the door. He stopped on the way out and shouted back, after pushing up the emergency bar,

'You're a lot of rotten dirty crooks. I won't come in here again, that's for sure.'

I was still standing by the table and I stamped my foot and banged my cue just like I was going to run after him, and he went down the stairs like a cork out of a pop gun. I stood the lads a cup of char each and went out whistling 'Colonel Bogey.' I'd had a good lunch, a few frames that showed me I hadn't lost the touch, and I'd taken Charley boy for a ride that he'd be too ashamed to admit to anyone. I didn't hang about though, because the lads was hovering around me like vultures. They knew I had some lolly and those lay-abouts had no pride. They'd think nothing of trying to put the bite on for a couple of quid. Well, they could get stuffed. Charity begins at home as far as I'm concerned.

If I'd known what I was letting myself in for I wouldn't have gone to that ballet, straight up and no kid. When we got to this theatre place right in the middle of the West End there was a whole lot of blokes and girls lining up on the pavement. Half of them seemed to know Pam because they all started nattering away and saying how lucky they was to be able to sit out in the cold getting piles. One bloke with a coloured college scarf was telling everyone how he'd been outside nearly all night. All the others looked at each other as if he'd just said he'd run a four-minute mile with his legs tied together – a proper birk.

'How long's this little caper go on for?' I asked Pam.

'Oh not long. We'll be going up in an hour,' she said like she was giving me some good news.

'What! You can stuff that. Here, you keep my place. I'll be back soon,' I told her.

'Where are you going, Auk?' she asked, all astonished like. She made it sound like I was turning my back on a gold mine.

'A tom tit, if you must know,' I answered. With that, Pam and all the others start shushing me as if I'd sworn out loud in front of the vicar or someone. Naturally, I didn't want to go but it was an excuse to get out of the queue. Just round the corner I found a decent pub full of market porters having a game of arrows. Now if I've got a few minutes on my hands there's nothing I like more than darts. So I joined in. Blimey, could they shift their wallop though. I must have downed about five pints before I realised it was time to get back.

As I got back to the theatre Pam was doing her teeny weeny because the queue was starting to go in and naturally some bright bloke had a moan about me trying to jump the queue. I was in no mood to argue with him – anyway he was chicken, and he just turned his back on me when I said 'You fancy getting filled in mate?'

Inside it was a real posh drum. Gold and red velvet seats, fancy curtains and a lot of people down below us in evening togs. I didn't go a bundle on our seats mind. We was so high up we could have shaken hands with the angels. But Pamela kept telling me that this was where the real ballet fans went. For my money the place to be though was down there with the stuffed shirts. If I'd been down there, I would have said the place to be was up in the gods. That makes sense. People who are well heeled will always tell the poor mutt who's worrying about his next nosh that he's better off poor.

Suddenly the big lights on the ceiling started going out just like in the flicks and the band under the stage started playing. And it was just as if we were outside again in the street because everyone including Pam starts shushing fit to bust a gut.

The story was a right load of old cobblers that wouldn't have kidded a half wit. It was all about some humpty backed old geezer who run a toy shop, only all the dolls were real people painted up and he went round the stage like a blue arsed fly pretending to wind them up. When he'd done that they all started jerking around like they had come alive. For my money they never looked like anything but real people all the time, and anyway you had to guess half the time what was going on because no one was talking at all. Naturally there was a bit more to the story than that, but I couldn't have cared less as the pints I had with the porters was putting on the pressure. So I nudged old Pam

88

in the ribs but she was so wrapped up in what was going on she didn't even feel it. It was only when the other people started moaning that she turned and asked me, 'What on earth is the matter?'

'If I don't get out of here pronto I'll cry my eyes out,' I told her. Would you believe it, she just squeezed my arm and said, 'I'm so glad you like it. It *is* terribly moving.'

'I'm talking about my bladder you nit,' I shouted.

Believe me, you couldn't say anything in that place. Everyone started griping and shushing again. One old tart even tapped me with her programme and said, 'If you don't like it why don't you leave and let us enjoy it.'

'Listen you old boot. That's what I want to do,' I said. 'Why don't you make your minds up? *You* want me to shove off while the others don't want me to even breathe.'

Pam of course went into one of her how-could-you moods, and started snivelling. Someone else joined in and was bawling, 'Call the attendant.'

Suddenly a torch was shining on me and some toff in a dinner jacket was pointing to the door and saying, 'Will you kindly leave sir.' At least he was on my side. It didn't help though that we was right in the middle of a row and everyone had to stand up to let me pass. The bloke at the end said all snotty, 'Good riddance,' as I passed. So I trod on his toe for a giggle. Still I made it and found a slasher on the landing. When I finished I got to thinking about Doris again and had to have a quick shufty to see that everything was all right. I could'nt see nothing and I felt a bit of a Charlie for still worrying about it. Anyway, I would never have thought about it if Shy Ronnie hadn't brought it up.

Wild elephants couldn't have dragged me upstairs again so I went down to the boozer again, but the darts boys had all gone. So I sat in the corner giving a quick gander every so often out of the window to see when the crowds was coming out. A century later they started. One of the first out was old Pam who stood on the pavement looking as worried as a mum who's lost her kid in a supermarket.

I shoved a tanner in a slot machine and swallowed a whole pack of those green tablets that takes away the smell of the wallop and ambled over to meet her.

'You've been drinking,' was the first words she got out. That didn't say much for the tablets but at least it proved there was nothing wrong with her nose which was something. 'You acted positively disgracefully,' she moaned. 'I even came out to see if I could find you. I just didn't know where to look.'

'Well, I waited didn't I? So I don't see what you've got to moan about,' I said to her. 'Not many blokes would have.'

'You must confess it wasn't very nice to leave me like that. Now say you're sorry.'

'O.K. I'm sorry,' I said. I wasn't really, but good manners never hurt no one.

'I'm surprised you didn't like it,' she went on. 'It's one of the simplest to follow – a fairy story really.'

'You're dead right there,' I told her. 'I've never seen so many fairies in one place in my life before. It's back to the walls when you go in there all right.' Pam didn't go much on that at all and started off again about how moronic I was.

'That don't upset me at all Pam, so stop trying to needle. If not liking to watch a load of queers prancing around makes me a moronic, that's O.K. by me. Now let's drop it. I'll take you for some fish and chips.'

I lashed her up to a whacking great piece of skate, a gherkin and a double portion of chips – which she ate two of and then started worrying about her figure. But it did the trick and when we were having a cup of rosy lee she held my hand.

While I was tickling the middle of her hand with my finger I whispered, 'Play your cards right Pam, and you can have me for nothing.'

She never even objected, so I offered to take her home which was a real mistake. Pam lived way out in the wilds – the last stop in fact on the Northern Line. Still, her old man's house was much better than anything anyone else I knew lived in. It had a garden in the front with roses and flowers and a posh name on the gate 'Chez Nous' which I

90

didn't know the meaning of. All the lights were off, so we had a little session in the porch. Nothing to write home about really; still it was more than I had expected and a good sign for the next time.

Not that I cared really because the old booze was working again and I kept staggering off of the doorstep. Once I bashed into a plant in the dark and poor old Pam got real worked up about that.

'Please be careful darling. That's daddy's favourite clematis.'

Well it takes all kinds to make a world, and if he could get all worked up about a flower then good luck to him.

After about ten million smackers on the nose, ears and eyeballs Pam went in, coming back to peep through the crack of the door to throw me a kiss as if she hadn't had enough. I know I had.

I'd got a long walk back to the station and I was bursting again. I felt sorry for the old man's pride and joy, but I had to go somewhere.

Chapter Ten

Although I never had to I called round at the office next morning. Old Pam was pushing and pulling away at the switchboard like nobody's business when I arrived. She still managed to spot me though, and called me over. Her mouth was moving and although no noise came out I didn't have to be no expert lip reader to know she was saying, 'I want you.'

When I got over she was all smiles and full of the night out. 'I really enjoyed myself. I hope you did.'

'It wasn't bad,' I said. 'The trouble was I went to kip on the train and went right to the end of the line. You ought to tell your old man not to live at the arse end of the world. You wouldn't get many other blokes prepared to go all that way for just a slap and tickle, Pam.'

'Shush,' she said looking round the showroom to make sure no one heard. She needn't have worried on that score, the salesmen were too busy selling death traps at killing prices.

As she stuck in a plug she said, 'Don't talk to me about Daddy. He was like a bear with a sore head this morning. He had such a terrible row with the neighbours. He said their cat had killed his clematis. He was so upset, I can't tell you.'

'I don't blame him,' I said. 'You tell him to get an air gun.' And before she could take it any further I was through the door and on my way up to Shy Ronnie's office. He was out, but Gorgeous was sitting in the armchair reading a big thick book about an otter. He was almost near the end and something had upset him rotten.

'There are some wicked people in this world and no mistake Auk. Did you know that some people hunt little otters? Not with little dogs that would give him a fair chance. Oh no. Bloody great shaggy things with teeth like donkeys that could take on a lion and still come up trumps. It's beyond me, it really is. Now tell me, what harm does a poor otter do to anyone? Eats a few salmon, that's all. With salmon at sixteen bob a pound, who would miss them anyway?'

And out of the open window went the book. 'What you do that for?' I asked him. 'Now you'll never know what happened to it.'

'I don't want to. I've made my own ending. That otter took on all those dogs and killed every one of them. And all the hunters got drowned trying to rescue them. According to my book anyway.'

'Can't say I care,' I replied to him. 'It's ages since we had any down our street mate. The rats don't do too bad though. I reckon they're the answer to your shaggy dogs. Send them down and our rats will have them for breakfast.'

'The trouble with you Auk is you're too thick. It's people like you who are responsible for upsetting the balance of nature. We wouldn't have any wild life if it was left to the likes of you, and that's a fact. No elephants, tigers, penguins, no nothing.'

'Stop it George, you're breaking my heart. Life wouldn't be worth living if there were no more elephants and tigers cocking their legs against the lamp posts down our road.' I said it with a real straight face too.

Gorgeous gave me one of his tender looks – the kind he reserved for someone he was about to work over with his shiv. 'You know something Auk, I don't much rate your chances of drawing the old age pension, but you're a dead cert for a disability one. No kid.'

'Can't you take a joke, George?' I said, realising I was pushing my luck over the edge a bit.

'Not when it comes to animals. They need protectors. They're not like us now, are they? They can't speak for themselves, can they? It'd be a different picture, oh yes, if the little otters and foxes could reply to all those geezers who say they like being hunted and eaten alive until they're dead. I know what they'd say all right. They'd say they

93

liked it about as much as a hole in the head. So knock it off.'

Well Gorgeous was an expert on protection, so perhaps he knew what he was talking about. Anyway, he never stayed on the animal lover kick for long.

'Tell you what Auk, Ronnie wants me to take you down to one of the clubs tonight. One of the bouncers was taken queer and had to go home last night. I reckon he must have got at some of the under the counter hooch they sell.'

'Suits me George,' I said.

'It don't suit me though. I had a date with a bird. We were going to a dog meet. Browned me off not being able to go. Especially when I heard the favourite had been nobbled and an outsider I was given was going to win. I can still bet on it but it's not the same as seeing your dog win with your own eyes.'

'You can still go George. You don't need to hold my hand. I'll cope, honest.'

He looked at me hard like and said, 'I reckon you could Auk. But as a special favour don't tell Ronnie I wasn't there. I'll take you down the club this afternoon and you can then tell him with all honesty that I took you. O.K.'

'O.K.,' I said.

'Let's go then,' said Gorgeous like he was the sheriff ordering the posse to chase an outlaw. Only he didn't have no horse waiting outside, just his big red motor.

On the way there I got to thinking of that slut Doris again and that didn't do me much good I can tell you. Next thing I knew Gorgeous gave me a terrific judo jab across the knee.

'You're sociable I must say,' said Gorgeous. 'Don't you like my company?'

'Course. Especially when you break my leg off of my body,' I answered back.

'Come off it. That didn't hurt. Anyway, I don't like people in my motor who don't want to talk. Makes me feel as if there's something up with me.'

'For Christ's sake Gorgeous, I was thinking. Can't a bloke think without having his bones broke?'

94

'Pardon, Auk,' he said as if he'd done no more than accidentally trod on someone's toe during a slow foxtrot. 'You got something on your mind?'

Now Gorgeous may have been a real beat up old geezer but he'd been around so I thought I'd put a feeler out about what was worrying me. 'As a matter of fact George, it ain't me. It's a mate. You see he went off with this bird when he was a bit loaded one night and he's worried that he might have caught a cold like.'

'Well, you tell your mate he'll know soon enough without worrying about it. When he finds he's slashing broken milk bottles he's copped it.'

'Thanks George. I'll tell him that. But what about the other?'

George left a bit of red paint on the side of a lorry and a private car as he went through a gap in the traffic. 'Tell him he's got two choices – the Foreign Legion or the Pox Clinic.'

We left a few more drivers effing and blinding before Gorgeous said to me, 'Look Auk, why don't you stop trying to con me. If you're worried about it, say so. Don't start telling me about some mate of yourn. Pox is like piles. It's always your mate who's got it, never you.'

'All right, so I was talking about me, but you don't expect me to stand on the street corner yelling my nut off about it, do you?' I told him.

'Don't you worry, Auk. Leave everything to Uncle George. I'll take you down the road. If you haven't copped you don't have to worry. If you have it's no worse than a bad cold. In fact it's better 'cos no one can see your nose running.'

Without warning Gorgeous did a U-turn that had every other driver hooting and shouting through lowered-down windows. Although we couldn't hear what they said we didn't get no headaches trying to guess. But with George at the wheel there was only two other kinds of road users – the quick and the dead.

Suddenly George slammed down his foot so hard that he must have taken a couple of inches off the tyre treads and I

95

could smell the stink of burning rubber as I nearly went through the windscreen. 'Here's the horses piddle Auk,' he said with his busted old grin.

'O.K. mate,' I said, feeling a bit narked. 'But you don't have to arrive like you was an ambulance driver with a dying patient, do you?'

The hospital was a whacking great dump with a big front door that had marble pillars and everything. Nurses with black capes and white caps were going in and out like pawnbrokers' parcels. They all looked like they washed twice before getting dressed. Through the glass doors I could see an old boy covered in medals writing things down in a book. 'I'm not going in there George. Supposing one of those nurses asks me what I want? What would I say?'

George tilted his trilby down over his eyes and eased out of the motor. 'I'll introduce you Auk. They know me of old. Listen, you don't have to talk to no one. You must amble down bold as brass till you see a door marked Special Clinic. They're so glad you called they don't even ask your name. Come on.'

Trust old George to get everything wrong. No sooner had we got through the swing doors than the old boy in uniform shouted, 'Can I help you gentlemen?'

'It's all right, mate. We want the Special Clinic,' he shouted so that everyone who was reading looked up from their papers and those that wasn't grabbed one.

'Why don't you just stick a big placard round my neck George,' I whispered to him.

'Belt up and nip in,' he said. 'I'll wait outside.'

The room was a little place with a hard bench with a row of blokes all sitting down studying form or trying to look like they was just sitting on top of a bus. On the other side of the room was a hole in the wall with sides round it like those new phone boxes to stop other people hearing what you said to the geezer behind. He had a big form in front of him and the first thing he says is 'Name please.'

'This is a ripe con if you ask me,' I told him. 'My mate, he told me you wouldn't want my name.'

'That's just for the record sir. After we have completed

the form I will give you a number and you will be known by that from now on.'

It all seemed a load of cobblers to me, but you can't argue with the welfare state. Anyhow, he'd got my name so that was that.

Gorgeous had briefed me on the line to take when I went in to the quack, so I wasn't really worried when my turn came to go in. It was just like seeing a proper doctor really, he had one of those things round his neck that they use to see if your heart's still beating and even a white coat.

'Sit down,' he said, and I could see the crafty so-and-so had already got the form the geezer had filled up in the other room. 'Why are you here?'

That seemed just about the most half-baked question I ever heard but I didn't jib, I just went straight into the routine Gorgeous had primed me with. 'I have been exposed to infection,' I said.

He wasn't going to help one little bit, I could see that. 'And who hasn't?' he said looking over the top of his bins. 'What symptoms have you?'

'What?' I said, wondering what the hell he was on about.

'Symptoms, s-y-m-p-t-o-m-s. A discharge or any other visible signs that have prompted you to call,' he went on with a sigh.

'No, I haven't anything like that. I just wanted a check up.'

'But there doesn't seem anything for me to check up on now, does there? We have plenty of work to do here without being bothered by every Tom Dick and Harry.' The way he said Dick I gathered was his idea of a killing joke.

'Look doc, every time I have a pee there's a notice above my head telling me to call in if I've been exposed. O.K. That's just what I'm doing.'

'Who was the woman?' he asked.

'Come off it. Surely you don't expect me to tell you that.'

'Of course I do. We don't want her to continue sending

us customers, now do we? It's merely a protection for the public.'

'Sorry, no dice,' I told him straight. 'You see this bird happens to be a very famous lady. If her old man ever got to hear about it there'd be all hell to pay. A general election or something.'

'I quite understand,' he said to me and wrote something down on the form. 'I'll protect the lady's reputation for your sake,' he said. 'I've just put down prostitute. I find I have to do that quite frequently as a matter of fact.' He let out one of his big sighs. 'All the years I've been here and no one has been ungentlemanly enough to name her. But there we are. I admire you for it.'

I thought to myself that there must be millions of doctors in the world and I have to get lumbered with a piss-taker. And I'm not trying to be comic either. Because at the time I didn't know he was going to ask me to go into a little room no bigger than a swimming-bath changing-box and have a leak in a jar.

I stood in the box with the jar in my hands and my trousers round my ankles wondering what the next move would be. Then I heard him shout, 'Aren't you ready yet?'

To tell the truth, by then I was in a bit of a flat spin. Not really thinking clear. So I shuffled in clutching the jar and feeling a real goon.

'And what do you think you are,' he said, all angry. 'Pull your trousers up man.'

I put the jar down on his desk and started heaving my pants up. 'Take that thing off my desk,' he yelled so loud that even old George must have heard it in the car.

Well, I didn't know where I was, honest. By the time I got my pants up he was holding the jar up to a light and muttering to himself, 'Clear as an archbishop's.'

After he had handed the bottle back and I had chucked it away down the sink he said, 'We might as well give you a blood test. Really, all your trouble is just worrying about it too much.'

I was feeling a lot better already until I had to go into another room and lie on a bed and squeeze a rubber dog's bone while some gink took ten gallons of blood out of my arm.

When I left I really felt like a secret agent. Now I was just a number on a green card. I stuck that in my shoe because I couldn't carry it in my wallet. The Old Lady often went through my clothes hoping to find the odd quid and I don't know what she'd have said if she'd found it.

The doc told me I'd have to call again to make sure everything was all right from the test. (And I want to say here that I did go back and everything was hunky dory.)

Gorgeous had stuck his car in the car park in a space marked Consultants Only, but he wasn't in it. I found him in a pub across the road ploughing into his tenth rum and black and trying to get the barmaid to sing 'Old Father Thames' with him.

'Have a drink,' he said as I walked in.

'You can say that again. I'll have a pint of the best,' I said.

'Good for you Auk. You must be O.K. If you've copped, the first thing you have to knock off is the wallop. That's the hardest thing about it.'

Standing by the side of the motor when we got back was an attendant with a pad, looking just like a copper about to book us. 'This your car?' he said with his pencil all ready to start writing. Gorgeous climbed in, switched on, then lowered the window and said, 'No. It's nicked.'

'Do you realise you have no right to be parked in this space. It is reserved for consultants, or can't you read?'

'Look general,' said Gorgeous, 'I don't know where you got all those medals from but I'll take a bet it wasn't in no intelligence test. Course I'm a bloody consultant. Don't I talk like one? Now, get your legs out of the way before you have to start crawling into your own hospital to get one of your consultants to sew them back on. O.K.'

The old bloke obviously wasn't in no mood to win any more medals for bravery because he said, 'All right, but you'll have to write your name and address in here first,' and he shoved the pad through the window. Gorgeous took his pencil, licked it and wrote down Sir John Thomas,

99

Special Clinic, and then let the clutch in with such a bang that the old boy went over the bonnet and ended up on his back still holding his book.

'You got to stand up for your rights these days Auk. It's getting more and more like a Police State.'

The club we drove down to was in Soho and Ronnie had spent a mint tarting it up. He was smart enough not to have his own monica linked with it so he had it run by a front man. Once it had been a shop, but Ronnie had turned the window into a showcase that was full of tit pictures and the doorway was made of three life-sized photos of naked birds that had been cut out and pasted on three ply. It was like the front of a cinema really. You know, with pictures outside to give you some idea of what was being offered inside. Two of the dolls were holding up the third one over their heads. Ronnie had paid a fortune to the three birds to pose and he really took his time finding them because he wanted to appeal to all tastes. The one lying on top was a real black bint with droopers, another was a long-haired blonde with rugby balls with spikes on. The other one looked like she was wearing a couple of poached eggs on her chest.

None of the birds outside was on show inside, but none of the suckers knew that. The wall of what used to be the store room had been knocked down to make it into one big room and round the walls were tables with that stuff you can't burn on the top. The lighting was so bad it made the snooker hall look like it was floodlit. It was early when we arrived and the place was empty but for two old dears who were on their hands and knees scrubbing the floor. The front – a Malt called Mick – was busy at the bar mixing the cocktails. As a drink it was strictly for the birds – and I'm not kidding. They was nothing but coloured fruit juice in fancy glasses that the customers had to pay 7/6d. a throw for. It was the only drink the girls were allowed and each time they had one they got a metal counter which they traded in at the end of the night for hard cash.

'Have a drink,' said the Malt as Gorgeous and me walked in.

'You must be out of your teeny weeny,' said Gorgeous. 'I

100

wouldn't drink that cats' piss if you paid me.'

'Thank the good Lord that the girls don't think like you,' he said. 'We'd all be at the Labour. No, joking apart, I meant a real drink,' and he pulled out a bottle of scotch that was not much smaller than a sixteen inch shell. 'Fell off the back of a lorry,' he said as he almost filled three glasses.

After George had told him who I was, the Malt said there was no real point in me being there that early, so Gorgeous and I went over to a pub where he started hammering the rum and black like we'd just been told the four minute warning had another sixty secs to go.

By the time it came for him to meet his bird and go to the dogs he had reached the stage of asking me who I was. He wasn't bad enough though to want to sing, and that's what worried me most, let's face it. Old Father Thames is strictly for the boat races as far as I'm concerned.

'It's nice to have met you mate. Maybe we'll have a drink together again. I can't stay though. Got a date with a cert,' said Gorgeous, giving me a real big wink.

'O.K. George. Enjoy yourself,' I said back. 'See you tomorrow.'

With that, George hit his head with the flat of his hand like he was trying to drive a nail into a three inch plank. 'Fancy me forgetting you Auk. You must think I'm potty.'

'Of course not,' I told him. 'It's just that you've got your date on your mind and want to be off.'

By the time we remembered where he'd parked the motor George had remembered too that I was with him. 'Don't take any lip from anyone down there Auk. Throw them out if there's any trouble. You won't have any comebacks 'cos most of the stupid suckers can't admit to anyone they were in a strip joint, least of all the bogeys. Their old ladies would skin them alive.'

Then George went off down the road reasonably careful. He wasn't doing more than forty when he turned the corner and only one back wheel went up on the pavement. I went back to the club which was now lit up with coloured lights and the sign outside saying *Les Filles* kept flashing on and off like a fag advert, although it was still the middle of the afternoon. Don't ask me why he gave it that monica. It had nothing at all to do with the ponies.

Not knowing me from Adam the bint at the door called out to me as I got near, 'Come on down darling. No G strings. They take it all off. You can have a lovely time afterwards.'

As I shouldered past her I said, 'If you're going to pop out of that doorway and frighten people to death you ought to have a hand bell to warn them. Blimey, what an advert for a strip club.'

'Don't talk to me like that, fancy pants,' she went on. 'I'm in the show later on.'

She sounded just like an actress who's been insulted on the way to the stage to collect an Oscar.

Once I got used to the dark I looked around for the Malt. He was sorting out a lot of music for the tape machine.

'I don't want to teach you your own business mate, but that bird on the door would put Jack the Ripper off.'

The Malt didn't even bother to look up. 'You could put a gorilla on the door, it wouldn't matter,' he said to me. 'They take a gander at the pictures and don't see the girl on the door. To keep her happy we let her take her clothes off in the finale of one number. Now don't laugh,' he went on. 'You'll never credit it but a bloke even tried to chat it up one night.'

The hostesses were all sitting round the walls dragging at fags and looking about as cheerful as a constipated camel. They were dressed real smart considering what a dump the club was. They all had party dresses on with low fronts and plastic flowers pinned on.

'Surely they don't expect anyone to come in so early?' I asked the Malt.

'You'd be surprised. I reckon we'd have some blokes in if we opened at eight in the morning,' he said without no expression in his voice. 'If it wasn't for the staffing problem it would be well worth it. Come over, I'll introduce you to some of the girls.'

He took me over to four of them sitting round a table

102

nattering; one of them was even knitting a jumper for a baby.

The Malt nodded his head at every one of them as he called out their names. 'Monica, Pearl, Samantha and Deirdre. Girls, this is Mr Grant who's keeping an eye on the place for us tonight.'

'Pleased to meet you,' 'Charmed,' and 'How do you do,' they all said, sounding about as thrilled about it as a fisherman who's just caught an old boot.

The one called Samantha pushed a packet of Yank fags over the table to me, 'Have a weed,' she said. 'A customer left them behind last night.' Before I had a chance to help myself she had taken one out and lit it for me from her own fag. That kind of thing may be all right when some luscious bird does it for Cary Grant on the wide screen, but as far as Samantha was concerned it was about as sexy as a baboon asking you to share a banana.

Still, I didn't want to moan on my first night so I took it and hoped I didn't end up sick of the palsy or something. 'What's your first name, Mr Grant?' she said.

'Call me Auk, everyone else does.'

'That's not your real name – come off it,' she said.

'So what, if your real name's Samantha then my knob's a bloater. Tell me, why do all you birds have to give yourselves fancy names? It don't make your knockers any bigger or better.'

Half of the fag disappeared as she took a drag and blew the smoke straight into my face. 'It's just part of the game really. My real name is Lillian – the other girls call me Lil so you can – off duty of course. But you can't expect customers to be happy about being fleeced by Lil or watching her dance Cuban Frenzy, now can you?'

Suddenly one of the birds jumped up and said, 'Oops, excuse me. We have visitors,' and walked across the room waggling her bum like two puppies in a sack. I looked up and saw two smartly dressed blokes coming through the curtain. They certainly didn't look like blokes hell bent on having a good time. They kept glancing over their shoulders and looking round like their wives was going to pop out from under the table.

The girl sat the blokes down at a table and straight away three other girls sat down with them.

'How about a drink darling,' said Deirdre who was the one who got her mitts on them first.

'Certainly, what'll you have?' said the younger of the two. Before he'd got the words out a waitress was at the table with a tray and five cocktails on it. 'That's two pounds please sir.'

He pulled out his wallet and if he was surprised at the price he didn't show it, I'll say that for him. 'And two large Scotches please.'

The waitress bit her lips with green teeth and told him, 'I'll have to have a word with the manager, sir.'

From the way the Malt moved in I knew it was something that happened every day of the week. He stood by the table and said in a real low voice, 'I'm terribly sorry gentlemen, but we do not serve spirits.'

'What the hell,' shouted the older man and he was on his feet so fast that the Malt had to push him quite hard to make him sit down again.

'Don't be hasty. I have a little something tucked away for our special customers.' When he came back he put a hip flask on the table. 'Just say you brought it in yourself if anyone should ask,' he said. 'Now relax and enjoy yourselves gentlemen. Delighted to have you.'

The two men smiled from earhole to earhole and said, 'Thanks a lot.'

The waitress wiped the smiles off when she said, 'That's three pounds please and two pounds for some more cocktails.'

'What goes on here?' said the older bloke. 'I haven't even got the top off this flask and you're on your second. Anyway, we only want two girls.'

'Stop worrying,' said the young bloke. 'We're out to enjoy ourselves remember,' and the dope shelled out again.

Deirdre was whispering in the older one's ear in a voice that you could have heard down in Trafalgar Square. 'Don't be silly darling. Just be patient. You can take us

104

home at the end. That's all part of the price of the drinks.'

The older one cheered up no end at that and even ordered another round and put his arm round Deirdre who snuggled up to him and said, 'I'm looking forward to closing time really darling.'

In about half an hour the place had filled up with a ripe old collection – Indians, Germans, Yanks and even a couple of Chinks. It looked like the United Nations on the razzle dazzle. They all seemed loaded with lolly and paid up, and even looked cheerful about it. No one seemed to care that every bird was trotting out the same old spiel.

Suddenly one of the Germans began hammering the table and shouting out, 'Ven do we haf the naked ladies please.' The Sheila with him pushed him away and said, 'Do you mind. I don't need a shower. I had a bath before I came along,' and she started wiping down her front with a hankie that wasn't much bigger than a table cloth.

I was kind of hoping that the German would start cutting up, then I could belt him one and chuck him out. After all, that's what I was there for and I was getting brassed off just sitting there doing sweet fanny adams. But he just laughed and grabbed the hankie and started to do a cleaning job where none of his spit could have got.

Then the Malt who was in tuxedo stepped on the middle of the floor and held up his arms like he was about to announce a big fight. 'Ladies and gentlemen, the floor show is just about to start. This is a respectable club so will the gents please keep their hands on the table when the fun starts. Our first turn is entitled Tahitian Temptation by Claudine. Now hang on to your hats and relax.'

I'll say this for the Malt, he could really put on the lingo when it came to it. He really must have sat up at nights wrapping his tongue round some of those words. Still, it went down well with the suckers.

Then the lights went down even lower and the old tape recorder started belting out some tune that was all tom-toms and liquorice sticks. Still, it sounded good in a sexy sort of way. The mob round the tables started moving in their seats just like people do when the big film is going to start.

Claudine came out of a door that was marked Stage Door – in fact behind it was a damp old room filled with big jars of the juice the Malt mixed up the cocktails from. The birds had to change in the middle of the room without even a screen or anything; come to that there wasn't even no mirror to look in.

When Claudine came in there was a bit of clapping and a lot of wolf whistles. She was a black bint dressed in a straw hat as big as a cart wheel, a long dress with frilly pants and an umbrella that would have been more at home on a golf course. A good old session at the Launderette wouldn't have done the clothes no harm, they were real tatty and sweat-stained, but the red spot light that the Malt shot on her hid most of the dirt.

Claudine wasn't of course her real name, and the hottest place she'd ever been to was the public baths in Notting Hill. She wasn't no Ginger Rogers neither, but she had what the customers had paid to see. Don't ask me why, but under that big hat she had a blonde wig on.

Personally, I found the whole thing a bit of a bind. She farted around for hours just taking one stocking off. Then she held it up at arm's length. If it was as scruffy as the rest of her gear I don't blame her for that. The nutters in the crowd tried to grab it from her but she whipped it away before they could get their paws on it. The same old routine went on with the other stocking before it ended up with its mate on the back of a chair. Next the dress ended up on the chair and I felt real sorry for any poor mug who ended up in kip with her because it didn't half take her a time to get skinned.

When the dress was off she was left standing there with the frilly pants and a bra. I'll say this for her though, she never looked like she come from some under-developed country. The slob of a German made a grab for the bra but only managed to add to his bill by knocking four cocktails off of the table.

When the pants came off Claudine was just in a G string

106

and everyone was getting a bit fruity. She didn't help things either by going round the table swinging her knockers under their noses like a couple of windscreen wipers.

At the end she stood there without a stitch on except the titfer but no one was looking at that. Everyone clapped, and Claudine picked up her clothes from the chair and went out the back with everything bundled under her arms. I thought the Malt ought to have rigged a little curtain up because the way she went off kind of spoilt the whole thing. It was just like someone picking up their togs to go into the bathroom.

There were about eight birds performing but once you'd seen one you'd seen the lot really.

The Malt was smart though. He had a long delay between each one so that the glasses was kept topped up. The girls who served the drinks had orders not to wait for the customers to call for drinks, 'Just keep filling the glasses.'

Most of the customers got browned off by the end of the strips and left but their seats were soon grabbed by other mugs. I only hoped I didn't get the job too often because it was a real chore. No one got shirty or gave you the least excuse to clobber them.

It was just before midnight that this odd bird came in. From her rig-out you could tell she didn't shop at Marks & Sparks. She obviously had loot and just from her face you could tell she was posh. She reminded me a bit of those old vintage cars you see around. They cost a fortune to keep running and seven coats of paint to hide the original dirt and scratches. But the Malt caught my eye and nodded towards her and I could lip read enough to know he was saying, 'Out.'

I ambled over to her, and told her blunt, 'Sorry love. No single birds allowed in. Up the apples now. There's a good girl.'

I might just as well have been trying to tap the Old Man for a quid for all the notice she took. She just walked across the room and plonked her fanny on a seat. I parked next to her and said, not even angry, 'Look cloth ears. No ladies without blokes, savvy?'

The bird who was about forty had a fair load of hooch aboard, I could tell that, but she could hold it well. 'My dear boy, I would be most grateful if you stopped pestering me. I am here for a serious reason. I am carrying out a social investigation. If you eject me I shall have to inform the police that you are selling alcohol here.'

I could see she had me by the short and curlies with that. Apart from anything else I was no match for the lingo she could trot out and that's a fact. Being the new boy I decided to let the Malt say whether she stayed or got the heave-ho.

'Let her stay Auk. She's probably a Les who wants to chat the girls up. Keep her in the background.'

When I got back the Duchess had already lined up two birds and was giving them a real ear bashing about their work. I parked beside her and said, 'The gaffer don't mind you staying so long as you keep in the background.'

Maybe the Malt was right because she was certainly a nosy bitch. She asked them why they worked there, how much they got, did they have it off with men, and didn't they mind showing off their bodies.

To get the answers she seemed quite happy to push the boat out so I left them alone. She saw the strip through three times with eyeballs sticking out like organ stops, and her arms round both the birds.

I'd be lying if I said I was sorry when it all ended as my eyeballs were stinging from the smoke.

The German was real plastered and making arrangements to meet a girl outside. She squeezed his mitt and said she was going for her coat. One by one the girls went out to the back to get their togs.

The Malt and I had a couple of stiff ones while he counted the money and stacked it away in a suitcase that he chained to his wrist. Then we went upstairs to the fresh air.

The German was walking up and down outside as the Malt locked up. He gave us both a shower as he asked where his girl was.

'I gafe her the money to sleep with her at home,' he moaned.

'She's gone off to bye-byes, mate. She's tired,' I told him. 'Anyway, you don't want nothing to do with her. She's got a full house.'

He moaned that it was daylight robbery and he waved his empty wallet under my nose. 'What you want me to do? Play the violin?' I said.

He was still pacing up and down when a big car stopped beside us. The posh bird lowered the window and called out, 'Thanks for a most enlightening evening. I've got some marvellous material.'

Although it was dark in the back I could make out the German's bint sandwiched between Claudine and another stripper.

I was so bunged up with smoke that I didn't even bother to get a taxi. I walked home. There was a lot of stars out and the streets was almost empty. I couldn't help thinking to myself that London takes a lot of beating.

Chapter Eleven

Though I'd been with Ronnie more than a year I was still padding with the Old Lady in the black hole of Calcutta. I was pulling down enough to have had a drum of my own, but it was too much trouble. It would have meant making my own bed, sending clobber to the laundry and sometimes cooking my own nosh. I didn't see no point in being lumbered with all that when the Old Lady took it on for a couple of quid a week. Also, every week the Old Man cleaned the car for five bob, which was cheaper than a garage. I could have got a kid to do it for less mind you, but I put it the Old Man's way as he needed the brass. That's what sons are for.

Mind you, there wasn't much room for all the togs I'd got by then. At a quick guess I'd say I had eleven suits, three of them light weights, and more shirts than a dog's got fleas. Some of them I'd bought myself but most of them came from Doris who I was still seeing from time to time. Apart from clothes she was also giving me things like gold cuff links and deodorants which I didn't take much as a compliment. It made me feel a bit like that bloke in a bowler on the underground who pen and inks so much everyone looks the other way. Which wasn't fair in my case as now I always went to the public baths once a week. And that's the god's truth.

One of the best things Doris bought me was a dinner rig-out which I used to wear when I had the club stint. I felt like George Raft.

Don't think though that Doris was the only bit of tail I had lined up. I was doing quite well in that line of country. Especially once I got to know the strip girls better. They obliged because they knew I could put a bit more work their way. It wasn't all one sided, don't think that. I did fix

110

them up and what's more I didn't take much of a rake off.

Don't ask me why but I was still knocking around with old Pam, though I never really got nothing from her except a slap and tickle. I suppose I only kept seeing her because she was a cut above the other sluts I dogged around with. At least she spoke proper and didn't make you feel ashamed when you was with her.

Personally, I would have said I had enough clothes for anyone till one morning I went in to find Ronnie looking at one of those black edged cards which means good news to some people and bad to others. He flicked it over to me like a kid with a fag card and said just like he was giving me a ticket to a trade show, 'Got a blue serge suit Auk, and a black tie?'

'Course I haven't,' I told him a bit narked. 'I'm not a chauffeur.'

Ronnie didn't answer, he just pulled a wad of notes from his back pocket and peeled off a few. 'Nip down to Burtons and get one off the peg. There's no point in spending too much. You may not need it again for donkey's years.'

I read the card but to be honest it didn't mean a thing to me, except a bloke in Camberwell called Cornelius Murphy was being stuck in the bone orchard in a couple of days' time.

'Who is he?' I asked, thinking I had a right to know who I was going to stand out in the cold for.

'Who is he? Who *was* he you mean,' said Ronnie. 'I'll tell you Auk. Con was the best getaway driver in the business. He drove the motor for Red Fred's outfit.'

That rung a bell for me right away because only a couple of nights before I'd read in the *Evening Standard* that this geezer had killed himself while being chased by the law after they'd pulled off a warehouse job. I also knew that Red Fred – they called him that because he was a Commie with a bonce full of up-the-workers crap – was in strict opposition. But they was both smart enough not to tread on each other's toes.

'I thought you hated his guts,' I said.

111

'I do, but we don't needle each other, and when there's a tragedy like this we're expected to pay our respects. Like the Royal Family really, they often have to go to funerals of people they don't like. Sometimes they can't make it, so they send a rep. In my case that's you Auk, and Gorgeous is turning out too.' He made it sound like a soccer team.

Down at Burtons I managed to get a reasonable outfit off the hook. It wasn't as good a fit as I normally go for but Con wasn't going to look at it so I didn't even ask for any alterations.

On the morning of the funeral I went to the office to pick up Ronnie's Silver Cloud because he insisted that everyone would be keeping an eye open to see how well he was doing. He thought the Rolls would give them some idea that he wasn't on the bread line altogether. He'd even managed to con a local hire car driver to do the motoring. He looked real posh sitting in front with a black suit and peaked cap on. I just wished that with that spread we was going somewhere a little more cheerful. Gorgeous was trying to fix a long strip of black ribbon on to the bonnet. He was wearing his usual rig out with a Sid Field overcoat that reached the top of his black suedes.

Piled up on the pavement and wrapped in cellophane was this whacking great wreath from Ronnie. It was made in the shape of a snooker table and about the same size, with different coloured flowers for all the balls. The black wasn't much cop really, it looked more blue, but as Ronnie said there was no such thing as a black flower. And the first gardener to grow one was on to a fortune.

'Con was a great one for a frame,' said Ronnie. 'I thought that would be a fitting tribute. I like the personal touch.'

It was so big we couldn't get it in the boot so we had to heave it on the roof by which time we'd managed to pot the black and lose a couple of reds. Not that it mattered really, it looked a bit more natural that way.

Out of his own pocket George had bought a long ladder made out of chrysanths and other flowers. That had to go on top of the snooker table.

Ronnie looked at it real puzzled. 'What the . . . no, I mustn't swear at a time like this . . . is that abortion?' he asked George.

George who never usually crossed Ronnie looked at him like he was a half wit. 'That, Ronnie, is a ladder to heaven. It's an old custom. I don't suppose you ever heard of it though. It's religious.'

'I hope it takes his weight,' he said.

Then he looked at the motor. I'll give Ronnie his due, he never said a dicky bird although it was looking more like a window cleaner's van than a funeral motor.

'It's a nice idea, George. But I reckon a lift would have been more use to take old Con down to where he's going,' he said and went off into one of his laughing routines.

On the way to Con's house George started talking like a bishop. He even got narked when I swore and kept telling me what a wonderful bloke Con had been although they never saw eye to eye.

'That man had spunk,' said George with a faraway look in his eyes.

'Con and me once had a set to in a back room when Ronnie sent me along to cut him down to size. We had a ripe old twenty minutes together whacking away at each other with our shivs. I'll say this for him, he gave as good as he got until I called in a bit of help. I was so impressed I drove him to the hospital myself.

'The cops tried to make him swear on oath it was me, but he wouldn't. He just told them he couldn't remember what happened in that little room as he was out at the time. After that Ronnie came to some arrangement with Con's outfit and there wasn't any more trouble. Con and I shook hands and let bygones be bygones. They ought to strike medals for blokes like him.'

From the outside Con's drum wasn't no better than our place, but inside it was done up a real treat. Not just little carpets on the floor but those ones that go from wall to wall. The furniture was just like that stuff you see in magazines.

In one corner of the front room a bloke in a white coat was serving drinks from behind a real smashing bar. It even had a little striped sunshade above it, although you couldn't see in there without the lights on.

Con was in his box in the middle of the room and a whole mob of men and women was walking past it slowly. Only his head could be seen and the top of that was wrapped up in a white cloth thing like doctors wear at operations. When the car piled up it took the top of his nut off as neat as a three-minute egg. But you wouldn't have noticed it. Someone said, 'He looks like he's asleep.' Well he certainly didn't look like he was in a hurry to wake up.

I went past and made a little bow, but George had to go the whole hog and overdo it. He bent over and kissed his old mate on what little you could see of his head. I thought he might have taken his hat off though.

Once that was over the bloke at the bar gave us a drink and Con's widow shook our hands and said how nice it was of us to come.

'You haven't changed a bit Gorgeous,' she said. 'Con would have been real pleased to know you could make it.'

Every now and then she would belt across the room and tell her kids to go upstairs until they was called for. She had certainly gone out of her way to give her old man a send-off. The kids – all six of them – were in white frilly shirts and velvet trousers, and she even had a veil on that she had to keep lifting to drink her port.

Apart from the drinks there was plates of grub everywhere but no one was eating. The whisper had gone round that the grub was for when we got back. She certainly knew how to throw a funeral. She'd laid on a spread that you don't expect to see except at Christmas. She must have been real fond of him to go to all that trouble.

I felt a bit lost there to be honest as I didn't know anyone and I didn't bother to chat any of the birds up as they were nearly all the dead bloke's age. Anyway, I wasn't forgetting it was a funeral after all.

Without making too much of a show of it, I grabbed a couple of stiff drinks then went to look for the bog. Like home it was out the back, but I couldn't be bothered to queue so I went and waited in the motor.

114

I'll say this for that street though, they certainly spread the ackers to give old Con a good send off. There wasn't many doors that didn't have flowers or a wreath of some kind nailed on. Wherever you looked heads were sticking out of windows and the crowd on the pavements was five foot thick.

As for the cars, they stretched the whole length of the road. It must have been a real field day for the wreath makers too. No one seemed to have any doubts about where he would end up. And they'd certainly gone out of their way to give him a leg up. Apart from George's ladder there was a big pair of wings. On top of one car was The Gates of Heaven made so big they would have looked all right outside Buckingham Palace. Then there was a big dice all made of flowers, the vacant chair, and a motor car with plastic windows just like real glass, red hubs and a steering wheel. Ronnie's snooker table got a pretty good hand too mind you.

I didn't have to wait too long before four characters came out carrying the coffin. I couldn't help wondering whether they had screwed it up in front of everyone. Don't ask me why but I thought that was a bit off. While the lid was open you kind of had the feeling Con was still around. When they came out you suddenly knew it was for keeps.

I forget the name of the place where they buried him in but you can take it from me they was in no hurry to get him there. We really crawled through the streets at funeral pace – and I'm not being comical neither.

There wasn't a proper church service which was a bit of a let down after all the Lord Mayor's Show stuff, but they'd laid on something in the Chapel at the graveyard. The drivers may have been a bit on the slow side but you couldn't have said that about the grey haired old vicar who did the service. Maybe he'd left something in the oven because he was in a real tearing hurry.

We all had a little card with the prayers and things on it but he romped through those faster than your eyes could follow the words. Not that I cared a fourpenny. I was uncomfortable on my knees because there wasn't one of those

115

pad things to kneel on. It wasn't as if I really knew Con anyway. I wouldn't have minded a touch of the old house-maid's for a pal.

Then the old boy gave five minutes of his time up to tell us what a lucky bloke Con was to be going *there* and how we shouldn't really be upset about it. Which didn't seem to cut much ice with his widow because she started to bawl her head off and that was enough to get the kids going too.

It ended up a bit cheerier with us all singing Onward Christian Soldiers and Gorgeous putting the rest of us to shame because he knew the words.

We wasn't able to take the motors down to the grave so we had to walk which didn't cheer me up. Not that I minded the stroll. It was passing all those graves that were covered in weeds and withered flowers in jam jars.

Con's missus had hardly left the grave before two blokes began filling it in like they were on double time for Wim-peys. All the flowers and things were laid out by the side with their little tickets on. Then it started to rain.

Gorgeous said to me, 'Come on Auk, back to the motor. It's all right for Con, he can't catch a cold now.' So we really hurried back to the dry.

By then the ink was running on the labels and I thought to myself how much Ronnie would moan because in a couple of minutes no one would know who had spent all that money on the snooker table.

Back at Con's house his missus did us real proud with platefuls of sandwiches and lots of drink. The kids were sent upstairs to change and were only allowed down after that to have some lemonade and bangers on sticks. I didn't want to stay too long. Don't get me wrong and think I was sad or anything. I wasn't. Everyone was talking over old times and there was one or two good giggles. But I was put off by Con's picture above the mantelpiece. It's hard to imagine a bloke's dead and buried when his picture's star-ing at you.

By the time it came to leave everyone had had a skinful but no one was tight. Con's missus saw us all off at the door and shook hands and said she hoped to see us all again soon.

And not to leave it so long next time.

Two of George's old muckers had cadged a lift back to town with us and the first thing Gorgeous did was to pull a bottle of rum out of the place you keep gloves or a torch in. He passed it round and we had to drink it off the neck which cheesed me. I hate sharing a glass with anyone, let alone a bottle with three others. What's more one of the characters kept wiping the bottle top with the palm of his hand and that was as black as Newgate's knocker.

It was this geezer who had the bright idea that we stop the motor at 'The Case is Altered' to drink a final last fling to Con.

Dirty Paws said, 'It was his local for years George.' I thought George was going to have a snivel. 'Don't I know it,' he said, and he really gave the old rum bottle a thumping.

When we got inside I twigged George was a little Mozart because he started giving us all a run down on the boozer. I can't remember now what he said, anyway it don't matter a lot. But it had something to do with the Crimean war that the pub got its name. As I said before, Gorgeous could get real worked up about nothing at times. Who cared what a pub was called so long as the beer was all right.

Dirty Paws put the first round up. I had a pint, George a rum and black and they had a couple of double scotches.

'What about you guvnor?' asked Dirty Paws.

The guvnor had a cup of tea on the bar which he pointed to and said, 'No thanks gentlemen. I'm just having a cup of rosy.'

'Listen,' said Dirty Paws. 'You're here to please the customers, right?'

'Naturally,' said the guvnor, wondering what it was all about.

'Then have a drink. Con was a regular here and we're toasting his memory. Because he's gone you don't want to know him, right?'

The guvnor looked at all of us and got the message that there was no sympathy coming his direction. 'I'll be delighted to join you. A small half if I may.'

117

Gorgeous patted him on the shoulder and said, 'That's better mate. Although I don't much fancy you being delighted about it. Do we look delighted now?' and with that he poured the tea down with the ullage.

The guvnor pulled himself a half and made matters worse by opening his big trap. 'You misunderstand me. No one is more sorry than I am that Con has died.'

If looks could have killed he'd have joined Con right away. 'What do you mean by that?' asked Gorgeous. 'Are you suggesting that we aren't as sorry as you? Us who've been his closest mates for years. If you ask me you're a bit of a liberty-taker.'

Dirty Paws' mate wasn't dumb after all because he spoke up. 'You're all words guvnor. We've shown our grief with money in your till.'

He didn't have to wallop the guvnor with a mallet to get him to see the point. 'Certainly gentlemen. What will you have on me ... to dear Con's memory. May he rest in peace.' He looked up at the ceiling which was covered with bits of silver paper the regulars somehow stuck up there with money wrapped inside for the Darby and Joan outing in the summer. The way his eyes went you would have thought he was expecting Con to come through for a noggin.

He got off light considering. Gorgeous settled for a double rum and black and the other two stuck to large scotches. I only had a pint and a single chaser. After the guvnor's arm had been twisted a bit more and he'd shoved the boat out twice on the trot I began to feel that I really knew old Con. He would have sure been happy to know he had such loyal muckers.

It was too good to last, you can bet, because suddenly a well-oiled Gorgeous leant over the bar and grabbed the guvnor's tie and started to twist it until his eyeballs nearly dropped in the ash tray. 'You're a real hard case, ain't you mate,' he said, and I could tell he was proper narked.

The poor old guvnor couldn't figure it out. 'For God's sake, what have I done,' he moaned.

'What have you done?' said Gorgeous giving his tie a

118

jerk. 'Just insulted the dead, that's all mate. And his griev-
ing friends. Now I can't think of a worse thing than that.
Can any of you?'

Dirty Paws and his mate nodded their heads, and for the
life of me I couldn't see how the guvnor had put a single
foot wrong.

'Let go of me tie and at least tell me what I've said,' he
croaked.

'It ain't what you've said mate. It's what you've done.
There's Con not even cold yet, and his best mates drinking
to his memory, and all you can do is stand behind the bar
and put a fag on.'

Gorgeous brought his left hand up like a flash of lightning and jerked the fag out of his mouth taking about an
inch of skin with it. Then he gave the guvnor a fair old
backhander that sent him flat on his bottle and glass. He
didn't even put up any opposition as the other two went
over the top of the counter and put the boot in.

I didn't agree with it at all, but I don't like to miss a
chance so I whipped over and emptied the till while they
was knocking some respect for the dead into him. I had to
be quick so I only went for the notes.

After he got to his feet and brushed his trousers they
made him pay for one for the frog and toad. Then George
had a word with him. 'Now listen cock, we don't want to
hear any more about this. O.K.? No phone calls or com-
plaints, see? If we hear you've been talking, some of our
mates will come round when you're closed. Then the next
drink we'll be having will be in your memory – and your
wife and kids, if you've got any.'

The guvnor said he was sorry and made it perfectly plain
to everyone that he got exactly what he deserved. In fact he
sounded rather grateful.

Mind you, it was a good thing that the hired driver
hadn't seen none of it. But George hadn't let him come in
for a gargle. Not because he objected to anyone drinking
and driving. It was just that he didn't agree with hired
drivers boozing with their clients.

After we dumped the Rolls back at the office George and

the others wanted to make a night of it and drink a bit more to Con's memory. I made out I was too upset – really I only wanted to count the money I'd nicked. It came to about forty nicker, which wasn't bad. Old Con hadn't done a thing for me when he was alive, but he hadn't done too bad after.

Before I caught a taxi home I bought an evening paper from the old girl on the corner and told her to keep the change out of a bob. I was chuffed to see a report and big picture of the funeral. One of the photos showed Ronnie's wreath up a treat. The words weren't much cop though, they went on about a gangland farewell to a notorious criminal. They was smart though. Only the dead man's name was mentioned, which meant that no one could do them for damages or defamation or whatever it is they call it.

Once I got home I took off the suit and tie and felt a little better because that whistle was giving me the heebie jeebies. Then I lowered my bed and crashed my swede for a couple of hours. There's nothing like a bit of Indian P.T. when you're at a loose end I always think.

It hadn't been a bad day really. Apart from the money I'd shown Ronnie I could be trusted to stand in for him at something important. I would have liked a wedding better. They're more sociable.

Chapter Twelve

It had always been whispered round the manor that Shy Ronnie was the brains behind a lot of the top robberies that were pulled off. He never went on them himself, naturally, he just did the organising. But as nothing had ever been said to me about it at the office I kept my north and south buttoned and my nose clean. I reckoned it this way: if he wanted me to know about it he would whisper in my shell-like.

When he did it caught me on the hop because it was the last thing I was expecting at the time. You see, Gorgeous and me was playing a game of pontoon in the office when in breezed Ronnie with this strange looking geezer.

Right out of the blue he said to me, 'Auk, I want you to meet Perce. He's an expert electrician who can bitch up any burglar alarm system.'

Now Perce didn't look to me like an expert at anything except starving. He was so skinny you expected to see runner beans climbing up his legs, and his adam's apple bobbed up and down like a yo-yo when he talked. It stuck out so much it was the only thing that stopped him slipping through his collar.

'Pleased to meet you Auk,' he said and slipped me a mitt that was just like a chicken's claw.

George must have known him already because he didn't bother to shake hands with him. He just nodded and gave his trilby a flick and said, 'How'stricks Marconi.' Ronnie went over and locked the door which I thought was a little odd to say the least. Then he sat down at his desk and said to me, 'You been here long enough to know a bit more about the organisation. From time to time we go in for a bit of villainy. Nothing shoddy and not too often. When we pull something it's worth while. I'll row you in if you're interested. If you're not, that's O.K. with me, you can leave here and no hard feelings.'

He hardly gave me time to think about it before he said, 'Well?'

'I ain't jumped out of the window in a rush to get away, have I?' I said to him.

Ronnie laughed like a sewer and knocked the wind out of Percy with his elbow. 'What did I tell you? I knew he was game. I'm a great judge of character you must admit, George.'

I felt a bit narked really because it stuck out like Schnozzle's nose that they'd been talking about me behind my back, so I said to George, 'You scared I would chicken out or something?'

George opened his trap but didn't get a chance to speak because Ronnie beat him to it. 'It's nothing like that really. George thought we ought to proposition you over a drink in case you weren't interested. Then you wouldn't be in an awkward spot with me. But I told him not to bother. I knew you'd want to come in on it.'

I must say I felt pretty good at that, just like I did at school once when I was picked for the cricket team.

Ronnie looked at us and said, 'Right, everybody comfortable. O.K. I'll begin. Here's the set up. The place we screw makes high quality jewellery, but it's not the tomfoolery we're so much interested in as the stuff they make it with. O.K.? Now this place is slap bang next to an empty shop where some bright spark has kindly hung a big sign saying it's due for demolition. Now next weekend's Bank Holiday when everyone will be out enjoying themselves, so why shouldn't we I say. It will give us two clear days to get through the wall and hoist the stuff out. By the time it's discovered they won't see us for the dust.'

You had to admire the way Ronnie went about things. Somehow or other he had got hold of a map of the burglar alarm system which he spread out on the top of the desk so Percy could work out where he had to cut it. He also had a lay-out of the jewel firm that showed every door and

122

window and the peter where the loot was kept.

Ronnie explained that there would be two other blokes joining us when we started, but there was no point in having them at the meeting because their only job was to knock a big hole in the wall, without making too much noise.

Then Ronnie said to me, 'Auk, I want you to do a bit of shopping as there's going to be five of you locked in above that shop for nearly two days. But don't buy everything in one shop – spread yourself around a bit. No one will remember little orders whereas they will a big one. O.K.? Once we've pulled this the cops will be pulling out all the stops to find out who did it.'

When he handed me the list I couldn't help saying, 'What we going to do, play Boy Scouts?' because that's what it looked like to me. There was sleeping bags, one of those gas things for cooking grub on, tin plates, campers' knives and forks, can openers, and a whole load of tinned grub. He'd even remembered a pack of cards.

So when the meeting folded Ronnie handed me a roll of lettuce leaves and I went home to pick up the motor. After the shopping spree I was to go to a little garage under a railway arch down at Lambeth where I would meet George and the others.

I did exactly what Ronnie briefed me to do. I went to Gamages first, then Selfridges and just for a giggle the Boy Scouts shop. All the stuff fitted nicely into the boot so there was no worry about anyone seeing what I had. After all that I went home, stuck the motor outside the house and went round to The Boot for a few pints. I was in kip by nine o'clock because I knew I had a long weekend ahead of me.

The next day which was the Friday I motored down to where I was to meet George. It was a proper creepy dump all dripping wet with damp and 'Go home Yanks' sploshed over the walls. The bloke who did the painting certainly wasted his time because it was so dirty no Yank would have set foot near. I had to nearly kick the door down before

123

George heard me and opened the door, which nearly fell off of its hinges. The lads were all sitting round one of those coke fires. I recognised Percy all right but the others was absolute strangers. All of them were wearing blue overalls. George said, 'This is Fred and Jim. They're a couple of the finest brickies in the country. They could make a hole in the wall at Battersea Dogs' Home so quietly that you wouldn't even hear a bark.'

Then he tossed me a pair of overalls and said, 'Get slid into them Auk.' As I was putting them on I noticed a blue van standing at the back with Public Health Department painted on the side in white paint. Then I realised it was all part of the job when George told the others to give me a hand with loading all the camping gear into the back of it. We stuck the sleeping bags and other stuff by the side of hammers, chisels, an electric drill, red and white poles and things to balance them on, and a row of those red oil lamps workmen use when they're digging up the street and car drivers love squashing.

When the loading was finished we had a big brew up with tea bags and sat on empty orange boxes smoking fag after fag, while George kept looking at his watch every few minutes as if he wasn't sure it was still going.

'Ronnie had the factory cased for about three weeks and they pack up at about 5 o'clock every Friday. The latest anyone has been there was six. So if we leave here about six ourselves we'll arrive with the place to ourselves.'

It seemed ages before he said, 'Right mates. Let's go.'

Once the van was out of the garage I had to back my own motor in. Then we all piled into the van and set off like we was going to Southend for the day. George shouted through from the driving seat, 'Now don't forget everyone. I'm the foreman. When I tell you to do something jump to it because everyone has got to think we really are workmen.'

I didn't say anything but it seemed to me that the last thing we wanted to do was look like we enjoyed work. Jumping when the foreman shouted was enough to make anyone suspicious and think we weren't real workmen. Still, it wasn't up to me to argue the odds.

George parked the van round by the side of the empty shop and the two brickies jumped out and set up two red and white trestles in the kerb and stuck the long wooden pole along the top.

After fiddling with a bunch of keys George opened the door of the shop and when the coast was clear we slipped in with all the camping gear. The next thing was to get all the tools in and as we were lugging them over the pavement a bloke came up and asked George for a light. As George lit his weed for him he whispered, 'Everybody's gone.' He'd obviously been planted to keep cave.

So we lugged all the stuff up flights of stairs into a back room and spread the sleeping bags and the grub over the floor. One of the brickies rubbed his mitts together and said, 'What about a cuppa, Auk?'

Trouble was it took me half an hour reading the instructions on how to work the primus thing before we even got it going.

While I was doing this the other brickie had drawn a great big circle on the wall just like an archer's target and laid out his tools like a doctor does before he carries out an operation.

Although there was no need for it we was all whispering whenever we spoke to each other. George took another dekko at his watch and said, 'We might as well all get a couple of hours' shuteye because we can't start working till about nine.'

It was a bit of a giggle really. We all struggled into our sleeping bags and started acting like we was a lot of kids on summer camp. I called over to Gorgeous 'Kiss me good-night Brown Owl' but he didn't think it was at all funny.

No one could kip properly because the floor was so hard and no matter what way you turned you always seemed to be lying right on a bone. So George got out of his bag and kicked the two brickies in the ribs which wasn't really necessary anyway as they weren't kipping any better. 'Come on you lazy gits, you might just as well start knocking a bleeding hole in the wall. With a bit of luck there might be a little of the holiday left for us to enjoy. Let's make it a rush job.'

Watching those two blokes at work was a real treat. First they got some sacks to kneel on so that they wouldn't get housemaid's knee. Then they started picking at the plaster so carefully you'd have thought it was their noses they was having a go at. They were certainly the cleanest workers I ever seen because they didn't leave a thing on the floor. Every little bit was swept up and put in a box. When they got down to the brickwork they started digging at the cement with long spiky things just like giant needles. The blokes who dig up dead Egyptians couldn't have been more careful, and that's a fact.

There was nothing for the rest of us to do but sit on our jacksies watching. As they worked the pile of rubbish got bigger and bigger, till Gorgeous said to me, 'We won't be able to move ourselves if we don't shift some of that soon. Come on Auk, give us a hand.'

Gorgeous had even remembered to bring along a couple of big baskets like you see demo boys filling up with stuff when they're knocking a dump down. We piled them full of plaster and that thin wood stuff you find behind and staggered down the stairs with them.

'We'll dump it in the road by the trestles,' said Gorgeous. 'One, two three, go,' he shouted, and we tossed it in the road right near the kerb.

You could have knocked me down with a feather – a sparrow's at that. Because when we turned round there was a copper standing behind us with his hands on his hips. Now when they do that you know you're just about to get your goolies chewed off. It was getting dark but not dark enough so he couldn't see our faces. I didn't say so, but I thought, 'Jesus, he's got us bang to rights here.'

The copper stood there just nodding his head like one of those car mascots and saying nothing, just as they do when a motorist has made a cock of things in a traffic jam.

He wasn't dumb though after all, because he said, 'And

126

just what do you think you're doing?'

I'll say this for old George, he didn't even look worried. Neither did he sound it, 'We're dumping this rubbish in the kerb, officer.'

'I can see that. I'm not exactly blind,' says Mr Plod. 'But why when everyone else has knocked off for the holiday?'

George lit a fag and offered one to the copper who brushed it away as if he'd been offered a stick of jelly to light. 'That's our van officer.'

The copper looked at it, strolled over and kicked the tyres to make sure it was real, then said, 'So?'

'So we're from the Public Health and we don't have no holidays,' said George. 'Like you officer, we work all the hours the good Lord sends.'

All coppers are bastards and they know it. So if you're nice to them they're so chuffed they would give you the keys of the Bank of England and stand bail if you got clobbered. George nodded over his shoulder at the shop and said, 'We're digging up the drains and water pipes in there. If we don't the whole neighbourhood will be down with typhoid or cholera or the black death even. The place is rotten because the sewage is all leaking into the drinking water. So that's why we're working when no one else is. As it is we may be too late.' He clicked his fingers together. 'The whole neighbourhood may go like that.'

The copper, who give him his due wasn't very old, looked a trifle windy. 'Tell me, can you pick anything up just standing on the pavement outside?'

George thought deep. 'I couldn't rightly say. Only the Medical Officer could answer that, and he'll be along soon. But it obviously ain't a picnic otherwise we wouldn't be getting danger money. Come in and have a look for yourself.'

'No thanks,' said the copper like he was being asked to feed the lions barehanded. 'I've got my beat to look after.' Then like all coppers he had to have the last word.

'I hope you're not going to leave that rubble in the road unlit so that some unfortunate motorist will drive into it

127

and break his ruddy neck.'

I hadn't said a dicky bird myself till then. 'No, we've got some lamps in the van,' I said, and darted off and came back with half a dozen and stuck them round the trestles. I started patting at my pockets but couldn't find no matches. Then the bogey tapped me on the back and handed me his lighter. 'Borrow this.'

He waited till I'd lit them all then he said, 'I thought our job was bad enough but I'm damned if I'd risk my life digging up a lot of germ ridden drains.'

Gorgeous shrugged his shoulders. 'We don't see it that way. It's a public service. Someone's got to do it.'

The copper started walking away at the regulation pace. 'Cheers,' he said. When he was ten yards away he started clearing his throat as if he'd swallowed a fly or some of the terrible germs George had been nattering on about.

I couldn't help saying to Gorgeous, 'That was quick thinking. I thought we was rumbled then.'

'No,' he said. 'That was the line Ronnie dreamt up in case we were interrupted at all. Tell you what Auk, those brickies will be hours yet. So lets you and me amble over to the boozer and wash away the germs.' In the bar a couple of blokes were playing cricket on the dart board. George called up his usual rum and black and got me a pint of bitter that had more collar on it than the Archbishop of Canterbury.

'Business bad guv,' said George in a voice that made it seem the guvnor was the other side of Wembley Stadium.

The guvnor was a bit thick about the short-measure hint because as he wiped his hands on the same towel he used to wipe the glasses with he said, 'No sir. As a matter of fact it's bucking up. I can't complain at all. And when a licensee says that you know things are rosy.'

'Well, what you serving short measures for then?' said George. 'My mate here has been fighting a war against contagious disease for the likes of bastards like you. And what thanks does he get? A pint of beer that would fit into a half-pint glass.'

128

The guvnor took one look at George's face and decided it wasn't worth arguing about, so he topped it up and tried to look like a little ray of sunshine.

'Fancy a game?' said George nodding towards the dart board.

'I'm easy but it's engaged,' I said, thinking the blokes playing wouldn't want to be interrupted. But George just walked over, took their arrows out and said, 'We've decided to give you a game. Any objections?'

The two blokes looked at each other then at George and decided they didn't have no objections.

'Three-o-one up wins. Nearest the middle for diddle is off. O.K.?' said George. George took hold of the arrows, weighed them up and then chucked them at the board like they was javelins. Two bounced out and nearly knocked my eyeball out, the other one just managed to stick in on the double top. George looked real pleased as if he had thrown for it and not the bull.

One of the blokes took his throw and hit the inner with his first throw. 'We're off I think,' he said.

As I took a swig I said to George, 'Don't think I'm carping, but you ever played this game before?'

'You being sarky?' he said. 'I'm a member of a team at the White Hart. We've never lost a game.'

'I'll take your word for it George, but I think I ought to go for our first double.'

I'm normally a nifty hand with the arrows as you know, but all three darts were grouped just outside the wire on the double nineteen, my favourite bed.

George ambled up, pulled the darts out and started writing down the score, 'One in, that's thirty eight, leaving. . . .'

He didn't have a chance to finish because the other bloke who hadn't thrown yet said, 'Sorry mate, but they were all out. Close I'll admit, but out definitely.'

George just about did his nut, 'You calling me a cheat? 'Cos if you are you'd better come right outside and repeat it. I don't take that kind of chat from no one, not no one.'

129

By then George had hold of one of the iron stools that was up against the bar by the leg, and he really looked like he meant business.

The bloke who had opened his trap pulled out a pair of bins from his pocket and stuck them on his eyes. He went and looked at the dart board with his nose half an inch away. 'My mistake. Pardon me,' he said. 'My eyes aren't so good these days. I ought to wear these all the time.' I don't know why he went through all that cobblers because there was no darts in the board by then.

We won two games straight off the row, and the two blokes bought the booze. Then one of them looked at his watch and said, 'Crumbs, my old woman will kill me. Look at the time.'

You could tell they was only making excuses to get away from George, who looked really surprised at them wanting to go. 'Don't shove off like that. I was just beginning to get my eye in. Tell you what, we'll give you a 101 start.'

The offer was too late. By then the two blokes were almost out of the door calling over their shoulders, 'Some other time mate. Thanks for the game.'

George called up a couple more and looked at me just like a kid who's been walloped for nothing does, and said, 'I can't understand blokes staying married if their old women terrify them so much. I think we'd just got the measure of them too.'

I didn't say anything except 'I can understand why the team you play for never lose a match George. You're unbeatable.' The crack went like a lead balloon.

By the time we got back to the boys the brickies had made a hole in the wall as big as a window. They were still chipping away though, and as a brick came away they stacked it neatly in a pile and swept up the dust like a couple of well-trained skivvies.

'Don't muck around clearing everything up,' said George. 'We're in a hurry.'

The brickie looked at him like he was a bowl of snot. 'If a job's worth doing it's worth doing well. I'm a craftsman,

130

see? Where there's no mess there's no muddle.' He showed George his union card too. 'Churchill held a card with us. We're not rubbish mate.'

George ignored them and said to Percy, 'Stick your nut through and have a look at the wiring.'

Percy disappeared through the hole and was away about an hour. When he came back he said, 'It's a doddle. I've cut out the alarm that goes straight through to Scotland Yard. The only thing we have to worry about now is the alarm under the carpets. If anyone treads on that they'll hear it in Timbuctoo. So give me ten minutes to cut it off. When I whistle you can all come down and have a knees-up if you like. There won't be anything left to go off.'

I thought Percy would never whistle because it seemed like he was away for hours. But he did, and George said, 'O.K. Auk, you and me will go down. You other two stay up here to grab the stuff as we pass it up.'

George had the trickiest part blowing up the peter where the gold blocks was kept. It didn't seem to worry him at all though. From the way he was acting it was no worse than lighting a little demon on bonfire night.

He fished out some jelly which he had in a jam jar and shook his head in disgust. 'It's sweating like a fat man on the job.'

It was all double dutch to me. 'Does that make any difference then?' I asked.

'Oh no,' he said in a way that was exactly the same as calling me a Charlie. 'It's just likely to go off half cock and blow us through the roof. That's all.'

The others seemed clued up about it though. They didn't even bother to come down. They just pelted us with the sleeping bags and blankets like we was enjoying a midnight pillow fight.

'Don't say we're all going to kip again,' I said.

'No we ain't Auk. That's to deaden the noise and also see the blast knocks shit out of the safe and not us.'

All the time he was nattering George was fiddling around with wires and odds and ends which he taped carefully to

131

the front of the safe.

'If these dets are as old as the jelly,' he moaned, 'we'd stand a better chance of blowing it with a couple of good farts.'

'Speak for yourself George,' I replied. 'I'm so windy I'd be scared to risk a fart.'

So while George was adding the finishing touches I dodged off up the far end. I knew it wasn't going to be no Hiroshima, but I was going to keep me swede well and truly down. When it did go there was dust everywhere, and the bang was so loud it would have woken up the House of Commons even. Me, I was strictly chicken chow mein and I didn't care who knew it.

Old George was laughing his head off when I did look up. 'Come and have a dekko Auk. I've had brazil nuts that were harder to crack.'

Those sleeping bags wasn't going to be much good for kipping in again though, but the door was hanging off its hinges. Mind you, George was a bit chokker. As he dropped the gold into the sack he kept griping. 'Not as much as we were told there'd be. Still, it'll pay the rent.'

We had a bit of a job passing the sack up to the boys because believe me there's a lot of truth in the saying 'worth its weight in gold'. Then George pulled a list out of his pocket. 'This is the rest of the stuff worth nicking. The other is junk or too hard to get rid of.'

In the shop there wasn't much light but we went round nicking stuff left, right and centre; George just kept saying, 'O.K. we'll have that,' or 'You can leave that load of rubbish where it is.'

I suppose it took us about an hour to lift all we wanted. Then George said, 'O.K. it's time to get out.'

On the way through the shop I passed a bench with a tray full of wedding rings. Some of them had little lovey-dovey messages on the inside. I helped myself to a hand-ful.

We went up through the hole like a couple of potholers. Outside it was pitch black so we were able to load up with-

132

out worrying too much about being seen. The only light came from the red lamps we'd put up ourselves.

George said to us all, 'Right, skedaddle. Go home. I'll take the van back on my own. One man in the motor won't arouse suspicion. If we're mob-handed someone might get a bit nosy and make a buckshee 999 phone call.'

As we dumped our overalls in the back George shook hands with us and said how he thought we had done a wonderful job, and Ronnie had every reason to be proud of us.

I don't know about the others, but I went home to change into the glad rags and decided to enjoy what was left of the Bank Holiday. I strolled down to The Boot to get as stoned as a raisin. I downed a few all right, but I kept worrying about whether Gorgeous had got away. In the end I couldn't stand it no more. Not that I really cared a four-penny about George, it was just the thought of my whack going for a burton. So I grabbed a taxi and went down to Gorgeous's boozer. I figured out that if everything was O.K. that's where he'd go as all the pubs had an extension.

Twenty yards from the saloon bar door I knew I needn't have worried because I could hear him singing 'Land of Hope and Glory' at the top of his voice. He spotted me as soon as I put my snout round the door.

'Come in Auk. What'll you have? Everything's on me. I'm celebrating. Yippee.' The way he was carrying on I could see us all landing up at West End Central nick.

'Take it easy George. You don't have to tell the whole world what we've been up to,' I whispered to him.

'What are you on about? I'm not talking shop mate. I'm celebrating I'm a godfather. Honest. I'm so choked I feel like crying.'

I looked around the bar, but as far as I could make out no one gave a toss what he was celebrating. They were just grabbing the ale and knocking it back as fast as George could buy it. They'd have been just as happy if George had

133

been drowning his sorrow.

'What's going on, George? What's all this crap about being a godfather? Spell it out for me.'

George said, 'Let me buy a drink for my friends first. Then I'll fill you in.'

After he had pushed the boat out again he grabbed me by the padding of my shoulders and said, 'You know when you all shoved off. Well I was just getting into the van when this bird grabbed me by the arm and said, "Quick, get a doctor. I'm having a baby. Quickly. My water's burst."

'I said to her, "Look lady, I've got a lot of perishables in that motor. I ain't got time to go looking for doctors or I'll be *doing* time."

'The next thing I knew she was on her back on the pavement yelling, "It's coming." Honestly I didn't know whether to shave or shampoo. There she was on the pavement and there was me with a van load of hot merchandise. Suddenly she shouted, "Cut the cord. For God's sake cut the cord." "Lady," I said to her, "If you can tell me how to cut the cord with a Georgian candle stick I'd be only too happy to oblige." "You must find something quick, quick," she goes on like she hasn't even been listening.

'Well I went through my pockets and I find my shiv. "Look lady, all I've got is a razor. That any good?" I'll say this for her, she certainly kept her nut. First she made me sterilise it with a match. Then she told me exactly what to do. Auk, I can tell you I was real scared the cops would come round the corner. Anyways, to cut a long story short she had the baby there and then. I piled her and the kid into the van and dumped her at the nearest hospital. On the way, you know what she said? She wanted me to be god-father. She even said she would call the kid after me. George. It's the first time I realised how nice my name sounds.'

I just said, 'I hope you didn't tell her anything that could lead to you being traced. Like an address or something daft; she must have spotted the stuff in the back.'

George gave me his old-fashioned look. 'You must think

134

I'm green. She sat in the front with me. What's more, I intend to be godfather. She's got my address and I don't care who knows. When a kid's born into the world like it is today he needs all the friends he can get.'

Chapter Thirteen

Next morning me, George and Ronnie sat reading the morning papers which had given us a pretty good write up. It was just like one of those old musicals when everyone stays up to read whether they've got a hit or not. Mind you I could do with some of the imagination those reporters had right now. I was there when we turned over the jewellers, but when I read about it I couldn't recognise it for the same drum. One paper had us as an international gang of jewel thieves. Someone else had us master-minded by Mr Big. Another paper called it a Rififi style robbery.

Naturally the big wheel leading the bogeys had handed out the usual tripe about having a vital clue which they wouldn't show out on in case it bitched up their enquiries. That was as good as saying they were up the creek without a paddle. Because you can take it from me the Mr Plods of this world are just the same as everyone else. When they're home and dry they can't stop talking about it, and letting you know what a lot of Sexton Blakes they all are. When they're knackered they don't want to know anyone. One paper printed an identikit picture which didn't help anyone except us. It looked exactly the same as every one the Yard issues. It just makes people think that one bloke is the geezer who knocks over all the banks, murders all the birds and rapes his way through Epping Forest.

I'll say this for Ronnie though, there were no delays when it came to the payola. I don't know what the others got and I didn't even ask. My cut was three hundred nicker, and I certainly never complained about that. Short of being a pop star I couldn't have done better anywhere else.

Mind you, picking up the money wasn't so easy at that. Ronnie had a set routine. He had to so that the Income Tax and the law couldn't pin him down. What we had to do was bowl along to this gambling joint in Mayfair. Gorgeous had done it all before so it wasn't any real problem for him. They knew we was coming anyway. We didn't even go near a game. We just went into a back room where a bloke shelled out our winnings. It was a good idea really because cops and other people get all suspicious if you start flashing a lot of greenbacks around all of a sudden. But there's sweet fanny adams anyone can do if you say you won it gambling and even name the club.

Of course, I had to be a bit artful at home. If the Old Man or the Old Lady had seen me loaded they would have put the bite on and no mistake. So the first thing I did was to ask them if they could lend me a fiver for a couple of days. I had a good half hour of how-hard-up they were and what a mean ungrateful son I was. Still, it was worth it. I didn't get the fiver but they honestly believed I was boracic and lint.

Ronnie was so chuffed at the way things had gone that he let me have a fortnight's holiday, and it couldn't have come at a better time because apart from me being so well heeled old Pamela was having two weeks off from work too.

Mind you, it took a fair amount of arm bending to get her to come on holiday with me. Not that she didn't want to. She was just dead scared that her old man might find out or one of her neighbours see us. As I've said, old Pam was a great one for what the next doors thought. She was like most birds who have been brought up proper. They wear snazzy briefs and bras and whiter than white slips in case they get run over, and not to give some boy friend a treat. I had to pave the way first though, so I took her to a decent noshery and filled her with grub and half a bottle of red biddy before she even began to get interested in being propositioned.

'I'd love to darling, really I would, but what will I tell Mummy and Daddy?'

She came as near as she'll ever get to having a bowl of macaroni dumped over her nut. I mean, what can you do with a dame who's always thinking her Daddy is peeping round the jolly horner with a telescope to see if his daughter's getting laid or not.

'Look Pam, your old man don't even need to know now, does he? You just tell him you're going away with a friend. I am a friend I hope, because if I'm not you're going to be lumbered with a big bill for grub.'

At the same time she was making a right mess of the spaghetti as I was talking to her. She was so worried about her manners that she wouldn't suck it up like I do, which meant that she always had some long bits hanging down. She was a trier though, I'll give her that. She kept at it with her fork and spoon, twiddling and twiddling it round like she was trying to bore a big hole in her spoon.

Pam was too polite to talk with her mouth full, so it took some time before she got around to what really griped her. 'I'd love to come, darling, honest I would. It's not that I'm old-fashioned either. If we were engaged it would be so different, but we aren't, are we?' she said.

You could see the way her crafty little brain worked. 'Look love, at this stage of the game I can't get ringed up. Much as I would love to. You see, Ronnie has me lined up for big things and that little caper would just about ruin it all,' I had to tell her.

Don't think I had anything against saying I would get engaged to her. I hadn't. If being engaged for a fortnight meant her giving the O.K. to going away I would have done it.

'Look Pam, there's a million or two million dolls who would jump at the chance of a holiday with a bloke who's not afraid of spending. You don't seem to be one of them though. So let's forget I mentioned it. I'll just have to line someone else up.'

That made her real shirty. 'Don't ever say a thing like that to me again,' she said, dabbing her eyes with her tiny hankie. 'I'll come, but only because I love you.'

'Well stop snivelling then, because I can't think of a better reason for you wanting to come.'

By the time we got round to the coffee it was all signed, sealed and delivered, and she even began looking forward to the idea.

At first I thought of going abroad to one of those hot places where the birds wear nothing but bikinis, and you can get sloshed for a couple of bob. Trouble is, you need a passport for one of those jaunts. That's easy enough in itself, but it means when you get to the hotel the bloke at the desk is going to tumble you ain't married and won't let you shack up in the same room.

So I plumped for Jersey which is abroad really because the only way to get there is by plane or ocean liner. I did it all proper through a travel agent too. I told him we was going on honeymoon and would he get us a cracker of a room at a posh hotel with a bar, dance hall and a front door step that was under water at high tide.

I even ambled down the Charing Cross Road and bought one of those books about shagging from a sleazy shop that sold jock straps for ruptures, pills for blokes who couldn't manage it, and dirty books for the geezers who were past the pill stage. Not that *I* needed the book, I just thought it might get old Pam going if I let her read it in bed.

The travel agent was real speedy and had the whole lot ready next morning. I picked up Pam in the motor in London – I didn't go to her house in case her old man rumbled – and drove down to Gatwick where we had to catch the plane.

Pam turned up in a nice blue outfit with a real smashing hat. She looked like she was going on a honeymoon. I had had a bit of a fling myself. Two suitcases, because I didn't have any, and a couple of oatmeal coloured lightweight suits, plus half a dozen shirts, and an imitation pair of leopard skin swimming trunks for the beach.

In the car old Pam gave me a wet kiss and said how excited she was. Before I put the motor into gear I slipped a wedding ring on her finger. That set her off grizzling because she was so happy. 'I'm never going to take it off, ever,' she said as if I was going to argue with her. As a matter of fact, it suited me down to the ground because then she wouldn't notice that it had 'From Ron to Edna with undying love' inside. What happened after the fortnight was over didn't matter a J. Arthur. Anyway, she had

139

to have a ring and there was no point in buying one if you had one you'd pinched.

I dumped the motor with a garage that laid on a driver who dropped us off at the aerodrome. He also agreed to pick us up on the return.

On the aeroplane it was quite a giggle because there was nothing but honeymoon couples who couldn't wait to get to their hotel. They was holding hands and nibbling each other like they hadn't eaten for weeks. I thought there wouldn't be much left of them at the end if they kept it up like that. It goes without saying that old Pam got into the mood quick and started acting just like they were. I never objected naturally. I only hoped the mood lasted a fortnight.

At Jersey the hotel had a little bus kind of thing waiting to pick people up. There was about a dozen blokes and girls all going to our hotel. On the plane they went out of their way to look like honeymooners, but once they got in the hotel they all started saying they had been hitched for ages.

When we went up to the desk to sign the book, an oily-looking cove in charge of the keys said, 'Would you sign the book, sir?'

You've guessed what happened – old Pam wrote down her proper name. .

Still there was no trouble. I just gave her a playful smack on the bottom and told the bloke, 'She ain't used to it yet. We've just got married.'

'That's perfectly all right sir, and madam. It's a delight to find a young couple who are so happy that they acknowledge they are honeymooners. Now, let me show you your room,' he said, making it sound like we wasn't paying and he was doing us a real big favour. The place was costing me a bomb but it was well worth it. They even had an old bloke to carry the suitcases up. Mind you, he seemed to like the room as much as we did, because when he dumped the bags down he didn't want to leave. He stood there rubbing his hands together and saying, 'Is that all sir?'

I got so browned off with him that I had to tell him

straight, 'Of course it is, unless you're thinking of sharing the bed with us mate.' I don't know what was wrong with him, honest.

Old Pam made a beeline for the window and was looking out at the oggin and saying, 'Do come and look, it's so gorgeous darling.'

Me, I was all in favour of pulling the curtains and having a short sesh. After all, it was costing me a mint and I wanted to make the most of it, but Pamela had other ideas. She started unpacking her gear and sticking it on hangers and putting it in the wardrobe.

That seemed a waste of time to me, and I told her, 'What's the point of unpacking after spending hours trying to get it all into the cases? Leave the gear alone, and take it out when you want it.'

Still, I let her have her way as there was no point in putting her back up so early in the game. By the time she had finished it was time to go down and eat; I was all for it because there's one thing you learn very quickly and that is a bellyful of beer and no grub are the two worst things on this earth when it comes to honeymooning.

Down in the restaurant everything was laid out like the Lord Mayor of London was coming. A proper waiter showed us to the table and even held the chair for old Pam. On a stage at the far end a mousy-looking bird with a fiddle was trying her hardest to ruin everything. She was getting bags of help from the piano player and another bloke who was torturing a giant sized fiddle between his legs. It was Palm Court in second gear, believe you me. But if you go to posh hotels you have to put up with that kind of stuff.

We hadn't been sitting down a second before a waiter wheeled up a trolley with a big silver bucket full of ice and a bottle of champagne. 'With the manager's compliments, and may you have many happy years ahead together.'

I felt a right nit, especially as the dame on the fiddle started to play the wedding march and everyone started clapping. It all seemed bonkers to me. Because there we was, the only two who wasn't on honeymoon pretending we

141

was, and all the others trying to act like they was Darby and Joan on their silver jubilee or something. I know I had a reason for lying, but I don't know what theirs was. Anyway, we got the bottle, not them. Which must prove something.

The grub they dished up was really something. I can't tell you exactly what it was as it had fancy names, but it went down a treat. After the grub we went for a walk along the front and I just had time to hire a zippy red two seater with a dial that went up to 120 m.p.h. It was show really as I reckon you would have to be a Stirling Moss to do that on the island. Still, I intended to give it a bash in the morning.

When we got back to the hotel the bloke behind the desk asked us what time we would want tea. I gave him a big wink and said, 'Don't ring me, I'll ring you.' He then wanted to know what papers we would like sent up. I noticed that some people had two or three down against their name. I settled for the *Mirror*. I'm not a great paper reader, but I know this much. Papers love to tell you how lousy things are, and how you ought to consider yourself lucky because tomorrow they're going to be a bloody sight worser. So why have more than one lot of bad news to wade through.

Up in the bedroom the maid had laid out my new cossack style pyjamas and Pam's new nightie. She'd never know what a waste of time that was. Then I gave Pam the book and told her to read it while I went down to the bar for a nightcap. I drew the line after about four doubles because I didn't want to spoil the first night.

As I was paying for it I took the lift up to our room although it was on the first floor. I believe in getting your value. Pam was sitting up in bed reading the book with her face all screwed up as if it was all about mathematics or something else brain crunching.

I let her carry on reading until I had stripped, then I pulled the book away and chucked it across the room. 'Don't look so worried about it Pam. I'll learn you the ins and outs in no time.' I thought it was funny, but she didn't even see the joke. As a matter of fact, she was trembling she

142

was so scared. As I slipped in beside her I tried to cheer her up. 'That book says there are seventy three positions, but we won't try them all tonight. There's still tomorrow.'

But all she could think of saying was, 'I do hope we're doing the right thing,' and 'You do love me, don't you?' I said, 'Of course, darling.' I meant it about the first question, but I wasn't so certain about the second. Like so many birds, Pamela couldn't do it with the lights on. When I switched out the bedside light she was a lot better but still shivering. Not that she tried to stop me feeling her all over, she didn't. On the other hand, she didn't do any roving herself. In the end I had to put her hand on it.

To be madly honest I can't say the first time was much fun. I almost ruptured myself, and Pam didn't go a bundle on it either. I never got narked though, because I knew virgins had to be broken in.

I'll say this for Pam, she took to it like a duck takes to water. Later that first night she even woke me up.

Don't think we spent the whole holiday in bed because we didn't. We really had a good time. The weather was pretty good and we went swimming a lot. At night we went dancing and gambling . . . black jack, dice . . . you name it, we played it. Old Pam was jolly good fun, believe it or not. She really let her hair down.

Once or twice she started talking about getting married and how lovely it would be. I didn't hold it against her though. After all, that's what most birds want.

I've never known a fortnight go so quick. Although it cost me a bundle it was worth it. We had a bottle of champers on the plane back – I was really getting the taste for it – then I drove Pam from the airport to the station where she caught her train home.

I knew she was happy because she kissed me real hungry like and said, 'I really did love it darling. I love you too, more than ever.'

Next she took the wedding ring off of her finger and kissed that too. 'Keep it for the next time darling. There will be a next time, won't there?'

'You kidding?' I said. 'I wouldn't mind turning round

143

now and going right back. But I couldn't even bail a drunk out right now, I'm so skint.'

Which was dead true because all I had left was about five quid. Not that it worried me. I knew I'd be back among the lolly soon.

Chapter Fourteen

It was about three weeks after being back at work that Pam dropped her bombshell. It happened as I walked in one morning and she called me over and whispered, 'I must talk to you. Can we meet for lunch?' I nodded and agreed to pick her up because I was really expecting her to have a moan. Since I got back I had been working so hard I hadn't even had time to get her across the back seat of the motor, let alone take her out for a nosh-up.

No sooner had we sat down at the table in the cafe than she said to me, 'You won't be angry, will you? Now promise me you won't.'

'Seeing as how I don't know what you're going to tell me I can't really say, now can I?' I told her.

She looked all round the cafe to make certain no one was listening, then bang, she let me have it right in the knackers. 'I'm overdue darling.'

I felt myself go real cold, honest. Just in the hope of hearing her tell me it was nothing serious I said, 'Come off of it. You could have made a mistake.'

'There's no mistake. I'm always so regular,' she said and out came the hankie. That didn't cut no ice because you could always bet your bottom dollar she would start snivelling at the drop of a hat.

'Just 'cos you're overdue don't mean you have a bun in the oven,' I said to her. At first I thought she might be trying the old come on. I know lots of birds who have told men they are in the spud line. Not because they wanted to get hitched but just to get them to cough up the dough to get rid of it. 'If you're trying to put the bite on you're wasting your time,' I told her real hard.

'How could you think such a thing. I really am. I want help. What on earth am I going to tell Mummy and

145

Daddy? We'll just have to get married.' She said it just like it was the answer to everything.

'Now just a minute. Don't I have a say in this? Just 'cos a bird finds she's harry preggers it don't mean a bloke has to marry her.'

'But there's no reason in our case why we shouldn't,' she said.

'Now look Pam. At the moment my plans don't take in marriage. In a couple of years' time yes, maybe. At the moment, no. I'm just starting to get on. I don't want to be lumbered. Anyway, I don't like kids.'

I didn't like to tell her also that if Ronnie knew I was tied up with a girl who worked for him he'd do his nut.

'I feel like putting my head in the gas oven,' she suddenly said. 'I really do.'

I didn't say anything to her, but I couldn't help thinking that it would be a good idea and the answer to everything, but you know from experience that birds only say that to make you feel lousy. They don't mean it.

'Look Pam, it's early times yet, so don't let's rush to panic stations. Leave it to Uncle Auk, and we'll sort it out.'

That cheered her up a bit, but not a lot. Still, she was not too worried that she wasn't dead scared about getting back late. 'I must dash,' she said after looking at her watch. Then she kissed me on the cheek like we was a married couple and said, 'I'm feeling much better now. I knew you would be able to do something.'

I might have sounded confident, though frankly I didn't have a clue what to do about it. Round our way there was a kind of unwritten law that if you put a bird in the bubble club you married her. They called it the proper thing to do, and no one ever held it against the bird who went up the aisle in white carrying all before her.

My own trouble was that I didn't want to get hitched. Me, I fancied a few years of the big time before I got lumbered with a pram in the passage and dirty nappies in front of the kitchen fire. And you can't blame me for that.

146

As I never had to rush back from lunch I got a taxi down to Gorgeous's local as it had struck me he might be able to come up with an answer. After all, he'd been around for years and if you could believe a word he said he had had more women than Henry the Eighth. So somewhere along the line he must have slipped up.

I figured it was a racing cert that George would be propping up the bar, and sure enough he was. So I walked up and gave him a smack on the back like he was the last person I was expecting to run into.

'Well, fancy meeting you here George. Here, let me call one up,' I said.

'Hullo Auk. I'll have a rum and black,' he said, as if I didn't know. He had a great big book under his arm and as I didn't want to show out too quickly on what I wanted I just asked him, 'What you got there, George?'

'Nothing. Just a book about elephants. I bet you didn't know that it takes a female elephant two years to have a baby. That's a long time now, ain't it? Especially when you consider it only takes humans nine months, and then they bitch.'

I was in like flynn. 'Then they don't always want it, do they George? Take this pal of mine now. He's put this bird in the spud line and neither she nor him want it. But do you think they can find any way of getting shot of it? Not on your Nellie.'

I tried to sound casual like. 'As a matter of fact, he asked me if I could help. I had to tell him though that I didn't have a clue. You wouldn't have any ideas by any chance would you, that I could pass on?'

George ordered another round and really looked like he was thinking and trying to help. 'To be honest with you Auk, I don't. The only time I got lumbered myself was with a bird I was shacked up with once. As a matter of fact, I didn't mind her having it, but we had a bundle one night and I knocked her down the stairs. She had a miscarriage but it wasn't on purpose. Anyway, you can't really get your mate to knock his bird about on the off-chance. It might not even work.'

147

We had a few more drinks together and after a time I began to feel like I couldn't care less about old Pam and the bun in her oven. There's one thing to be said for the sherbert, it certainly helps to solve your worries.

If it hadn't been for George I wouldn't have said no more about it. But then out of the blue a bird he knew came up to us. She was a big peroxide with more rings on her fingers than a hoopla stall at Battersea Fun Fair.

'I'll have a Vera Lynn and tonic seeing as how you're buying, George,' she said.

George turned and instead of being narked he put his arms round her and nearly managed to lift all twenty ton of her off of the floor. 'Elsie, you old bag. How are you? You're a treat for sore eyes.' He held her away from him so he could have a real gander. Which was comic really as she was so big you couldn't have missed her from a mile away.

It turned out that they had known each other for years. So we went to a corner table where she really caned the mother's ruin. It was George who brought up the question again. 'Auk, why don't you have a word with Elsie about your mate. She might be able to help.'

Well, to cut a long story short I told her about this mate of mine who was behind the eight ball because of this girl he had put in pod.

She patted my hand with this fistful of rings and said, 'You go and tell your mate to stop worrying. Getting rid of them is just a little bit harder than making them. Mind you, it's not so much fun. Now listen to your Auntie Elsie and just tell your mate to buy her a bottle of gin and get her to swig it down in a real hot bath. And I do mean hot. She won't feel so wonderful in the morning, I'll say that, but she won't have to be worrying about letting her skirts out.'

I felt real chirpy after that, and although I was still short of the necessary I stayed with them till closing time. We stood nattering outside for a while, then George went off arm in arm with Elsie. 'Come on Elsie,' he said. 'I'll give you a bottle of gin if anything goes wrong.'

Elsie laughed like it was a jolly good joke. 'Isn't he a

scream now? I'm a bit too long in the tooth to be caught out now, but I'll still have the gin. You tell your mate not to worry. It's no worse than a glass of senna pods – and it tastes better.'

Next day I took old Pam out to grub again. She looked real awful like she hadn't slept a wink all night.

'I don't know how you can be so cheerful, honestly I don't,' she said.

'I'm looking chuffed sweetheart because you don't have to worry any more. It's all sorted out, see?'

I explained to her exactly what Elsie had told me. 'You don't even have to worry about the gin. I'll buy that,' I told her.

There was I thinking everything would be hunky-dory. But no, old Pam has to go finding difficulties. 'I know you're trying to help me darling. Honestly I do. But how on earth can I lock myself in the bathroom at home with a bottle of gin? Mummy and Daddy would get suspicious. If I stayed in bed next day they would insist on calling in the doctor.'

I could see it was no good arguing with her. It wasn't her fault really that she had such a couple of awkward parents. But it narked me.

'I don't like to be a worry to you darling,' she said. 'I really don't. But don't you think it would really be best if we got married? I mean, we wouldn't exactly be the first people who have had to. People are much more broad-minded these days.'

I really blew my top then. 'It seems to me that you don't give a monkey's about my career,' I told her straight. 'Can't you get it into your thick head that marriage is out? For the time being anyway.' I added that last bit because I thought if she still had a bit of hope she would go along with me.

'It's not as if I'm asking you to do anything risky. I'm asking you to get sloshed in a hot bath. Some birds would be eating out of your hand for the chance of getting stoned in comfort.'

It's all very well for people to say if you've made your own bed lie in it. I don't go along with that. I'm glad my

149

Old Lady decided to have me, otherwise I wouldn't be here. But after all those years with the Old Man I'm not so sure she wouldn't rather have opted for a bottle of Gordons.

It took a fair old time to get Pam round to agreeing. In the end she did though. She phoned up an old mate who had a bed sitter in Kensington and arranged to spend a couple of nights with her. I dropped her round the corner from her old man's house while she went in to collect her tooth brush and other gear. It turned out she had nothing to worry about because her old man wasn't even suspicious about her going away for a couple of nights. It just showed you what a worry guts old Pam could be at times.

I even drove her round to her mate's flat, but didn't go in. I didn't want her mate to cotton on that I was to blame in case anything went wrong.

It wasn't until three days later that I learned Elsie had been talking through her fundamental. Pam turned up looking like death warmed up and I could see straight away it was going to cost me another lunch.

'It just didn't work, darling. It didn't. And it's no good blaming me. It wasn't my fault,' she sobbed.

'Well, it certainly wasn't mine now, was it?' I said. 'You sure you did it right?'

'Of course I am. I was just terribly sick, that's all,' she went on.

'All right,' I told her. 'But you sure you've given it time? I mean, it might have worked without you knowing like.'

'Don't be silly darling. I would know if it worked. It didn't. Can't you understand that? I do wish you wouldn't be so horrible about it. I did try.'

There was no point in arguing. I could see that. It was right back to square one. She didn't help matters a lot by having to be sent home by one of the firm's cars later on because she said she felt ropy. My mind was made up too, that once I had sorted this little lot out that was the end of Pam and me. It was getting so I couldn't think of anything else but getting shot of the kid.

When I got home to kip that night I couldn't sleep from thinking about it. I just tossed and turned trying to think of a way out. As a matter of fact, I made so much noise that the Old Man hammered on the wall with his boot.

'For Christ's sake shut up. If you can't sleep spare a thought for them that can. You playing on the one-handed flute?' he shouted.

It had been quite a day for me, and I was in no mood for the Old Man's sarcasm. 'Get stuffed or bung your earholes up,' I shouted back. That only woke the Old Lady who joined in with her usual bitch about working her fingers to the bone. All she managed to do though was wake the people upstairs up. So they started pounding on the floor with a broom handle. If only Pam could have known the trouble she had caused.

Funnily enough while I was lying there I got a brain-wave. Doris. If anyone knew what to do in a spot like this she was the one. I could have kicked myself for not thinking of her before. It was such a relief that I fell fast asleep even though the Old Man was still having a slanging match through the ceiling with the people in the flat above. Knowing him though he probably enjoyed it more than a good night's kip.

Because of her job, I knew Doris didn't get up early but I couldn't have cared less about that. What are friends for? So soon after eleven I was taking the key which she left under the mat for her daily and letting myself in.

Doris was dead to the world in her great big bed, and judging from the look of her business was on the up. She really looked like she'd been clocking up the overtime. When I slid my hand under the sheets she woke up with a jump.

'Knock it off, will you?' she said. 'It's early closing. The shutters are up.' When she saw it was me though she looked really pleased. 'What a lovely surprise. I'd given you up for lost. Where have you been hiding, loverboy?'

I started making excuses about working hard, but she wasn't even listening. 'Don't just sit there. Come in and keep me warm,' she said.

Although I didn't feel like it, I knew it was the best thing to do, especially as I was counting on her to get me out of

151

the cart. So I got in beside her. I can't say I was sorry when she said, 'No. Not just yet darling. Just keep me company for a little while.' In the next breath she asked, 'What's the time?' When I told her she just said, 'Good, we'll have a cuppa in a sec. The teamaker'll be going off any minute.'

Doris was a right mixed-up kid. She just wanted to be cuddled, honest. As we lay there drinking tea she gave me a knowing look and asked, 'What brings you round here at this time of day, darling? Trouble?'

'You could put it that way,' I told her. On the way round I had worked a line to shoot which wasn't strictly the truth, the whole truth and nothing but the truth. But it was near enough to win her over.

'It's like this Doris. I'm up to my knackers in trouble and I don't mean maybe.'

'You run up against the law?' she asked me.

'No. It's nothing like that,' I said. 'It's something where only a real pal like you could help me. I've gone and put my best mate's missus in the family way.'

'Charming,' she said, trying to make me feel like a heel. 'And your best friend doesn't go much on it. Right?'

'Stop micky-taking. It's not like that at all. He don't even know,' I told her.

'I don't fancy your chances when he does, either,' she said, sounding real huffy. 'Honestly, you ought to be ashamed of yourself.'

'Look, Doris, you got it all wrong. I'm not pretending that I'm not ashamed. I am. But it isn't like you see it; you see, my mate's in the army serving abroad. Now I was at a party a few weeks ago and his missus made a bee line for me. I was shanted up, otherwise I wouldn't have done a thing. But you know how it is. She kept on and bang. Now she's telling me that he'll kill her *and* me if he finds out.'

Doris took it all dead calm. 'I'll say this for you cock. When you find trouble you don't muck about, do you? You have it real big. So you've come round to me to help her get shot of it.'

There was no point in beating about the bush. 'That's just about the score Doris. She's had a bash at the gin and bath routine but it never worked.'

Doris made a noise like she was disgusted that anyone would even try it. 'Look, you take a tip from me and leave that witch doctor stuff alone. Another thing, you keep this girl away from those back alley old cows and their knitting needles. Otherwise you can take it from me you'll find yourself in Court explaining why a dying girl has been dumped on your door.'

As she poured out more tea and put a couple of biscuits in the saucer she told me. 'Now listen to me. You got the poor girl into trouble. You'll just have to get her out. It will cost you money, but that's the decent thing to do. If you will go dipping your wick where you shouldn't you must face the consequences.'

The last thing I needed right then was a lecture, but I put up with it. I had to.

'Now listen to me carefully. I can arrange this for you without any trouble. It takes a bit of time because you have to make certain there are no come-backs. I'll send her to this doctor who does it all above board. He examines her and then gets one of those brain experts to say she mustn't have a sprog. Then the law can't touch him. It'll cost you about a hundred quid. Cash, on the dot. I suppose you've got the money? If you haven't, you can forget all about it.'

'As a mater of fact Doris, I'm stony at the moment. I don't suppose I could borrow it from you for a couple of weeks?'

'You suppose right lover. You just listen to me. I've been real good to you, but I'm not going to shell out money to get you out of a nasty hole brought about by yourself. I'll make the arrangements, but that's as far as it goes. Now come and relax and don't worry about me falling for anything.'

It was at least a couple of hours later that I crawled out of Doris's kip.

'Come on loverboy, out you go. I can't stay here all day enjoying myself. I've got work to do.'

That may sound real screwy, but that's how Doris looked

at things. Business and pleasure were two different things. She never thought of it as a busman's holiday.

Seriously, I wasn't over worried about the money angle. With a little thought I would soon think of a way of getting my hands on a hundred. So I went along to The Boot to get the old grey matter bubbling.

There was hardly anyone in the pub so I got a pint and a whisky chaser and sat down in the corner. It's not that I was being nosy, but two blokes on the other table were having an argument and I couldn't help hearing what they were on about.

They was talking about money, so I naturally became all ears.

One geezer called Sid was saying, 'Look Mike, appearances don't mean nothing. There's a bloke at our factory who buys all his clothes off the second hand stall. He don't drink, he don't smoke, and he's never had a bet. I'll tell you, he once told me he even experimented to find out at what height the gas boiled the kettle quickest. What's more, as he never drunk more than two cups that's all the water he put in.'

Mike said to him, 'So, what does that prove? That he's real tight?'

'All I'm trying to point out is that there are some blokes who look like they haven't got two ha'pennies to rub together. Yet they're rolling in it. Like the one I mentioned. On the other hand, you see some real flash harrys who would have to write out a dud cheque to go for a pony and trap.'

'Look. One swallow don't make a summer, now does it? You've mentioned one bloke at your works. Just one, that's all.'

The other geezer took a long swig at his wallop and went on, 'All right, you don't have to look any further than the end of your own nose to prove my point. Take the old Jew boy in the fag and sweet shop. To my knowledge, man and boy he's been there forty odd years. Now he might not be running Selfridges, but he does all right. A packet of Woods here, packet of Weights there. The odd Players,

154

sweets, envelopes, writing paper. It all adds up. Yet you ever seen him in here? Course you haven't. Ever seen him even go out? It's no again. So it stands to reason he's got it all stashed away. I'd bet you a pound to a pinch that he don't bank it either. That kind never do. The authorities might start taxing them. Mark my words mate, it's in a sock somewhere.'

All of a sudden I realised they was talking about the old boy who shopped me on my first run in with the law. As a matter of fact I couldn't remember his name, but you didn't have to bash me over the noddle to make me get the message. I'd found the money for old Pam's little visit to the quack.

Chapter Fifteen

After giving the shop a good eye-balling I realised it wasn't exactly the Bank of England I was breaking into. I decided to play safe and turn over the old boy's pad late at night when I knew he would be fast asleep. I figured it this way. It would be a doddle to climb over the wall at the back and shin through the window. I could remember the lay-out of the old boy's front room, and that seemed to be the most likely place where he'd keep his lolly. I put on my fur-collared shorty overcoat because it gave me more leg room to move and stuck a nylon in the pocket to pull over my nut. I had tried it out with a stocking before, just for a giggle. Honest, you should see what a difference it makes. No one would ever recognise you.

Then I stuck the Spanish flick knife in my pocket. Don't ask me why, because I don't rightly know. I suppose it just made me feel a bit better.

I'd bought it off a geezer when I first started at the clubs, although I had never had no reason to use it. Mind you, I had practised drawing it and flicking open the blade in front of the Old Lady's mirror. And though I say it myself, I was quite a dab hand at it. I was real quick on the draw.

To pass the time, I went down to The Boot till closing time, but didn't do no serious shanting. With a skinful I might have fallen off the wall and broken a leg or something daft. Also I took a torch with me that had a round bit of cardboard with a slit in it stuck over the glass. It gave enough light to see where you were going but not enough for some nosy parker to get suspicious over.

When I was leaving The Boot I started singing and annoying people by butting in to their talk, and staggering like I had a real load on. Everyone was carping about my

156

carrying on, and in the end the guvnor grabbed hold of me. I knocked the iron girder out of an old girl's hand, and she screamed, 'He's knocked me Guinness over.'

'Come on Auk, be a good lad,' he said. With that, he heave-hoed me through the door. I hit the deck like a sack of wet cement, and laid down till he went back in. As you might have guessed, I only did it to cover myself. If anything went wrong the cops couldn't feel my collar. There was a million people who would swear on a stack of bibles as high as Nelson that I was elephant's trunk.

When I got round near the shop I had a good gander to see if any lights were on. I took my time. There wasn't, so I went round the back and nipped over the wall.

Frankly I didn't need to be no pussyfoot cat burglar to get in without making a noise, because the silly old git had left the top half of the kitchen window wide open. So all it meant was going through and just making certain I didn't step on the cat if he had one. Then stuff me rigid, the old boy hadn't drawn the blinds in the front room, so I had to do that before I could really get down to having a good goosey goosey. Well I looked everywhere. Down the back of the sofa and armchairs, in all the vases, behind the pictures, and even the sideboard. But I didn't even find a dud Thomas Tilling, let alone enough money to get old Pam fixed up. By then I was so cheesed off I didn't bother with the torch no more. I just switched the blooming electric on. After half an hour I knew there was nothing for it except to turn the old boy's bedroom over. I went in there like a cat with corns, I trod so soft.

The old boy must have had something wrong with his chest or something, as he wasn't lying down in bed – he was sitting up in it with a couple of pillows behind his back. And Jesus, was he snoring! It was as noisy as a tube train coming in a station and just as windy. Well it just wasn't my night. Everywhere I looked was a dead loss.

That left one thing. The bed. If it was anywhere it was there. The idea didn't thrill me a little bit, but after all the trouble I'd been to I wasn't going to chicken out at the last minute. First I started feeling round the pillows. Then I

157

almost rolled him out of kip to get under the mattress. Honest, I could hear my old ticker banging away like the clappers. Which was saying a lot, considering the din the old boy was making himself. In the end I sat down in a chair, lit an oily rag and had a good think, which didn't help at all. I very nearly jagged the bloody lot in, but I couldn't see how those two blokes in the rubber dub dub could have got it all wrong. Anyway, in for a penny in for a pound I thought. The old man would have to be woked up and asked point blank where he kept his money. It wasn't as dicey as it sounds though, as I still had the stocking on so he couldn't recognise me. Also, the only light was from my torch anyhow.

The first thing I did was stick a hand over his mouth to stop him shouting, but a couple of hefty shoves still didn't wake him. So I had to give him a real twister of a pinch that nearly sent him through the ceiling. When he opened his eyes, he got the torch light straight in them.

'You just keep quiet and there won't be no trouble,' I told him. The old coot started mumbling away, but that was a dead waste of time as my mitt was still covering his mouth.

'All you got to do is tell me where your money's hid and you won't get hurt,' I told him.,

It meant taking my hand away, but he looked so dead scared I wasn't running any big risk.

'I do not have any money you foolish person,' he said. 'Why would I have money here where there are banks? Answer me that please.'

'Because two blokes in a pub told me you keep it stashed away up here, you mean old bastard. That's why,' I told him.

Then I shook him like he was a dice in a crap session. That did the trick all right. 'Please stop. It's over there, by the window.'

'Look mate, I'm not a cat. I can't see in the dark. Where's over there?'

And that's where I dropped a real clanger. I got off the bed and shone the torch under the window. The very next minute the room was lit up like Southend Pier because the silly old fool had switched a light on. I'll tell you this for free. Nylons are about as useful as a doctored tom cat. Because the old boy gave me one dekko and yelled like a sergeant major.

'I know you. The Grant boy. Now leave here before I call the policeman.'

'Look Ikey,' I said. 'You behave yourself and show me where the money is. Then I'll leave pronto. Anyway, my name ain't Grant, it's Jones.'

Believe it or not, he rubbed his hands together and looked like he had just answered the sixty-four dollar question on TV.

'Of course it is you. And why have you that silly thing on your head? I notice you straight first time, see young man?'

Things were getting to look real daft, I can tell you. There was me standing by the window with me useless disguise, and there was him in bed acting like we was having a happy little guessing game together.

'Listen to me, you crazy old basket. I want the money – honest.' Again he spread his hands out like Jews do and said, 'You have been told. It is under the window. There, in the shoe box.'

Sure enough, there was a box under the window. Just as I bent down to open it, I heard this noise and coming across the room like a number 16 bus was the old boy.

Actually, it was more like one of those bullfight films. For a fat old gink he could certainly get a wriggle on. Me, I was taken so by surprise that before I knew it the flick was out and in my right hand. Then I really did look like a bloody bull fighter.

He was crazy as a coot though. Even the sight of the flick aiming straight at his Derby kelly didn't stop him. Straight on he came and grabbed me like he was a grizzly bear wanting a waltz.

Thinking back on it, I know it wasn't the smartest trick to pull. But I let him have the knife three times in the guts. Even then he hung on like grim death. Which when you come to think of it is exactly what it was. And that's not trying to be corny, either. I was really cheesed. I never wanted him to croak because that can lead to real trouble with the law.

There was no point in moaning about it though. The damage was done all right. The place was in a fair old shambles I can tell you. I must have hit a big vein or something, as claret was all over me, the floor and him. And it was still coming out like a treacle tin without a lid.

As for me, I looked like I had been working in a slaughter yard. My shortie coat was drenched, and it was down the leg of me trousers. It was a fair bet that my new Italian style shoes would never be the same again. Even so, it was no time to start worrying about the whistle. I had to get out, and pronto, so I took a chance and went straight out through the shop door. There was no one to stop me anyhow. But no sooner had I opened it than a bell started clanging away. Which I thought was a real liberty and a bit of a cheek. After all, who needs a burglar alarm when there's nothing to nick.

Lucky for me, I only lived down the street so I could nip in before anyone had time to see what had happened to set the alarm off. My luck held out when I got indoors too. The Old Man and Woman were in Kippsville.

Chapter Sixteen

When I turned the light on in the kitchen I had to whistle out loud as I was in a right bleeding mess, and I really mean that both ways. My best white leather Peckham Rye was so soaked with blood it was a write off. The shoes I could clean up under the tap with the saucepan brush, but I figured they'd still look like a couple of overdone kippers by the time I dried them out in the oven. Even by setting it at Regulo One, which was pretty low, the one the Old Lady used for stews, it would take a couple of hours. And how would I explain baking my shoes to her if she happened to wake up?

Only the dry cleaners could tackle the flute. It looked just like I had rolled in it. The overcoat wasn't much better neither, and as far as my shirt was concerned, and the socks too for that matter, I'd have to stoke up the copper in the wash house and send the lot up in smoke. Still, that wasn't too much of a loss. Fifty bob at top whack. Never mind, you still get fond of things.

One of my first jobs was to give the flick a good wash and drying. It was much too good to chuck away, so I really had to scratch the hat rack to think of a place to hide it safe. Then I had a brainwave. I remembered an old bloke who was in the Andrew during the war used to put his watch in a french letter when he was in enemy water. Then if he got sunk his watch would be O.K. So I stuck the knife in a Durex and went out to the back and lifted the top of the bog tank and put it in there. I only hoped it wouldn't go wrong like it so often did, and some nosy parker would find it. I mean, it's not the kind of thing you expect to find in a lav.

It seemed to take hours to get the fire going, and even then the gear wouldn't burn properly. So I gave that up and went back in again. I was dead bushed when I clocked off. And for what? I hadn't made enough dough for a hot cross bun, let alone getting rid of the one old Pam had in her oven.

The alarm clock was set for eight, but I switched it round to ten. It was much too early for me to get up the way I felt. Anyway, it wasn't really meant for me. It was for the Old Man, and who cared if he was late for work. He only stuck it in the kitchen – where I kipped – because he knew it made me get up and switch it off. I always went back to kip, but he was happy just having needled me. It set him up for the day. Because he had to get up early he thought everyone should.

As it turned out, no one needed the alarm. We was all got up by what sounded like someone trying to kick the door down with hob nailed boots.

The Old Lady was the first to wake up. 'Answer the bloody door, you in there,' she shouted in her best violets they're lovely voice. 'They'll have the house down.'

'Answer it yourself,' I hollered back. 'It ain't for me.' And with that I stuck my noddle under the pillow again. The Old Man came in then wearing only his shirt and I knew he'd had a rough session the night before, as usually he only kept his vest on when he hit the sack. When he kept his shirt on it meant he was too sloshed to bother to undress himself, he couldn't have managed it.

'Do as your mother says,' he went on. 'It must be for you. Probably some of your lairy friends.'

It didn't take me long to realise the callers was for me. 'Open the door please. We are Police Officers. Otherwise we will force an entry,' shouted a voice. 'Now be sensible, Grant.'

The Old Man nearly broke the sound barrier with the speed he crossed the floor at. He was brought up in the hard school that believed coppers loved bashing doors down just for the fun of it.

'Hang on, I'm coming,' he shouted.

He looked real comic, like wee willy winkie in his long shirt. He hadn't reached the door before two hard-faced blokes came in, and you didn't have to look at their boots to know they were bogeys. They was wearing real smart suits, hand stitched round the edge that were a bit square, and trilby hats that went out with oil lamps.

'Let me put a pair of trousers on,' he said, all hurt like. 'Anyway, what you want me for?'

'We don't,' said one of them. 'We want to speak to your son.' The Old Man rushed to my help.

'That's him, there. If you can get him up you're better men than I am.'

'Thanks, Dad,' I said, sarcastic.

The noise must have needled the Old Lady because she started off too. 'Who is it? What do they want?'

So the Old Man shouted back, 'It's the law. It's all right. No need to get up. They don't want you or me – only him.'

The big copper who was obviously the boss man said to the Old Man, 'Why don't you go in and get dressed, Mr Grant, while we talk to your son.'

'You're right,' he said back. 'I'll catch a death of cold standing here like this.'

When he'd gone, the other copper came over to my bed and said, 'Right lad, let's have you. Out you get.' Although he never laid a finger on me, I could tell from his voice he expected me to jump to it.

The boss man who talked rather posh sat on the corner of the kitchen table all relaxed and not sounding at all tough. 'Grant, I'm Detective Superintendent Blakey, and this is Detective Sergeant King. While you're getting dressed, I'll explain why we want you to come down to the station and help us with some questions. We are making enquiries into the death of Mr Glickberg. We think you can help.'

'Who?' I asked as I got out of kip. That's being honest. When he mentioned the name to me it didn't even ring a bell. Not at first, anyways.

'The old gentleman who ran the sweet shop on the corner. Now come along. Hurry lad, and pull your finger out.'

Jesus, I thought to myself. They've got around to it

163

pretty sharpish. Still I wasn't worried. I had made certain last night that there was nothing left to pin it on me. The old man was past picking me out in an I.D. parade. That's for sure.

'Oh,' I said. 'That's a shame. What rotten swine would go and murder him?

The Super didn't raise his voice at all. 'Did I say murder, Grant? Well never mind. I'm sure we'll get to the bottom of it with your help.'

When I got out of bed I crossed over to the suit which was hanging on a hanger behind the door.

The Sergeant just said, 'Not those clothes, laddie. That is, not if you were wearing them last night.'

'Please yourself,' I shrugged. 'It makes no difference to me. I have got another whistle, believe it or not.'

While I was dressing the Super chatted away like a bloody old washerwoman. 'If I recall, Grant, you were in trouble yourself some years ago with Mr Glickberg. That's what made us think of you.'

'Me?' I said, sounding all surprised, though I knew what he was on about, but it seemed sense to play it cool. Then I banged the front of my head like I had suddenly remembered something. 'Oh yes. Now you mention it. I was put on probation. But that was years ago.'

The Super lit an oily and just said, 'Ben. Have a look outside, will you? Try the wash house and any other likely place.'

The Sergeant said, 'Right sir,' and went out. Me, I wished him luck. He would need it, because there wasn't much out there for him.

My chin was a bit rough so I run the electric razor over it, tied my Peckham and was all ready to go to the nick. The Super, calm as anything, took my suit and even picked up my shoes. Then he walked to the Old Man's bedroom and clobbered the door like the Old Man was mut and jeff.

He called through, 'We're off now, Mr Grant. If there's anything you ought to know later I shall send an officer down to you. Good morning.'

164

Back through the door the Old Man yelled, 'Righto, and thanks for calling. I hope he can help. It's about time he helped someone. He certainly don't around here.'

There was a handful of nosy parkers on the pavement, all waiting to see what the squad car was doing outside. I played it real cool as I strolled out, looking like I was Humphrey Bogart, always being pulled in by the law. I wished I had lit a fag up – it would have made me look tougher like. Bogy always did in a touch spot. The Super spoiled it with his good manners. He opened the door for me like I was a dame. When I got in I saw another dick sitting in the back. When the Super got in I felt just like a slice of ham between two bits of bread.

'We won't wait for the Sergeant,' he told the driver. 'You can come back for him.' A tap on the shoulder and we were off like he had a train to catch.

Like all nicks, this one was a proper dump. A cracked blue lamp outside and the usual board full of 'Wanted' posters was on the railings. Inside it looked like a three-star dosshouse. Dirty old paint and that picture thing showing you all the dogs there are in the world, stuck on the wall.

We went into a room that had a desk in it, and a couple of chairs and a big cupboard with cups and shields in it for boxing and football. It didn't look like a place where they got to work with rubber hoses. That cheered me up a bit. First the Super hung his hat and coat up, then said to me, 'Sit down Grant.' Next, he pressed a bell and a uniformed Mr Plod came in and said, 'Sir?' He sounded just like the Old Man at a British Legion reunion when an ex-sergeant talked to him.

'Send us a jug of tea and some cups please, constable.'

For all the good I was doing there I might as well have stayed in kip. The Super just ignored me and started reading through a lot of letters on his desk. The crafty sod hadn't forgotten me though. When I lit a fag he didn't look up, but just said, 'You'll find an ashtray on the window ledge behind you.'

After what seemed hours, but was in fact only five minutes, he blew his breath out like someone who has just finished a chore they don't like. 'Thank goodness that's over. Hate paper work. Trouble is, it gets worse and worse,' he said. 'You shouldn't have joined,' I told him.

When the tea came in he poured me a cup and one for himself. Then he brought the bowl over and said, 'One or two lumps?'

Me, I didn't go a bundle on this tea party touch. Any moment he was going to give me an orange and a paper hat. 'Look chief. What's all this about? Why the kid gloves? You rush me down here. Then don't want to talk.'

'Now what do you mean by that?' he said, sounding real hurt. 'Is there any reason why I should treat you otherwise? You haven't done anything, have you?'

'Of course I ain't,' I told him.

'Then why should I act differently?'

'Look, you asked me down to help you about the old Jew. So start asking me questions. Otherwise I want to call my mouthpiece.'

'Come, lad,' he said, and got up and put his hand on my shoulder. 'You can take my word that if at any time there's need for you to speak to your solicitor arrangements will be made. I'm sure there's no reason why you should want one. Or is there?'

'Course not,' I told him. Suddenly I began to get an odd feeling that he wasn't either so stupid or big-hearted as he was trying to make out to be. 'It's just that I want to get out of here and get to work. I'm losing money. So if it's not too much trouble, let's get it over with. The way you're carrying on your pension will be up before you get around to it.'

'It's not quite as easy as that, Grant. You see, I can't ask you questions without my Sergeant being here. That would be unfair. So we'll just have to be a little patient, won't we? Another cup of tea?'

Then it went all quiet again. Honest, it was worse than if I had a light shining in my eyes and a bloke grilling me who I couldn't see.

'Have a look at the early edition of the evening paper while we're waiting,' the Super said out of the sky blue, and tossed a paper into my lap.

Bang, there it was. Right on the front page. The *Evening Standard* bloke had a full story about the old boy being found dead after someone had reported the alarm going off. I didn't go a bundle on the bit about a hunt for a maniac killer though. Still, the last thing I could do was complain.

'So how can I help you?' I asked. 'I hardly knew the old geezer. I kept well clear of him after what he done to me before. Anyway, I was stoned last night. Ask anyone in The Boot, they'll tell you. I was given the heave-ho from there.'

It seemed I had done myself a bit of good with that, because he didn't answer. Why should I worry, I thought to myself. It wasn't as if I didn't have a cast iron alibi.

A good half hour must have gone before the Sergeant bowled in. He also went through the rigmarole of hanging his hat and coat up before talking. Then he only said, 'Sorry I was so long sir, but it was worth the effort.'

It was only then I noticed he had a carrier bag. He put it down on the desk and mate, that's when I got the wind-up. When he emptied it on to the table there was a plastic bag with what was left of my shirt, socks and tie. Even though most of it was burned away, there was enough left for me to know they was mine. That didn't worry me a lot though.

It was the F.L. with the flick in it. Only a louse of a copper would have the kind of mind that would go snooping around the khazi.

Still they said nothing. The Super just rung his bell again and this time a uniformed three-striper came in.

'I want all this stuff sent down to the Yard's forensic lab straight away,' and with that he handed over my suit, shoes, the remains of the shirt and tie and the knife in the dreadnought.

'Look after that french letter mate. I might want to use it,' I called out just to show I wasn't worried at all.

Joking apart, I could see we were going to get down to business. Sergeant King took out a notebook and sat cross-legged just like a bird in an office who does letters.

'A post-mortem is being held at this very minute,' said the Super looking at his watch like an army officer about to go over the top of the trenches. 'Soon we shall have the full picture. But we can say this already. Mr Glickberg died from knife wounds that were not self-inflicted.'

'Brilliant,' I said. 'No wonder you're a top dog in the force, mate.' The Sergeant came over and gave my tie a yank that made my eyes water. 'Behave yourself lad when the Superintendent is speaking to you.'

The Super just said, 'Cut that out, Sergeant. No rough stuff. To continue. We also know that the shop was broken into and that attempts were made to remove property belonging to the deceased.'

Even at a time like that he had to talk like a television copper.

'Now would you like to tell us where you were between 11.30 p.m. last night and 2 a.m. this morning . . . approximately, that is.'

'Simple. No trouble at all. I was dossing. As I told you, I got tight and went home to sleep it off. There's no law against that yet – or is there?'

After he had written it down, the Sergeant came over and pulled my hair back. 'Explain why you have a flick knife – an offence in itself – concealed in a contraceptive and hidden in a toilet cistern?'

Once again the Super interrupted. 'Knock it off, Sergeant. There's no need to ill-treat the lad.'

Now you didn't need it in letters six foot high and lit up to know that the two coppers were up to the old, old game of playing hardy and softy. Everyone knows they do. One is a real hard bastard who wants to ram your teeth down your throat. The other is a nice guy who's on your side. Usually blokes get so brassed off with the hard nut they cough everything to the bloke who's playing it gentle.

Me, I was too old in the tooth to fall for that. 'Don't worry about me, Superintendent. I know you coppers must have your fun.' The Sergeant just said, 'The knife.'

'The knife?' I said. 'Well, that's simple. You see I was given it and knew it was a crime to have one. So I hid it.

168

My mother wouldn't want me to have a thing like that round the house.'

On and on it went, with the questions all being asked over and over again. It went on for hours, honest. If they asked me something once, they asked it fifty million times. And all the time he was writing it down. I thought he'd end up with writer's cramp.

Even though I say it myself, I didn't crack and I never dropped a clanger.

Then just when I thought it would never end, the Super said, 'O.K. Let's call it a day, Grant. I cannot release you just yet. I am going to detain you here for the night on a charge of possessing an offensive weapon, namely a flick knife.'

At least that was a weight off my mind. Possessing a knife wasn't that bad to be lumbered with.

Trust the cops to make a song and dance about it though. First they charged me. Then I was cautioned that I didn't have to say anything, but if I did they would write it down and use it in evidence. That was all a waste of taxpayers' money, because I didn't say a dicky bird. Why should I, it was a fine at the most.

Like I said, nicks are not the poshest places on earth, and the cell they stuck me in was real ropy. The bed was just a couple of boards and the bog was just a cut out hole at one end of it. There was a sliding thing in the door to talk through, and a bell if I wanted anything.

Still, they did have the decency to give me a hot meal. But they left the light on all night which didn't make kipping too easy. Also, they took away my tie and belt.

Early in the morning I was bundled into a van and driven down to the magistrates' court, and stuck in another cell. After about two hours I was pushed up the stairs into the dock.

The clerk read the charge and the beak asked me if I understood it. When I said I did he told me to sit down and pay attention.

Super Blakey went into the witness box and swore to tell the truth the whole truth and nothing but the truth. He didn't bat an eyelid either when he said it.

But it turned out he wasn't going ahead. 'We are asking for a remand in custody in this case as there are enquiries to be made into a far more serious matter.'

So the beak told me to stand up again. Then he asked, 'Have you anything to say after hearing the officer?'

'I'd like bail, your lordship.' Now I knew he wasn't a judge. I'm not that daft. I just thought it might make him feel a bit better and let me out.

'Bail refused,' he said. 'Remanded for a week in custody.'

It was on the way to the remand prison that I first got a touch of the squitters. The screw, a chatty bloke, gave me a fag and said, 'This is just a holding charge, you know.'

That tasted like a salt biscuit to a thirsty man, as Gorgeous had once explained that a holding charge was what they stuck on you till they could slam you with a real big one.

Still, I slept all right. After all, *they* might want to pin something on me, but as far as I could see they would never be able to make it stick. From my point of view I had been a shade too smart to get lumbered.

That week on remand went pretty quick. The jug wasn't a bad place at all, but best of all the cops didn't come near me so that made me feel a bit like the cat who got the canary. If they had anything they would have been round to see me sharpish.

Things never work out though the way you see them. When the week was up and I was driven to the court the Super pulled out a real dirty stroke.

As I was waiting in the cell to be called, he came in with his Sergeant. 'Good morning Super,' I called. 'You sound full of the joys today, lad,' he said.

'Well you know Confucius he say, "Man with hole in trousers feel cocky." Not bad for this time of morning, eh?'

He smiled at that. The smile was still on his face when he charged me with the murder of the old Jewboy. And he even had the cheek to go through all that tripe about me not needing to say anything. I hadn't said anything last time, but it never helped.

Back in the court again they didn't even bother about the knife charge. When the boss man went into the box he just said, 'At the rear of the court this morning I charged the accused with the murder of Samuel Glickberg while in the pursuit of a felony. Namely robbery.'

Again I asked for bail. The beak looked at me like I was a nut case for having the nerve to ask. At least they cared about me enough to give me Legal Aid, which was something. Then it was back to prison and a sleepless night for me wondering what the rozzers had got up their sleeves.

For the life of me I just couldn't see how they could have got enough evidence to pin it on me. Obviously it was a diabolical frame-up.

I mean to say, I had been dead crafty from start to finish. Not that that helps a lot. If coppers don't have the evidence they just make it all up. But they don't always get away with it. That's what lawyers are for, and at least they had promised me one of those. Which was a good start.

Chapter Seventeen

Now there's never a day goes by without some bishop, parliament member, lord mayor, judge or copper saying in the papers or on the goggle box that the thing that makes this country so wonderful to live in is the fact that you're innocent till they find you guilty. Well, you can take it from me, it's the other way round.

You can understand the church blokes and perhaps the labour and tories saying it, but the cops and judges should know better. Yet they say it more times and louder than any of the others all put together.

It's a fact, and you can ask anyone who's been in porridge that it's a proper load of cobblers. When you're nicked you're nicked, and until you prove you're innocent you stay nicked. Bail is like a bullet in a war. Something the other bloke gets, never you.

Just look at most of the court cases where the geezer does get off. He's so pleased he starts kissing his old woman if he's got one, and shaking hands with the jurors and what have you, and writing thank you letters to the judge.

He forgets it cost him a bomb to prove he never done it. Also, you can bet your bottom dollar outside the court he'll say he always had faith in good old British justice. But does anyone rush around to give him some money to pay for the time he spent in clink while waiting to prove he didn't do it? Not on your Nellie. He's just told how lucky he was to live here and not some horrible other place where you're guilty till proved innocent.

The real truth is most people will say, although not to his face, that he was dead lucky to get away with it. If you hadn't done it you wouldn't be in court in the first place.

Certainly that's the way I felt about the law. Because in my case the law let it be known that they thought they'd got me by the short and curlies.

Just like I said earlier on, a Sunday newspaper had got interested in my case, and as I told you it all fell through. So there's no need to go all over that again.

Apart from all that being mucked up, I still kept the same solicitor. What a crumb. The first time I saw him was when he came to see me in the jug to talk about the case.

'Grant, I want to be perfectly frank, brutal if need be. You face a serious charge. The most serious there is. It is a capital offence.'

'Look,' I told him. 'Cut out the horse manure and speak king's English. Now just what is a capital offence? Murder's bad enough without you adding to the agony.'

He looked at me like I deserved everything that was coming. 'It means you can hang for it. Hang. H.A.N.G.,' he shouted, and sounded quite pleased at the thought.

'I'm not daft. You don't have to spell it out. I know what topping is. The police admit that nothing was stolen though. So that means it's not a topping job. O.K.?' It was like talking to an idiot. Jesus, and he was defending me.

'Grant, the charge says in pursuit of a felony. That means a robbery was contemplated, not necessarily accomplished,' he said, using words he knew bloody well was over my head.

I ask you. What was the use? Lawyers always talk round and round the mulberry bush. That's why they make so much money I suppose.

'Listen. I've never said I did it, and I don't think they can pin it on me unless they start bending it.'

Then he was at it again. Talking to me like I was dead bonkers and blind. 'Grant. We don't know till the lower court just what the evidence against you is. But we have our little ways of getting to hear bits here, bits there.' He looked round the room as he said it as if the 'bits' were dotted all over the place like clues in a treasure hunt.

'Candidly, I don't want to upset you unduly. But from what we have heard they have a strong case. A strong case, and not circumstantial.'

If it hadn't been for the writing I was doing I would have

173

got bored stiff with the whole issue. Time after time I was hauled up in court and the cops trotted out the same old story. They had more enquiries to make. Their enquiries was nearly finished, but not quite. Soon they would be ready to go ahead. All it really added up to was another remand, and more visits from the solicitor. And all he did was lay it on with a trowel what a fix I was in.

'Look, you may be the legal eagle, but don't try and put the fear of Christ up me. It may be a topping job, but they can't do it to me see? I know the law. They don't hang anyone here till they're 21, so there.'

The lawyer looked at me very odd. 'Grant, I have something to tell you. You have the facts a trifle wrong. Here they will not let you vote until you are 21. Our enlightened community hangs people at 18. That, unless my calculations are wrong, makes you eligible.' He sounded quite pleased to be telling me I was wrong.

I'll tell you straight, that was a bit of a blow. 'And they call this a civilised country. You must be crackers. Anyway, I'm still not worried. They've got hardly nothing on me, and that's a fact. Well, ain't it?'

All he said was, 'Grant, all is not lost,' and he patted me on the back in a way which showed he didn't believe a word he was saying.

As far as I was concerned though, I wished he would get lost. He was about as cheery as a cold hot-water bottle.

Still, if they made things sound too easy they wouldn't get the bills paid. So with a case like mine which was a cinch for a 'not guilty' it was natural he would make it sound like he had a tough job ahead of him. The law's a bit like the motor trade in a way. You go in to get the battery charged and they tell you the engine needs a rebore. You can't make anything sound too simple where lolly is concerned in it.

One day the solicitor told me, 'This is the last time I shall see you before the lower court. I shall be there. Don't worry about it unduly, it's a mere formality. It gives us a chance to hear their case against you. Then all we have to do is get our Q.C. to pick holes in it. We aren't beaten yet,'

174

he said, giving me a slap on the back.

I really liked that *we* bit. Personally I would have been happier if it was true. He might have put a bit more zing into his work.

You ask anyone who's been lumbered with a serious charge, and he'll tell you the same thing. His own lawyer said the magistrates' court was nothing to worry about. It's just like being given a chance to look at someone's hand before you start playing a game of cards. All legal too, and jolly good fun if you happen to be a lawyer.

Only when you go into that dock you find out with a jolt that this is a game of cards where the cops deal from the bottom of the pack. They also have a full house and the fact you've seen it don't help a lot.

At least that's the feeling I got at the end of the first day, and they told me it would need another one to finish it.

Two screws sat on each side of me when I went into the dock. I suppose that was a bit of a con to make everyone feel I was a dangerous criminal who would try and hoof it out of the door at the first chance.

The beak who sat under one of them shield things with a lion and a horse with a horn on its head was the same geezer who had sat through it before, but that didn't make no difference to him. Although he knew what it was all about, he still gave it the works. Stand up, sit down. Do you understand? Read out the charge. A fat chance I had of a square deal if he'd forgotten what it was all about in such a short time. After all, he'd known for three weeks what the charge was, yet he still wanted it read out to him again.

Never mind, I had a pretty good turn-out. The court was crowded and the reporter blokes were so squashed together they hardly had room to write. The only person I knew though was old Pam. She sat in the front seats and waved as I came in. Just like people do at weddings. It was the first time I had seen her since I got nicked, although it wasn't her fault. She had wrote to me saying her Mummy and Daddy wouldn't give her the O.K. to come and see me, as she was under age. There was sweet fanny adams I could do about that. Her letter also mentioned that the pea was still in the pod. I had enough troubles of my own without getting lumbered with hers. After all, if it hadn't been for that I wouldn't have been in the dock.

After some copper had shouted 'Silence' Christ knows how many times, we was all ready to kick off.

A fat-looking bloke in a black coat and striped trousers stood up and said, 'I am appearing for the Director of Public Prosecutions in this case. My opening will be brief. The evidence I shall call is so overwhelming that I submit you will have no hesitation in committing the accused for trial.'

Like all lawyers, his idea of keeping things short was to chat for more than a couple of hours. I can't remember everything he said, but in a nutshell I was a right mean bastard and had done the poor old boy in with a flick knife. Well, he was entitled to his view.

The first bloke in the witness box was a copper who had done a drawing of the shop and room where the old boy copped it. It was a lovely drawing all right, but it didn't mean I killed him. So I wrote him off as a dead loss.

After him, there was another copper who took pictures of the place with the old boy stone cold dead on the carpet. Again it didn't point nothing at me. I noticed though that half the people in the gallery almost broke their necks trying to get a dekko of the old boy lying stiffo.

Then the Sergeant went in and told the beak how he had called round to my pad and found me in bed. Next he produced my suit. Then the burnt gear. There was a long pause while a copper tied a luggage label on each and wrote a number on them. Every time he shouted out the exhibit number like it was a bingo session.

When it came to showing the Durex with the knife in it, he didn't bat an eyelid.

Everyone else thought it was a bit of a giggle, and the usher bloke had to charge around shouting 'Silence' and looking like he would clock someone.

The old beak warned everyone he would chuck them all out if he had any more of it.

I couldn't resist it, so I asked, 'That include me?' That set everyone off again, and the reporters all wrote it down.

My own lawyer nearly did his nut. The beak gave me a ripe bollocking too, and said I should realise how serious it all was. Still, it brightened things up a bit.

Lots of the people who gave evidence seemed to have nothing to do with it, but the bloke in the flash coat and pants who was gunning for me said they showed a pattern of events. Whatever that means.

Then a grey-haired bloke with a monocle went in and said he was the pathologist who had done the examination on the old boy. He said he was a well-nourished man with nothing wrong with him except a bad chest. He had died from stab wounds. I would have thought they all knew that.

Next he was shown the flick and said it *could* have been that knife what did it. It was identical to that one which was used.

What it boiled down to was he *thought* my knife did it. But thinking it was is one thing. Proving it was another. Anyway, there were thousands of knives exactly the same as mine knocking around.

One bloke was talking right over my head. He came from the forensic place they kept nattering about, and talking about nothing but blood groups. After he was handed all the clothes, he said the blood on them wasn't mine but the same group as the old man. I don't know what he hoped to make out of all that jazz. Everyone has blood and it's all red, except those earls and dukes who have blue.

My bloke certainly wasn't doing much to earn his corn. Sure he wrote down a lot in a big book. But he never asked no questions. He just stood up when everyone finished and said 'No questions at this stage. Cross-examination reserved.' It was money for old rope.

So the first day ended. Pam gave me another wave and blew a kiss, and my lawyer said he was ashamed of me.

Honest, the only time anyone looked happy was when the lawyers all asked for some lolly for turning up. They smiled. The beak smiled. The clerk smiled. It was the one time they had agreed about anything all day. Then they all bowed to the beak and called it a day.

Before it started up again next morning the Old Man came to see me in the cell under the court. I could have done without that, honest. His trousers hadn't hit the seat before he was off: 'A fine fix you've put your mother and me in,' he said, looking all hurt. 'Everywhere we go they look at us like we was dirt. I don't know what made you do it, straight I don't. The only good that's come out of it is the money your mother got from some pictures she sold to a paper.'

'Here, hold on,' I told him. 'I hope she hasn't been dishing out those soppy pictures of me in my birthday suit lying on a cushion. You'll make a bloody laughing-stock of me.'

I might have guessed. Not only had he flogged those but ones of me at school and another I had taken standing by the motor looking like I was a hoodlum.

It was only the copper saying 'You two haven't got much time before the court rises, so I shouldn't waste too much time rowing' that stopped me from hanging one on him.

Frankly, I was browned off with him and the Old Lady. None of them had bothered to come and see me since I was nicked. And I told him so point-blank.

'Look son, it's not that we didn't want to. I can't afford to take the time off, and your mother's been up to her eyes in it. But don't worry, we haven't forgotten you.'

'Well thanks a lot. That's made my day,' I said.

'Now don't get touchy. There's plenty of time left for us to come and see you. Honest, we'll be up as soon as your mother gets something decent to wear. After all, you wouldn't want her turning up like a ragbag, would you?'

The real trouble was we didn't have anything to talk about really, and I began to wish that the court would start again. It seemed ages before the screw said 'Time's up, Mr Grant, I'm afraid.'

He sounded real sorry. Actually, both the Old Man and me were pleased. We never talked at home, let alone in a cell.

There was only one witness left to be called, I found out

when I got in the dock. That was the Super. Mind you, he kept at it till lunchtime.

He went rabbiting on about the knife, my clothes, the post-mortem, my blood, the old boy's blood. How it all showed I did it.

Still, when it came to the crunch he had to admit that I hadn't said a dicky bird. And that's what counts, after all.

The beak decided that there was a case to answer. My bloke stood up and said, 'He pleads not guilty and reserves his defence.'

So the beak sent me for trial at the Central Criminal Court – the same as the Old Bailey really.

Then the two lawyers stood up and asked for some more loot and got it, naturally.

My bloke came down to see me before I was driven off. 'I shall be along to see you with the Q.C. who will defend you. Till then, keep in good heart.'

Before he shoved off I asked, 'How's it look? I mean, do you think you can swing it?'

'We'll do our best, Grant. And no man can promise more than that.'

He hadn't exactly sounded like a boxer who was asked how he fancied his chances before a big fight.

Still, as they say, you die if you worry and die if you don't. So why worry at all? It certainly killed the cat.

Chapter Eighteen

There's another thing to be said for the good old English law, only lawyers say justice. It don't believe in pulling its finger out and getting a wriggle on. After the beak was finished with me I was sent to a different nick to wait for my trial. My lawyer told me it would be weeks before it was due up.

'But don't worry, Grant, you'll be well looked after on remand and we shall be along to see you frequently to discuss the defence.'

The thought that I would be seeing even more of the bum made me realise what they meant by crime doesn't pay.

They took me down to the new nick in a Black Maria handcuffed to the biggest screw you ever did see. Though he wasn't a bad bloke. He didn't like the bracelets any more than I did because it was such a bind whenever he wanted to light up a weed. There was he feeling around in my pocket for the matches while I had one of my hands in his groping for the fags.

The prison I went to was more like one of those olden days castles you see in those films about Robin Hood, with whacking great oak doors and big towers. Only there was iron bars on all the windows and no Maid Marian leaning out waving a hanky. You knew it was the jug all right though because there was a big wooden sign on the wall telling you how much time you'd end up doing if you chucked anything over the wall to someone outside.

I'll tell you this though. Getting into a prison is a bloody sight harder than getting out. When the van pulled up outside the main gate the driver hooted on the horn and a bloke slid back one of those peep holes in the door and really gave us a going over. Mind you, he had every right to be sus.

There was nothing to prove it was a police van – except the name on the side and the uniform of the driver who did the trip three times a week. Having made sure it was no one breaking in he ordered about six screws to open the gates and let us in. Right in front of us was another big gate but they wouldn't open that till they had closed the other one behind first. Which was all show really and a waste of time as I noticed there were a lot of prisoners working outside anyways.

Like all blokes on a murder rap I went straight to the hospital wing. But don't go getting no wrong ideas. It sounds like I had a little bed in a comfy ward with smashing nurses trotting round with cups of rosy, and when no one was looking whipping the old screen round the bed for a short session to take your mind off of your worries. It wasn't like that one bit.

I can tell *you* it wouldn't force Butlins to close. I think they called it the hospital wing to con everyone that you was being well looked after. Only what it meant really was that the head-shrinkers could keep a good watch on me and see I didn't wriggle out of nothing by acting potty or pretending I didn't know what I was doing. That was just another con for the sake of the public too. Because if I had run around on my hands and knees barking and frothing they would still say I was as sane as them. Which, when you look at it, doesn't mean much anyway.

The first thing I had to do there was to have a medical, which took all of five minutes. The way the saw-bones touched me you'd have thought I was a sweaty sock or something. He didn't even let me reach the door before he started washing his hands. Which was a bit of a cheek seeing as how he had rubber gloves on most of the time. Then I was marched off to meet the Guvnor in his office. The way he went on you would have thought he was running a private school for the sons of dukes. He kept on and on about the team spirit and how everyone liked it there, and how we was all to pull together.

Naturally he was a paid-off army wallah and dressed like one in a tweed suit and brown shoes you could see your face in. I bet he got some poor convict to do the polishing. I sussed him straight away though when he asked me if there was anything I would like to do while I was waiting, and I told him I wanted to get this writing thing done.

He was all in favour of that he said, and anything I wanted would be laid on. Pencils, paper, and even a rubber.

But he gave himself dead away when he said, 'Good may come of it, Grant. Remember Oscar Wilde wrote a masterpiece in prison.'

Now it's a funny thing, but so many blokes seemed to keep mentioning that old queer. If you were knocked off for a crime, the head shrinkers blamed poor old Oscar. And if you ended up in the nick the Guvnor seemed to think he'd help you in there too.

It sounds like I'm always bitching. To be honest, remand wasn't all that bad. I got plenty of exercise and a bottle of beer every day and a bath at night. I didn't need it every night, but I had to go along with them. They was mad about keeping clean. I reckon if you worked in a laundry they would still want you to bath every night. From that point of view, it was better than at home when you had to do it in a tin bath in front of the grate.

Also, there was always this bind of being seen by some doctor or head shrinker. But I got used to that, and after a while didn't worry about it. Sometimes they was from the prison, sometimes they was on my side. It was all a game really as the prison blokes seemed to spend all their time trying to prove I had the sharpest brain outside Oxford and Cambridge, while my blokes tried to make out I was dimmer than a Toc H lamp.

I got to the stage where I just let them get on with it. Life's too short, I say. I didn't know whether I was expected to be Frankenstein or Einstein.

I was stuck in what they called a 'room' which was just another cell really – with another bloke. There was curtains at the window, but when you pulled them back you still found iron bars and a lovely view of a high wall. It was just my luck to be lumbered with an odd ball.

Apart from him it wasn't too bad. There was a screw in a

white coat on duty all the time, but the first thing he said to me was, 'Look, Grant, I can make life hell for you. Trouble is if I do that I make life hell for myself. So let's play ball. I don't mind you doing stir, but I'm against doing it with you. O.K.?'

We agreed and shook on it, and as a result I was able to listen to the radio and sometimes watch the telly. Some of the things that were on though he wouldn't let me look at like the news or talks where people didn't like the cat or topping.

But to get back to this other bloke. He was a real pain in the neck. The very first time I met him I knew I was in for trouble. I had just put on the pyjamas they had kitted me out with and was climbing into the pit when this bloke with a bald nut poked it out from under the sheets in the next bed.

'You must be Grant,' he said. 'Pleased to meet you. I'm Harper but everyone calls me the Eel.'

I took a good gander at him and said, 'I can understand that mate. You look pretty slimy even from this distance.'

Far from belting up and being narked, he roared his head off.

'You got it all wrong. They called me that because I was such a slippery customer. They could never catch me. Slimy, oh I like that.'

'Seeing as how you're so clever, what you doing here then?' I asked.

'What am I doing here? What a daft question. I'm doing time. Four years. It happens at the moment I'm not too well. That's why I'm in dock.'

'Prison getting you down then?' I said, in a micky-taking way.

'That'll be the day. I've been inside more nicks than you've had birthdays. So keep a civil tongue, see?'

'All I can say is they'd have been real stuck for a name to call you then if you'd have kept outside,' I said.

Then he stuck a pair of bins on and said, 'You look a lot older than your age, mate. Pity. It might go against you. A young face can make all the difference to a jury. You see, in a topping job they really go out of their way looking for an excuse not to give the hangman a morning's work. Pity that. Your looks, I mean.'

'Look mate, my looks is my own affair. Now belt up, I'm going to kip,' I told him.

With that, I stuck my head under the clothes and pretended I was sleeping. But it was no good, he just came round the side and pulled the sheets off of me.

'That won't help cockie. You're stuck with me whether you like it or not. Morning, noon and night. Unless you feel like dropping a line to your M.P. saying you object to the company and could you please move into Windsor Castle.'

He really thought that was funny. He creased up with laughing so much and said, 'Quick, bash me on the back.'

I didn't need no invite. I really gave him a fourpenny one that sent him flat on his mush.

When he got up he shook my hand and said, 'Thanks. I can see you and me is going to get on fine.'

'I ain't stuck with no one. Let's get that clear,' I told him. 'What's more, if you keep boring the pants off me I'll bust you one right on that red hooter of yours. See?'

'Grant, that would be bonkers. That's all these people here are looking for. You wallop me, and it will go straight down in the little book they are keeping about you. Fart and its jotted down. Hit anyone and it goes down in red ink and underlined. That's what they like. A rough handful. It makes them feel better after you've been topped.'

'Knock it off, mate,' I said. Not that I was worried, but no one likes to hear a crank writing you off even though you know they're wrong. 'I ain't even had my trial yet.'

'It doesn't matter, Grant. Your trial is just a formality.' Then he looked down to see the screw wasn't listening, and said, 'I shouldn't tell you this, but I manage to get hold of the newspapers. As an expert, I've read your case and would say you don't stand a monkey's.'

'Get stuffed. All you've seen is a report of the beak's case. You ain't heard my side of it yet,' I said.

Slimy looked me up and down and said, 'I hope you're right for your own sake. It's not for me to go putting you

184

off. Where there's life there's hope, I always like to think. Even though it don't always turn out that way. I'm the last person to want to think of you ending your days strung up for an hour like a turkey in the shed. Because, believe me lad, that's how long they leave you hanging up there after you've been topped good and proper.'

'Look Slimy, I ain't exactly got the wind up, but on the other hand you're not going out of your way or mine to cheer me up. What you say we drop the subject?'

With that old Slimy went off into one of his side-busting routines. 'You're a card lad, and no mistake,' he said when he got his breath back. 'Let's drop the subject. Oh, I like that. Was that meant to be funny, lad?' he asked.

'No it wasn't. Why should it?'

'Well, I mean drop the subject. Very witty. Or didn't you know that they call it the eight o'clock drop? Always done at the same time you know,' he said, talking like he was an expert on the question. 'Not one minute before or afterwards.'

Gradually I got used to old Slimy, but no matter how hard he tried he kept coming back to the question of topping. He seemed to have a real bee in his bonnet about it. Then after a while he got to remember it didn't happen to be my favourite subject and you can understand why. Then he always said he was very sorry to bring it up again, and he wouldn't no more. But he always did.

Every morning, him and me was allowed to go for a walk together, but it was a real drag as we was only allowed to walk round this concrete path which was round like a miniature dirt track.

One morning we was ambling round it and nattering about nothing really when I asked him, 'Slimy, why do they make this round like this? I'm getting bloody giddy.'

'It's no accident boy. It's done on the purpose. You see, they don't want anybody to be able to go straight when they leave here. It stands to reason, don't it? If everyone went straight all these screws, guvnors and whatnots would be out of work. They're just like the coppers. They like crooks because if there wasn't none they would have to find something else to do. And, let's face it, this job is money for old rope.'

And that was all the old fool needed to get back on to hanging. 'Talking about rope, Grant, I bet you never knew that they never use the same bit twice. That little bit of rope with leather round the noose must never not be used on no one else. That's the law.'

'Look, Slimy, I thought you and me agreed that we wasn't going to talk about it no more.'

'That's true lad, but I just thought as you were so closely concerned with it you'd like to know the facts. 'Cos I'll tell you this for nothing, when you get in the death cell you won't even know you're in it. They really go out of their way to hide it. You'll just think it's the best peter in the place with your own bog and bath, and two screws with you all the time. Not to mention the Guinness a day. And no one will ever tell you that the door you always have to sit with your back to is the execution shed.

'Mind you, it only takes them from 5 to 10 secs to get you in there and pull the trap.'

'Listen Slimy, if you keep going on like this I'm going to cut you dead. I'm not having this every day of the week. I keep telling you anyway that I'm not going to be lumbered with it.'

Well, we finished our stroll round without talking no more about it. We just kept on about how lousy the grub was.

You may think this a bit screwball, but after a while I got to like old Slimy a fair bit. And to be frank, I started asking him questions about topping, because the whole thing had kind of got me. I mean, it wasn't as if I was in any real danger myself.

I mean, if it hadn't been for him I would have never known that the hangman had to know your proper weight and height before he could do the job. And he only found that out by taking a good look at you through the spy hole in the cell door. Some of them got so expert at it they was as accurate as a weighing machine. Also, that they even took the trouble to have a P.M. after a topping so that the

186

coroner could say how you died. Which is the nuttiest thing I ever heard, because it must be pretty obvious what had happened.

One evening while we was having a game of crib I asked Slimy how the other cons took to a topping. 'You'd be surprised how bad they take it. Yet you'll find people saying how hard the average crook is. Nothing is further from the truth. Three days before a topping you can cut the air with an axe. The funny thing is that they know more about what's going on than the bloke who's due to cop it.

'When the time's near you see two screws take the poor soul for a stroll round when it's not his normal time. He don't know, but everyone else does, that that's when the hangman goes in to test the gear. He's a hated man. He does the shittiest job for money. For a double topping he lands sixteen quid and eleven for a single.

'And on the actual morning everyone bangs on their cell doors with their mugs. The din is something awful. When it's over, everyone goes right off of their grub. They know he's out in a hole in the yard being eaten away by quicklime. Still don't let me put you off, lad. I've really got to like you.

'Mind you Auk, don't go thinking they rush. They don't. Three clear Sundays you'll get. Plenty of time for a pardon,' he said. 'Trouble is you can't get the padre off your neck. He spends all his time trying to get you to make your peace.'

Well, I didn't toss and turn at night thinking about it. Slimy and me spent most of our time together and we got quite pally, but one morning when we was legging it round the old treadmill he really narked me and no kid.

'You know something Auk,' he said. And that just shows how chummy we was because he was calling me by the name only my mates use. 'I don't think they are going to top you.'

'Well, that is good news coming from you. Because believe it or not, I don't go a bundle on the idea myself, and that's a fact,' I told him.

'No,' he went on. 'You know why? Because I don't think

you did it.'

'You're dead right there. I never,' I said.

'You never did because you haven't got the nonce or the guts. You're all wind and water, mate.'

Pals or not, I was not having him talking to me like that. 'Listen Slimy. I did it right enough. Don't have no doubts about it. What's more, I'll tell you how, and this is straight from the horse's mouth.'

With that, I really filled him in with the whole lot, including Pam and all the trouble I had with the old boy trying to find where he hid his lolly. I could see he was impressed, and that he was really on my side.

'Good for you Auk. He deserved it. I just wasn't giving you the proper credit due,' he said, and we shook hands on it.

The trouble was, he was moved out next morning before I was even awake. I was glad though that he went knowing the full score. I liked him and wouldn't have wanted him to go thinking I was chicken.

Chapter Nineteen

I was allowed to get as many letters as I wanted, which I'm not sure was doing me a big favour. As first I had to answer them which was a real chore. Second, they was all opened before I got them, of course, though the screw said that was only for my own good. Cranks and oddballs liked to get in on the act, he said. Also newspaper blokes wrote pretending they was old buddies and saying how they remembered you at school, and what a lovely geezer you was. And do please drop them a line. Not that they wrote on office paper. All they wanted was your letters for free so they could stick them in the paper when it was all over ... one way or another.

To be straight, none of the screws ever cut nothing from the letters I got, and they always said how sorry they was to have to read them. They said they didn't like it no more than me. If they was speaking the truth, they was bored to death by them. I know I was.

To give old Pam her dues, she was the one who wrote most. She must have worn out a whole lot of pens and spent a mint on paper. I could have done without them, but I didn't like to be too off-handed as, after all, she was doing it all in the right kind of spirit. She wasn't to know her letters browned me off like.

So long, and full of moans. They sounded like them letters to Aunt Mabel in the women's magazines.

Like this one she sent me. It started off like this, as if we was sweethearts.

'My dearest darling.' (Now that alone was enough to start me thinking she wanted to get me all hitched up to her. Still, here's what she wrote.)

'I hate to trouble you with my problems when you have more than enough of your own. Daddy has been quite

189

horrid about the whole thing and turned me out of the house. His own daughter. I ask you! I was desperate at first, but I've now been taken in by a charity society who run a home for unmarried mothers.

'Although I consider we are man and wife in God's eyes, I pray for you and our baby every night and morning. Although I am told to do that, I would in any case.

'I still keep up my job for the time being. Honestly I don't show much yet. How long I can stay working is a question. There are some lovely clothes in the shops now which help to hide my condition. Now, don't go thinking I am ashamed of it. I'm not. It's just that some of the customers don't like it, and I do need the money.

'I spoke to Mr Ronnie yesterday and asked him to help. He was very rude and not like him at all. He said that what you did – I quickly pointed out that you were innocent – was not done in his service, therefore he felt no obligation to help. Also, he did not want the police breathing down his neck. Which was something I did not understand at all.

'Your friend George (so-called) said the selfsame thing, and I was disgusted with him. He had the cheek to say you should know the score, whatever that meant. He sent his best wishes, and I told him point-blank what he could do with those.

'We don't need the likes of them. When it is all over and you have proved you could not do such a horrid thing, we can move away and start a new life with our own baby.'

The thought of that nearly made me throw up, I can tell you. Nappies and titty bottles didn't figure in my future plans.

'Daddy as I said is really upset and quite hysterical about it. He says he can't look the neighbours in the face any more, and everyone at the bowling club says they are sorry for him. Just because of that he won't go any more.

'He said he had tossed and turned for nights now not being able to get a wink wondering how a daughter of his could get involved in a thing like this. He called you a bad lot with black blood, and I burst into tears. Because they were his actual words.

190

'One night he even cried and said he was not an ignorant man and had tried to be fair. He said he had read lots of books about bringing up children. He got so cross he smacked Mummy, a thing he has never done before.

'He said she had brought up a daughter who was sex mad (although those were not the exact words he used) but you will understand how strongly he feels.

'I suppose he can't help feeling old-fashioned in his outlook. But it's awful to think he has no faith in his own flesh and blood, or you. Thank God, I told him, he was not on the jury.

'He said that I should let someone else bring up the baby who did not know the background. I refused, and we had an awful row. Mummy was crying when he turned me out. She did help me to pack though, and gave me ten pounds. Daddy must not know about that.

'I know you are not in a position to help, but do not worry. I had some money from a newspaper which wrote a nice story. "I am happy to bear his child." And I am truly. There was a good picture of me and they have promised to send me copies. I will send you one as normally I do not take a good picture, but this is quite good, even if I say so myself.

'What's more, they have offered me £100 for the first picture when our baby is born. Mummy said I should not do it as I am cheapening myself for money. I don't care, I'm proud of you and our baby.

'The baby and I send you our dearest love. I only wish Daddy would let me come and see you, but he still refuses to give permission. I must close now. Your ever loving Pam.'

There were so many crosses on the bottom it looked like a perm across eight on Littlewoods.

I wrote back to her a funny letter, just to make her happy and stop sending me another boring one. I had enough to think of without her.

I sent to her, 'Dear Pam, I'm dancing with tears in my eyes for the girl in my arms is a screw. Joking apart, the screws here are quite decent. I liked your letter but maybe

191

your old man has got something when he says to you to farm it out. After all, do we really want it when I come out?'

Then just for a giggle I wrote her a letter which was just nothing but pop songs. Even though I say it myself I was pleased with it and it took some time to think out. I can still remember it. I got the idea from a TV bloke who sang a lot of songs strung together and made a kind of story of it.

'How much do I love you, I'll tell you no lies, because I'd like to get you on a slow boat to China, because memories are made of this. So wrap your troubles in dreams and look for the silver lining, as in eleven more months and ten more days I'll be out of the calaboose, and then we'll get lit up when the lights go on. Some day we'll build a home on a hill top high and have a blue room for two room in our mountain greenery home.

'So don't worry too much about me Pam. It won't be long before I'll be seeing you in all the old familiar places. Just remember that a kiss is still a kiss and you will always be the girl of my dreams and my funny valentine, so until I'm walking my baby back home I'm going to buy a paper doll. Love Auk.'

I only put a couple of kisses on the bottom though as I never wanted her to get too many ideas of what I aimed at when I got out. No matter what she said, I was heading right back to Ronnie. I knew he couldn't step out of line and help. So I didn't hold nothing against him.

Believe it or not, the Old Man also wrote. He must have been stoned, that's all I can think. There was no thin up and thick down with his writing. It looked just like he had dipped a bandy spider in the ink well.

He said, 'Dear boy, Sorry your Mum and me have kept you hung up so long for a line and we haven't managed yet to pop along. Its hard as you know to fit everything in.

'I hope you wont mind but I have now sold your motor for a good figure. You could not have got a better one yourself which is saying something for me as a salesman what.

'I had to do it as there was moans about it being left outside day and night with the kids getting in and out. Anyways the tax was about up which I could not pay and also as you know I do not drive nor have a licence. I did in the army but I dont expect you would like to know about that just at this minute. Though it was pretty exciting and dangerous I can tell you straight. Some people got medals for less.

'Since you got into your little scrape we have been getting piles of letters through the door. Some of them have had money in which was nice. Others were not so, and I wont tell you about them as they say things like hanging is too good for the likes of you. I ask you what a thing to say to a boy's mother and father. What you have done is your own look out so why pick on us. That's only fair. I'm sure you agree.

'The reporter people keep coming round asking if we have had a letter from you so please write. They promise not to use anything till its over. They are offering hard cash for every one so if you have a few minutes to spare you can earn yourself a few bob. We can split it down the middle when you come home if you like.

'Mum sends her love and says don't think she has forgotten you. The papers was full of the case and people at The Boot say I am looking on the black side when I say things aren't looking too rosy for your Mum and me. Still dont worry we'll be along some time soon.'

I didn't know whether that was a promise or a threat from the Old Man. Mind you, I was real narked about the motor. He had no right to do that.

I wrote him back twice and asked him to hold out for a good sum for the letters. There's no point in doing things on the cheap.

Chapter Twenty

It turned out that I was to be weighed off in Number One Court at the Bailey, and there's no doubt about it that's where the best cases go. I was being put in the selfsame dock that many other famous people had sat in before me. Although I wouldn't claim to be in the same class as all of them, at least it showed that they thought my case was important.

It was much posher than the beak's court, and the dock had a glass screen all the way round. The public gallery, a bit like the gods at the threepenny rush, was packed with birds in fancy hats and swell clothes, and there was another mob of sightseers in the seats of the court itself. Altogether it was quite a turn out.

The judge was a purple nosed old fart with a pair of them specs on that only had half a bit of glass in each side. He kept looking at me through the part that had no glass in, as if he was worried that I would rush off any minute. I didn't blame him. If I had my way I would have.

On each side of him sat a couple of blokes in fancy dress holding bunches of flowers. They had these fancy pants on that buckle at the knee and white stockings below.

Right in front of me were the legal eagles in their black cloaks and white wigs. My bloke, a Q.C., had the tattiest cloak of the lot with a big rip down the back. But my lawyer told me not to worry about that as it showed just how good he was. It seems when you're at the top you go round ragged arsed. Only the dead beats look ritzy.

Now a funny thing had happened on the way to the Bailey. The screw who was looking after me said, casual like, 'I hear old blue nosed Jeffreys is taking your case.'

'No, it's Judge Briggs,' I said. 'My mouthpiece told me.

He said I was certain to get a fair trial with him.'

'Briggs is his name, but we in the trade call him Judge Jeffreys,' he said.

'Why's that, mate?' I asked, really interested.

'If you don't know lad, it wouldn't exactly fill you full of beans if I told you.'

Well, you pays your penny. As for me I couldn't care less what his nickname was so long as he was rooting for me.

The screw said, 'I'll tell you one thing, Grant. Watch him closely. When he starts digging the wax out of his ears and tipping his wig over his eyes, you're guilty. So watch him like he was the lodger sniffing round your sister.'

I only mention that because after the usual bowing and scraping they started swearing in the jury. They looked a fair enough bunch to me, but my lawyer objected to a couple of women and they were chucked out and their seats were taken by two more men, who looked like they might have a bit of form between them.

Whilst it was all going on I had a gander at the old judge. Would you believe it, he was digging away at his earholes like he had just had a ton of coal shot down them. Also, he was tipping his wig over his eyes as if he was bored to the armholes before we even started.

I reminded myself to tell the screw at lunch time just to show the know-all how wrong he was. Me, I hate blokes who try to put the wind up you for no reason at all.

When the jury was all sworn in and a foreman chosen, the bloke who had the job of screwing me stood up. He was a long streaky git with about four side kicks to help him.

I never got to know his full name as everyone called him Sir Ralph. Even the judge too. I expect they were pals off of duty.

By then it was already time to have some grub so there was a bit more hammering by the usher bloke and a couple of hundred shouts of silence. Then the judge went off to some posh noshery no doubt. There was only an hour's break and I reckon it took him half of that to get up out of his throne and reach the door.

195

Me, I had to put up with a crummy old meal in the cells. As luck would have it, the same screw watched me nosh to make sure I never swallowed a mills bomb disguised as a baked spud and blew the lot of them up. Not that I didn't feel like it. It's just that I didn't want to go too.

I said to the screw, 'You ain't being fair to the old judge. He was having a go at his earholes while the jury was being sworn in.'

The screw swiped one of my spuds with his fingers and said, 'No. I ain't wrong. He's made up his mind. You're guilty. I'll take six to one on that.'

Although I knew he was wrong, I didn't take him up on it. Lady Luck hadn't been running for me too good lately.

After grub the prosecution bloke put up a little folding table thing on the bench in front of him and covered it with sheets of paper. All along the bench by his side were great big thick books on the law. I only hoped he wasn't aiming to go through them all because if he was we would be there for a couple of years.

Sir Ralph who kept tugging his cloak to make sure it was still there started off with a big spiel about the murder. As a matter of fact, I don't know why they bothered to call no evidence because he went through the whole lot.

After about half an hour I noticed a couple of the jurymen were nodding already. I was having a bit of a job to keep awake myself. Sir Ralph really had it in for me all right. 'I will call evidence, gentlemen of the jury, that will show beyond all reasonable doubt that the accused and no one else did this dastardly thing.' Now I was supposed to be getting a fair crack of the whip.

He named all the people he was going to call and kept saying that they would provide stuff that would fix me good and proper.

And all the time my bloke was sitting there writing down stuff and whispering over his shoulder to his side kick. I'll say this for the old Legal Aid system, they did give me two blokes. And judging from the way my geezer was going I'd

196

need them. He didn't look as though he would last the course.

Now one thing about the Bailey is that it's all very nice and proper. A bit like a game of cricket. When my bloke stood up, Sir Ralph sat down. When my bloke objected to something he said how sorry he was first. All the time Sir Ralph kept telling the jury that if there was any doubt about anything I should get the benefit.

I got the feeling that the legal eagles also thought it was a bit of a competition really. The winner being the one who got the most points. A bit like all-in wrestling really. Only it was all fixed before, but they made it look good.

Before he finished his talk to the jury, Sir Ralph called for the flick knife. 'This is the weapon that killed. A killer's weapon,' he said, and with that he pressed the button and out flew the blade.

'It cannot open by accident. Pressure is required. Not much, and it springs out like greased lightning.'

I thought he was overdoing it a bit, but the jury was lapping it up.

'Then I submit the accused plunged it several times into the body of his victim.' Good old Sir Ralph stabbed in and out like he was really enjoying it.

'Then, as quickly as he opened it, he closed it. Just one quick movement.' And with that he closed the blade. Obviously he had been putting in a bit of practice because he could do it nearly as good as me. Not quite, but nearly.

So the first day ended and it was back to the nick for me.

The next day was another long bind with lots of people being called. Most of them had sweet fanny to say, but they still managed to take a long time getting it out.

The hard bastard of a sergeant took ages to tell how he found my burnt clobber in the copper. He read it all from his little book, and everything was handed to him as he read out what he found. The shirt, tie and wot not.

As he was shown them, he said each time, 'Yes. That is it.'

197

On and on it went until it was clocking off time again. My bloke had asked a load of questions, but it didn't seem all that important to me. As far as I could make out, nothing had been said to pin it on me.

The next day was pretty much the same. It looked at one point as if things was really going good for me. During the evidence on the blood, and that seemed to go on for hours, I noticed a couple of the jury having a crafty doze. Which was perfectly all right with me as my legal mouthpiece had said the blood stuff was going to give him a real headache.

So it only stood to reason if it sent them off to kip it wasn't cutting too much ice.

When the top copper went into the box to give his side of it he had to admit that when he saw me next morning I had never owned up to it. In fact, I had always said I never did it, he said. That must have stuck in his throat a bit.

He went a bundle on the knife though. Trying to make out how simple it was to open it and close it. My bloke made him look a real liar though.

The old judge had said to him first, 'Take off the condom.' Just trust him to have a fancy name for a F.L.

When the cop took it off he said in that this-is-honest way they have, 'With one simple press, it is open. Another closes it.'

My bloke said, 'Pass me the knife officer,' and he turned it round looking at it like it was some object from space. Then he made a right old pig's ear of trying to open and shut it. Then in a whisper that the jury could hear he said to Sir Ralph, 'I can't get the darn thing to work.'

Ralphy grabbed it off of him like it was his own nicked gold watch being shown to him. He did a real quick job on how it worked. But by then my lawyer had conned the jury into thinking it was a put-up job. I mean how easy it was to work the flick for one side, and how hard for the other. My legal then handed it back to the cop and said, 'I'm sorry I don't find it quite so easy. But then it's been in your possession some time now. Like so many things, practice makes perfect.'

With that, he sat down sharpish. The copper started to moan about my bloke being unfair, but it didn't get him nowhere as my bloke was already squatting. And the rules of court say you can't argy bargy with a lawyer when he's parked his jacksie.

Right from the dock I could hear my bloke saying to Sir Ralph, 'Honestly, I just could not do it.' Sir Ralph was griping that it was cheating, which only proved once more that it was just a game to them.

Naturally the judge had to poke his hooter in. He asked my eagle if he had no objection to me seeing the knife. My bloke said he had. But the judge slashed on him from a great height and said I was to have it anyway. Which shows just once more how bonkers the law is. Because why did he bother to ask him in the first place anyway, if he'd already made his mind up.

So I had to step down from the dock and go in the middle of the court where everyone could see me clear. Then I was made to wear the overcoat I wore on the night.

I stood there like a nit as he said, 'Take the knife out, open it, then shut it please.' I liked that please bit. I knew he only said it to make me feel he was trying to help. When all the time I knew full well he was trying to trap me.

Well it just wasn't on. I took it out like a crippled snail and worked real hard to open and shut it. The jury was all leaning forward looking very carefully.

Then Sir Ralph stood up. 'No doubt Grant you have seen people draw knives such as this with great speed.'

'Oh sure. Some are real dab hands at it. Villains, that is,' I told him.

'Well, just show the jury how fast a villain would operate it,' he told me.

I really pulled a fast draw and opened and shut it in a flash. Then I realised too late that the cunning bastard had conned me.

Still, I don't think it mattered. Because he didn't smile and say 'Got you' or anything like that. He only, 'Thank you' and sat down.

Not even my own bloke said anything. Which was sure proof that it hadn't rated. If it had he would have done something about it. So I never worried. Anyhow, the jury still looked brassed off.

Then come the real hard shock. I felt real sick inside me.

Sir Ralph stood up and said, 'I have a fresh witness to call. I must apologise for not having been able to warn the defence before.'

Me, I naturally wondered what he was up to. My own bloke obviously didn't know because he was on his feet and objecting before he even knew what he was moaning about. Again, it never did him any good. He might just as well have cried in the ocean for all the notice the judge took of him.

So Sir Ralph said, 'Call Mr . . .' Then he mentioned a name I had never even heard of before. So I thought it couldn't be too bad.

But I sure recognised old Slimy when he went into the box, and took the oath like he always slept with a pile of bibles under his pillow every night. It was a turn up for the book all right.

What's more, he had really dragged up for it, with a new whistle on and stiff collar just like a clerk's. There was a lot of giggling though when he gave his prison address.

Sir Ralph told the jury, 'Before he gives evidence, I must warn you that he is not a man of good character.' Old Slimy looked really down in the dumps at that.

'But that doesn't mean he is a liar or unable to tell the truth. He is here on oath,' said old Ralph almost with the same breath.

Well, I nearly fell out of the dock then because some of these lawyer blokes are real dumb. They always think that just because someone takes the oath he's going to tell the truth. Well, even I know that nearly everyone lies his head off in the box. And why not? I can't remember anyone being struck by lightning at the Bailey yet.

Well, Slimy really put the poison in all right. He said

200

that on exercise one day I had told him I did the old boy. Worse, he remembered word for word what I said to him.

Even the jury decided to wake up then and listen. You can imagine what a shock it was to me. The only thing I could think of was to shout, 'You double dyed lying bastard. I never said that at all.' I put on a real shocked look too.

The judge did a little bit more banging with his wooden hammer and my lawyer shook his finger at me and waved his head to show he thought I'd mucked it all up good and proper. The trouble was the jury saw him too and probably thought the same thing.

Sir Ralph then went into top gear. 'In prison, were you able to read anything about the Lower Court hearing? By that I mean the Magistrates' Court.'

Slimy looked real shocked at being asked such a thing. 'Of course not, sir. I was not allowed to see them. I was in the hospital wing with him and we wasn't allowed them in case he saw it and got upset.'

That for a start was a diabolical lie, but proving it was another thing. I knew myself he got the papers every day.

Sir Ralph gave his old black gown thing a tug and came in double handed for the K.O.

'So anything you have said here could only have come from the accused. Unless of course you are gifted with second sight.' With that he gave the jury a sick grin that meant that they would be off their rockers if they thought he had.

'Unless of course you made it up,' he went on, to make it sound fair.

Slimy looked like he had been asked if he slept with his sister. 'I would not lie when a man's life is at stake. On my mother's grave I am telling the whole truth and nothing but it.'

My bloke looked sick. Even his voice sounded as though he was only going through the motions for the lolly. Still,

201

he had a half-hearted bash.

'What promises have been made to you to give this evidence?' he asked. 'A reduction in sentence?'

'No sir. I done it for the sake of my conscience and the public safety,' said Slimy.

'The public? Come come. You have been an enemy of the public most of your adult life. Let's just look at your record.'

With that my bloke went through all the form that Slimy had picked up. He had done the dirty on me all right, but you had to give him credit where it was due. He had a record as long as the M.1.

'And with a record like that you have the nerve to come here and say Grant has confessed to you. All this time he has denied it. Why admit it to you?'

Slimy hammered another big nail in. 'He was just boasting about it. I never asked him to tell me. When he did I was real shocked. I've met some hard cases but he has them all beat. And I'm not saying no more.'

My bloke said, 'We will hear the truth when Grant goes into the witness box. He has nothing to hide. If he had, I would have advised him not to.' I thought to myself there and then, what a hope! If he thought I was going to tell the truth and stand old Slimy's story up he had another think coming.

The old judge looked at his gold watch then although there was one as big as Big Ben on the wall, and decided it was about time we knocked off again.

Down in the cells while I was waiting for the van I found out that the screw who was running a book on the verdict had changed the odds to five to one against me. Which shows just how helpful Slimy had turned out. The rotten nark. Still, there was the next day left and I didn't kip too bad after a decent nosh.

My screw told me not to worry when I told him about the odds. He said that it was the screw's own lookout if he wanted to chuck his money away. Everyone else thought I was a cinch to get off. Or at worst get life.

I did a jump for joy at that; at least it would mean I'd be out in ten years at top whack. My own view was that no decent bloke could believe a word of Slimy's. Without him I still thought they didn't have much to go on. So I would walk out scot free.

Chapter Twenty-One

As soon as I opened my eyes I knew that it was shit or bust day for me. Somehow or other the word had got round to the screws too, and they kept coming in to my cell on tip toe like people visiting someone on a hospital deathbed. They wasn't a bad lot, and they all shook me by the hand and wished me 'Good luck' as if I would need it real bad.

I wasn't feeling too down in the dumps though as I still felt I was going to skate it. I mean I had the most to lose of anybody, so I wasn't looking at it through rosy specs, don't think I was. But for the life of me I just couldn't see how they could whack it on me. After all, I had sat through the whole case and even if I hadn't understood everything what was said, I was clued up enough to know that they didn't have me on ice and dead bang to rights. The clothes and knife and everything didn't help my case I'll admit quicker than anyone, but they still didn't cinch it. No one had saw me do it.

So I was driven down to the Bailey feeling far from down, which was more than I could say for the screws there. When I got into the cell they all started out again on the good luck kick and handshakes all round.

Sir Ralph started the ball rolling by saying he had no more witnesses to call and sat down.

Then my bloke was up on his plates of meat, gave his gown a tug that made the tear down the back a little longer, and shouted, 'I now call the accused.' He said it in a way that suggested a whole army was going to try and stop him.

I walked out of the dock and went into the witness box where the usher handed me the bible and a card with the oath on it. I promised to tell the truth but believe you me I had no intention of even getting near it. Just for show I kissed the book and got a rocket from the judge who made me do it all over again – 'without the theatricals'.

Then believe it or not my bloke asked me my name and address and what job I was doing. That took the cake because it just showed how much attention everyone was paying to what was going on if they had to be reminded at that stage of the game what my monica was.

The first question he asked me was a simple one to answer. 'Grant, did you kill this man?'

'Course I didn't,' I said, and my voice didn't even shake as I said it. Then he asked me where I was when the old boy was clobbered. That was easy too as we had that all worked out between us.

'I was stoned at The Boot,' I said. 'The guvnor had to chuck me out I was in such a state.'

The judge looked over the part of his bins with no glass in and said, 'Members of the jury, the accused is telling you he was inebriated.'

That got him a laugh, and he tried real hard not to show how pleased he was at everyone for realising what a comic he was. Well, he had the nose for it all right.

'You are not proud of your condition that night?' my bloke asked.

'No, I'm not,' I told him.

'You were in a disgusting state.'

'Yes. I couldn't stand up straight.'

'You were in no fit state to break into a house and murder anyone?'

'No. I was only fit to hit the sack and sleep it off, sir. After the fight that was.'

'Fight? You had better tell the jury about that,' he said. We'd gone over it before, so I knew what to rattle off.

'Well, when I was tossed out of the pub two blokes tried to roll me. They must have thought I was an easy touch in my state. But we had a punch-up and I whacked one of them across the nose and his blood shot all over me. I thought I had duffed him up real rotten, that's why I tried to burn my clobber.'

'Do you know these men?' he asked.

'No. I never set eyes on them in my life before. They was a couple of rotten layabouts if you ask me.'

Then he asked me about the flick and that was a piece of cake too as I knew what he wanted me to say.

'I hid the knife because I was scared my old woman would find it. I also knew it was against the law to have one. I've never used that knife on anyone. I never threw it away in case some villain found it and did something wicked with it, see?'

Well, we went right through the evidence and I don't think I done too badly even when he asked me about Slimy.

I got all hurt and worked up when I said what a rat Slimy was. I licked my fingers, wiped it and drew it across my throat. 'See it's wet, see it's dry, cut my throat if I ever tell a lie. Honest, I never said a thing to him about doing it. He kept asking me to own up, but I said why should I when I never done it.' I could tell from the looks on the faces of the jury that they was bending over backwards to believe my story. And I'll say this for my mouthpiece, he *acted* as if he really believed everything I was saying. Well, if he ever gets the sack from the law there's a good job waiting for him at the Old Vic.

What I didn't realise was that old Sir Ralph would be able to have another go at me, which he did in such a nasty way you'd have thought the dead old boy was his dad or something. While he didn't exactly call me a lying git in so many words, his voice managed to get the message over. If he had worn a gas mask he couldn't have made it plainer what he thought of yours truly.

'You are saying you were so intoxicated that night you were incapable of killing a helpless old man?' he asked.

'That's right,' I told him.

'But you were quite capable of fighting two perfectly fit men who tried to rob you?'

'Well if I hadn't they would have probably killed me. I was fighting for my life.'

He just looked at the jury and gave a sick kind of grin. 'As you are now?'

206

I didn't answer that because to be honest I didn't know what to say.

Then old Sir Ralph sounded all chummy dick. 'Tell the jury, Grant. Are you a law-abiding citizen?'

'Oh yes sirree. I don't hold with villainy of no kind at all.'

'I'm so glad to hear that,' he said. 'But why in that case didn't you tell the police you had been savagely attacked? And why try and destroy the clothing that was the one thing that could support your story?'

'Well, it's like this,' I said. 'If I had gone to the bogeys and tried to put two blokes in lumber they might have taken it into their heads to have another go at me. That was the last thing I wanted – more trouble I mean.'

Sir Ralph sounded real puzzled. 'But, Grant, you routed them. Their blood was soaking into your clothing. Do you seriously suggest they hadn't learned their lesson?'

Well honest, I could see I was on to a hiding to nothing from him. He asked me a question and then when I gave him an answer he went out of his way to make out I was lying.

Anyways, he went on and on about the clothes and wanted to know why I hadn't told the cops about it in the first place. Then they could have checked up to see if I was telling the truth. As it was it just looked like it was a cock and bull story I had dreamed up at the last minute.

Well it was, but I just hoped the jury were not all suspicious like him.

Then he came to the knife and got real nasty. He made it as clear as a bottle of gin that he didn't believe me.

'Explain if you will, Grant, how this knife happens to have bloodstains on it. Bloodstains of the same group as the dead man's.'

'That's something that's been baffling me, to be quite honest,' I said. 'I can only think it was used before I had it – on someone else I mean. Not the old geezer.'

'And by a strange chance it exactly fitted the wound. Come, come, Grant. You killed that old gentleman now. Didn't you?'

I thought the time had come for me to give them a touch of the Oliviers. I lowered my head and started sobbing and bashing the box with my clenched fist.

But old blue nose just said, 'Come, come Grant, pull yourself together. You're not helping yourself at all.'

All out of breath and talking like I was real upset I said, 'I can't help it. I never done it, honest. But no one here believes me. You're all against me. You're dying to see a innocent bloke topped.'

It cut no ice with the judge or Sir Ralph.

The judge said, 'You must get this clear, Grant. Neither Sir Ralph nor I have any personal interest in this. The decision rests with the jury. He is here just to present the facts. I am here to advise on the law, no more, no less. Now pull yourself together and be a man.'

Old Sir Ralph looked pleased with himself when he finished which is more than I can say for myself or my mouthpiece.

Then my bloke was up again with what he called his address to the jury. I must say he did me real proud and earned every penny the Legal Aid people was paying him. He was like a walking dictionary.

Once again he went through what every witness had said and tried to pick holes in it.

The coppers came in for a real old ear-bashing. He said they had been unfair in the way they had questioned a poor young man who was scared and didn't really know what was going on. That was me he was talking about.

Slimy got it even worse. He called him a stool pigeon who had made up this fantastic story to get himself out of nick quicker.

He was almost shouting when he said, 'Members of the jury, I ask you to ignore what he said. It will be on your conscience if this young lad were to die through the words of a self-admitted rogue.'

It was a pity – old Slimy wasn't there to hear it. I'd have loved to have seen his face.

He said without Slimy they didn't have no case worth talking about.

My bloke was talking for nearly two hours before he sat down. He looked at me and I gave him the old thumbs up because I honestly thought he deserved it.

Sir Ralph didn't take half so long, but he really piled on the agony. He didn't have a good word to say for me, not one. I was a cold-blooded killer who did it for gain. I was a hard-hearted scoundrel. I was a lying git. You name it, he said it.

Then he pointed his long skinny finger at me and said, 'Not one word of remorse has come from his lips since he entered that dock. Not one.'

Which struck me as being proper daft. How could I say I was sorry, as that would have meant owning up. As I hadn't it meant there was nothing for me to be sorry about.

He didn't see it that way at all. From the way he rabbited on you would have thought I should have gone to the old boy's funeral with a big bunch of roses and tears dripping down my face.

He also praised Slimy. He was a wonderful geezer who had at last showed there was some good in him because he had broken the code of the underworld and spoken up like an Englishman. He seemed to think an Englishman was God or something.

Then in the next breath he was telling me that if they didn't want to believe old Slimy they didn't have to. The prosecution was not relying on him. He didn't matter a fart to them.

After a quick shufti at the clock he said, 'I am nearly finished, gentlemen of the jury.'

Which meant he would only go on for another hour. Which he did. I must say that the way he saw the evidence wasn't the same as I did. When he sat down I was dead scared because I knew that if I was in the jury I would have gone along with him all the way. If only to stop him nattering.

Even then it wasn't over. The judge said we would knock off for lunch and when we all got back he would sum up, whatever that may have meant.

You don't need to be told that I didn't feel like grub,

209

although they sent out to a café over the road and brought me back half a roasted chicken, with peas and chips.

I let the screw have it, and I'll say this for him, there was nothing wrong with his appetite. Still, he didn't have as much on his mind as me.

Only a few minutes was left before I was put up again, and I didn't mind about that, I just wanted to get it over and done with.

The screw had a quick look round to see no one was spying on us, then he pulled one of them little miniature bottles of scotch from his pocket.

'Gulp it down, lad. You'll need it,' he said.

It went straight down into my guts like a hot fag end, and on the empty stomach I felt quite dizzy when I went into the dock again. The court was jam full for the ending, and I don't think I've ever seen so many reporters in my life before. Most of the birds with fancy hats had also turned up again to see me weighed off one way or the other.

But blind old riley, if I thought it was nearly over I was in for a real shock. The judge brought out a whacking great book and started the case all over again. Only he made quite clear what side he was rooting for, and you can take it from me it wasn't mine.

It wasn't exactly what he said but how he said it. Like when he came to my evidence he said, 'You saw him for yourself. If you accept his evidence that is the end of it.' I reckon he would have loved to have sprinkled me round his roses.

Now when you read his words it sounds like he was being fair. When he spoke it, he made it sound like the jury would be a bunch of loonies if they thought I could shout help without lying.

Old Slimy came out of it with everything but the Victoria Cross. The judge went a real bundle on him. I reckon if old Slimy was ever to come before him he would get a pound out of the poor box and an invite to dinner.

It was nearly dark when he shut his book up and said he was finished. Then he told the jury to nip off out and get

210

their verdict. Though he didn't say hurry up, they must have got the message.

Some bloke in a black rig-out but no wig was swore in and made to promise that he wouldn't let anyone get at the jury and nobble it. As if that was possible. I didn't have that kind of money and anyhow no one was pitching for me on that score.

I stood there with the old fingers crossed as they went into their little room at the back of the court. One of the screws tugged my sleeve and nodded with his head for me to go down below again. I wished they had a lift as it was getting bloody boring going up and down.

The first thing the two screws did was to lay on some tea which I needed real bad as my mouth was all dry and stuck together. I couldn't even make any spit come into it. I didn't try and talk because I would have give the game away that I was scared.

All I could think of was those blokes in their little room working out what should happen to me. For all I knew some of them might not have liked the look on my face. And it's for sure the judge hadn't fallen over backwards to give me a good reference.

The two screws poured the tea out and the same one as before slipped another slug of scotch in it.

'Come on, have a game of cards,' he said. 'They could be out a long time. The longer the better for you. That means they can't agree. So cheer up, lad.'

Well, we played cards but I didn't really care. It wasn't because we wasn't playing for money. I didn't mind that. It was just that I couldn't think clear about my hands. But fair do's, they didn't bitch when I loused a round up.

The clock on the wall had one of those big second hands, but even that seemed to be crawling round.

One of the screws said, 'Stop looking at the clock, laddie. As I told you, the longer they are out the better it is for you. Wouldn't you agree?'

His mate nodded his head and said, 'I'm not a gambling man, but I'd say that you'll be all right son.'

When the jury first went out it was around half past four,

and the next time I looked at the clock it was nearly seven.

'Jesus,' said one of the screws, 'they're certainly taking their time. Look, you promise to behave, Grant, and I'll rustle up some sandwiches.'

I don't know what he expected me to do while he was away. But his mate explained that it was a rule that I should never be without two men.

About ten minutes later he came back with a pile of ham sandwiches but there wasn't time to eat them as a bloke yelled through the peep hole, 'They're coming back.' Not that it bothered me at all as I never felt like eating.

I was stood up in the dock. People were standing everywhere. First the judge came in and then the jury came in. I figured something was wrong because none of them looked at me, which was odd because all through the trial they had kept doing nothing else.

Then the jury was asked if they had got their verdict. I can't exactly remember who it was asked. The judge or the bloke in black who always held the bible up. Not that it mattered.

In a very soft voice the foreman said they had. He was asked what it was, and he said guilty. Funny, but I somehow knew it was coming. I didn't feel anything. Just nothing at all.

Then they was asked if it was the verdict of them all, and the foreman said it was.

Suddenly there was a lot of clapping from the gallery and then some boos. But the old judge soon put a stop to that by having the lot – booers and cheerers – chucked out on their necks.

Then he made a big fuss of putting a little bit of black cloth on top of his wig. Then he sentenced me to death. I didn't catch everything he said, but there was a whole load of mumbo jumbo about taking me to some place and hanging me by the neck till I was dead. Which I thought was not necessary as everyone, even me, knew what he had in mind. In fact that screw was right on the first day. The old bastard had made up his mind in the back of his Rolls-

212

Royce on the way to the Bailey. He said he hoped God would have mercy on my soul and a clergyman said 'Amen'.

I was bundled down the steps into the cell and given a cup of tea and a fag.

It wasn't long before my legal eagle came down to see me. The funny old geezer was really upset and I could see he was not far off of having a snivel.

He put his arm round me and said, 'I did my best, Grant, I honestly did.'

'Not to worry,' I told him. 'It's not your fault the other bloke was dealt a few more tricks.'

'All is not lost, Grant,' he went on, and believe it or not he wiped his eyes. 'We shall appeal straight away. We have good grounds.'

I didn't like to put him off. It seemed better to let him have his way. Me, I didn't have too much hope if all the judges was like old Jeffreys, or whatever his name was.

We had a couple of quick hands of solo while waiting for the van to come. When it drove out there was a big crowd outside the Bailey with coppers arm in arm holding them back. Again there was boos and cheers. I could see them through the blue glass but they couldn't see me. I knew that because some of them shook their fists and spat on the wrong window.

When I got back to the nick it was just after nine o'clock, so I knew that by now Pam and the Old Man and Woman would have heard the news on the wireless and telly.

Chapter Twenty-Two

They whipped me straight off to the condemned cell and it didn't need no sign outside to let you know what it was. As far as prison cells go it was the best in the whole building, but you can take it from me if they had stuck a big 'To let' sign outside the Judas hole it would have stayed there and rotted off. Still, they did let me have a good night's kip before the guvnor come in next morning with something to tell me.

The two screws who were on duty jumped up and one of them shouted for me to stand up too. Then the guvnor told me the date for my topping had been fixed. He sounded like I ought to be grateful, and for some soppy reason I even said thank you to him.

That day went real slow for me as I couldn't really take it in proper. I still believed honestly that something would turn up and I would be all right in the long run.

Sure enough the next morning the guvnor was back again to tell me the date had been cancelled as my appeal was to be heard. He patted me on the back and told me not to worry as he was sure everything would turn out trumps. I just couldn't make him out. He seemed just as chuffed as on his last visit, when he gave me the date.

Well, to be fair to them it didn't take long to fix my appeal up. But then it didn't take long for them to turn it down either. Just to make certain I didn't get away with it they had three judges lined up against me.

There's not really a lot to say about that. One morning they came in with my clothes and I was allowed to change out of prison gear and go down to the Law Courts in the Strand. The screws called it that although the lawyers called it the Courts of Justice.

Two screws took me up the back way and I was stuck in

a balcony kind of thing way above everyone else. Frankly I don't know why they bothered to have me along as I wasn't asked to say anything and no one said anything to me or even bothered to look up.

I noticed that old Sir Ralph was there ready to do the dirty on me, and my own bloke had turned up with more books in front of him than the public library.

The thing was heard in the Lord Chief's own court which was just a little bit bigger than the Albert Hall. Don't ask me why, but every other lawyer seemed to have taken the morning off and turned up in his wig and gown to hear what was said. Some of them didn't even bother to sit but just lounged around like regulars in the public bar.

My lawyer had a fair old go at the three judges, one of them being the L.C.J. himself. I'll say this for my bloke, he wasn't scared of them one bit. He said the judge at the trial had led the jury right up the garden path by leaving out the things which were on my side and hammering home the things that went against me. Which was true. He also said the verdict was all a load of cock as the evidence was all against it.

It took him all morning to put it across and he kept going to these books he had in front of him and talking about other blokes in other cases. They had nothing to do with me at all, but I suppose he had something up his sleeve. Whatever it was it didn't cut no ice with the three big-wigs.

When old Ralph stood up to say his party piece they told him to sit down as there was no need for him to answer back. Which just proved whose side they was on.

The other two then had a little huddle round the L.C.J. and whispered to each other for about five minutes.

Then the L.C.J. told my bloke that the verdict was right and that old Judge Jeffreys was a wonderful bloke who had gone out of his way to help me. My bloke looked proper browned off with that. Me, I kind of expected it. No one in his right mind would expect three judges to say that a mate of theirs was wrong. I just wondered myself whether they knew about his dirty habit of picking at his earholes to signal when his mind was made up. They might have had second thoughts about the whole thing. Although I don't think so. Birds of a feather and all that jazz comes first with them.

So it was back to the condemned cell for me. Once more the guv came in to see me. This time it was to tell me that the date he had told me about in the first place still stood. But he told me not to give up hope as I could still ask the Home Secretary to give me a reprieve if I wanted to. I told him I did, naturally.

Now life in the condemned cell is pretty boring as there's not a second of the day when you can call your life your own. I mean the set up don't allow it. When I tell you that the bed wasn't too bad and that I had all mod cons and a private visiting room next door, it sounds as if they had booked me in the Savoy. But the light was never allowed to be turned off even at night, and there was always two screws with me morning, noon and night. When I had a wash they watched me. Every morning they gave me my razor and soap to shave with, but took it away as soon as I had finished, just in case I did the hangman out of a job and his eleven nicker. And you'll never credit it in a month of Sundays, one even watched me when I had a tom tit. Well, all I can say is some blokes will do anything for money.

Mind you, it wasn't always the same two screws. There was a team of six of them who did a straight eight hours on each time. I used to nark them by saying they was the death watch beetles.

I'll say this for them though. They was a decent bunch of blokes who really went out of their way to cheer me up. I must have seemed right ungrateful at times to them.

All the time they tried to take my mind off of the cart I was in, but the way things was run made that hard. For instance, I never saw no one else at all. Prisoners, that is. For all anyone cared I could have been on a desert island. What's more, I wasn't allowed to even listen to a wireless or read a paper. I could have as many books as I wanted though, but I had done without them all right so far so I didn't see the point in taking it up at this stage of the game. Anyway, crime books was out and that's what I read when I

216

did, which wasn't often.

So all that was left was ludo and cards and some other corny games they had got their hands on. I felt sorry for them at times, because if things was hard for me they wasn't no better for them. Even smoking was out for them, although they never tried to stop me having a drag when I felt like one.

There wasn't even no window in the place and the only time I got any fresh air was when they let me out for exercise. Believe you me, I know now why a dog wags his bloody tail when he's taken for a walk. The place I was led to for a stroll was a little yard with a whacking great wall round it, but at least I knew the sky was still there. The trouble was I was only let out twice a day when no one else was around. Once when the others were at grub and after tea. They worried that the others might shout at me or even worse give me a cheer.

The screw I liked best was a bloke called Sidney who was a fat old boy who was due to pack up in a couple of years' time. Him and me become great buddies.

But even he would never tell me straight what was in store for me. I asked him once which way out I would go if things went wrong, but he wouldn't show out.

'I won't tell you boy for the simple reason I don't think you're going to have to worry about it. You just think about the good times ahead when you eventually get out. Because you can take it from me, the Home Secretary will grant a reprieve.'

I also learned from him that thousands of people had signed a form to send to the Home Secretary asking him not to top me as I was so young. Sidney should never have let on to me about that, but he did and it made me feel a lot better I can tell you. If it hadn't been for him I would have been right down in the dumps. But when you know you're still in with a fighting chance you don't feel too miserable.

Another thing he told me was that when they finished duty they had to fill in a book about what I'd done and how I'd been during the day and night. He let it drop that none of them had put in a bad word, which would cut a lot of ice with the guvnor who could actually ring up this Home Sec bloke if he felt like it, and say for him to call it off. Because as Sidney said, 'He's only got to tell him that he thinks a term of imprisonment – a long one mind you – will be enough punishment in your case and he'll give the order.'

Well, when you hear things like that every day you can't help being a bit cheerful.

Another geezer I got to like was the prison sky pilot who came to see me every single day. He tried hard at first to get me to own up to doing it. But when I told him point blank not on his Nellie as I never did it, he stopped putting the pressure on. He said a few prayers every day and I didn't mind that too much as although I don't go great guns on the church stuff he was at least putting a good word in for me up there.

As the days went on I began to get a bit worried as there was still no word from the Home Secretary bloke. So whenever the guvnor came down I asked him if there was any news, but he just shook his head and said no there wasn't, but he was still full of hope. Which was more than I was, as on my reckoning there was only about three days to go before the bloke with the rope would be sizing me up through the peephole.

I could tell that the screws were getting a bit worked up too. They started trying to tell me funny stories which was a thing they had not done before. Also they seemed to be ignoring the rules and having the odd fag when they wanted one. Sometimes they got a big niggly with each other but to be fair never with me.

As for me, I was beginning to wish they would get the thing over with one way or another. I wanted to live all right, make no mistake about that. But I was getting the view that they had been stringing me along all the time.

It was one Thursday morning the guvnor came in and I took one look at his face and knew it was all over. He didn't beat about the bush, and I was glad about that. He just said the Home Secretary could not see his way clear to stop it. So that was that. Don't think I'm boasting, but I felt glad in a funny way. It had dragged on too long for my liking.

You can be messed about too much.

When the sky pilot came in for his usual session he said he had been told of the bad news and would I now like to pray for forgiveness. Well I know it was going back on everything I had said before, but I told him I would. So we both knelt down and asked God to go easy on me. I did that because I knew it was no good trying to kid myself no longer. To be honest, I still hadn't made up my mind whether there was a heaven or not, but if there was I wanted to get up there. And who can blame me for that? So I played it safe.

You could have cut the atmosphere in the cell with a lawn mower after that. Even old Sidney seemed to have had the stuffing kicked out of him. I asked him if he would come in with me when the time come, and he looked real shaken up. But he shook my hand and said he would, and I was glad of that because there wasn't nothing left but to go out showing them I wasn't chicken. Without Sidney I'm not sure I could do it.

All the time old Pam was still writing letters, but I had give up answering. There didn't seem a lot of point. If she wanted to kid herself it was her lookout.

Out of the blue a real funny thing happened. The guvnor come in and said that the Old Man and Old Lady had dropped in to see me. Well, better late than never, I thought, and went in to see them in the waiting room.

The Old Woman was tarted up to the nines in a black suit with a new hat and even gloves on. The Old Man was as smart as he was the one day every year for the Cenotaph parade.

'Blimey,' I said to him. 'You've forgotten to put your medals on.'

The Old Lady gave me a kiss and said how sorry she was that things had turned out the way they had, but she and the Old Man had done the best they could for me. And they couldn't honestly see what made me do such a wicked thing. 'We'll live it down,' she said. 'I just wish they'd give me the chance,' I told her.

The Old Man must have realised he wasn't going to see

me no more because he pulled his fags out and left them on the table and told me to take one whenever I wanted. Before, he had been like a miser with no arms when it came to offering fags around. So I made the most of it. I bet he was sorry he came.

There wasn't really a lot to talk to them about, so I just said, 'Well, how is everybody?'

The Old Man said, 'It's funny you should say that, but your Uncle Ken came round last night. There was this knock on the door and you could have knocked us down with a feather when we saw him standing at the door. He told us that he had planned to have a real right booze-up if you got reprieved. Coming from him that was something, as he hasn't touched a drop for years now. But he realised after what the Home Secretary bloke had said that there wasn't no hope so we didn't have a drink. Still we had a nice evening going over old times, and he sends his best.'

The Old Lady was having a quiet snivel, which made me feel a bit stupid like as the two screws were in there with us and I didn't like them to see her showing me up in public.

'I sent a telegram to the Queen this morning,' she said. 'So I don't see why he should keep going like that. There's still time for her to stop it. So there.'

The Old Man told her to shut up. 'There's no point in leading the boy on like that. You know jolly full well she won't even see it. It'll go straight in the paper basket of someone in her office. So don't go giving the boy any false hopes like that.'

After about an hour the Old Man looked at his watch and said it was time for them to go as a newspaper had driven them up and they didn't like to keep it waiting too long.

'They're putting us up in a nice hotel tonight,' he said. 'So that no one else can bother us in the morning. I think it's jolly good of them as all they want in return is a little chat when it's over. You don't mind, lad, do you?'

'Why should I mind?' I said. 'By then I'll be past caring. Have yourself a ball.'

So they both stood up and got ready to go. The Old Man shook my hand and the Old Woman gave me a kiss which was something she hadn't done for donkey's years. Next they both shook hands with the two screws.

At the door the Old Lady turned round and blew me a kiss. 'Keep your chin up tomorrow, boy,' she said, and started snivelling again. I thought to myself that only she could say such a soppy thing. But then I don't suppose the silly cow even thought about it.

Postscript

James Grant was one of the last people to be hanged. Capital punishment was suspended for a trial period of five years in November 1965.

But since then the controversy has still gone on. During the period of suspension a nation-wide petition has been circulating urging its reintroduction. This will be presented to Parliament when the trial period is up.

Mr Digby Parry, Q.C., M.P., a leading abolitionist, during the course of preparing evidence for this occasion, called on Mr Grant, Snr, in an attempt to obtain ammunition for the debate.

Mr Grant was unable to assist but he handed Mr Parry an unopened brown paper parcel which had been given to him with his son's personal belongings after the execution.

The parcel contained the manuscript written by James Grant.

Mr Parry purchased it and arranged for its publication. For legal and humane reasons some names have been altered. Apart from these, no changes have been made.